'This is **a book that should not be missed**.'

Guardian

'... the and lingering sna... of miller womanhood . . . Though unsettling at times, the unrelenting rawness of *Shelf Life* forms its brilliance. The novel is **a bold and uncompromising addition to experimental women's writing**, exposing truths at every turn.'

The F Word

'Structured around a shopping list, the non-linear narrative is **as droll as it is disarming**. The playful form gives a new, distinctly millennial shape to perennial struggles of love and dating.'

Culture Whisper

'Franchini dissects ideas of love, dating and identity in a way that feels both ruthless and humane. **I loved it**.'

Sophie Mackintosh, author of *The Water Cure*

'*Shelf Life* is **dark and disarming**. It wryly explores hunger and denial and the play between pleasure and power in an honest portrayal of the complexities of desire. Franchini's voice is **sharp and clever** and her debut novel tells us truths about how and why we love.'

JESSICA ANDREWS, AUTHOR OF *SALTWATER*

'*Shelf Life* is so intimate. It's **like riding the bus home with a friend** as she confides her secret hopes and fears. Each raw emotion is carefully delivered. Franchini has created a protagonist who feels achingly real.'

ROWAN HISAYO BUCHANAN, AUTHOR OF *HARMLESS LIKE YOU*

'A novel that explores the precarities, fragilities and tendernesses of modern life – **it scintillates**.'

ELEY WILLIAMS, AUTHOR OF *ATTRIB. AND OTHER STORIES*

'*Shelf Life* is **a truly unique read**; a book so thoughtfully and articulately written it draws the reader deep into the painful heart of a fracturing relationship. Ruth, the novel's central character, is crafted in such a believable way, I felt every one of her disappointments keenly. I was rooting for her throughout. By the final page **I felt like we'd been through something monumental together**.'

JAN CARSON, AUTHOR OF *THE FIRE STARTERS*

Shelf
Life

LIVIA FRANCHINI

BLACK SWAN

TRANSWORLD PUBLISHERS
61–63 Uxbridge Road, London W5 5SA
www.penguin.co.uk

Transworld is part of the Penguin Random House group of companies
whose addresses can be found at global.penguinrandomhouse.com

Penguin
Random House
UK

First published in Great Britain in 2019 by Doubleday
an imprint of Transworld Publishers
Black Swan edition published 2020

A CIP catalogue record for this book
is available from the British Library.

ISBN
9781784164805

Typeset in 11.04/14.7pt Bembo MT Pro by Jouve (UK), Milton Keynes
Printed and bound in Great Britain by Clays Ltd, Elcograf S.p.A.

Penguin Random House is committed to a sustainable
future for our business, our readers and our planet. This book
is made from Forest Stewardship Council® certified paper.

1 3 5 7 9 10 8 6 4 2

For Gesuina Bolis;
freguj

Sugar, flour, kippers, greens
sugar, sugar, sugar
'Kew Gardens', Virginia Woolf

Here are some things I know about weight. A pound of feathers weighs as much as a pound of bricks, but a pound of bricks is easier to carry. A pound of flesh may be used as payment or taken as forced retribution. A pound cake is made using a pound each of four ingredients: flour, eggs, butter and sugar, which actually means a more exact name for this cake would be four-pound cake. Most things you buy in the supermarket come in a standard shape, a fixed weight, which makes them feel familiar. For example, a one-litre bottle of sparkling water, the brand you like to drink, weighs exactly one kilo. The weight of the measure of oats that you enjoy in your morning porridge fits perfectly in the palm of my hand. The weight of your suit jacket on my shoulders, when I get cold because I have forgotten to bring a jumper, is exactly the same weight as the end of that night, which is felt in the knees, in the light grip of a migraine nudging at my temples, and is easily assigned to a specific hour, between eleven and midnight, just before the last train home. The weight of your arm, draped across my waist when we are lying in bed and you are falling asleep, and how long it takes for that weight to turn into a different kind of weight, the dead weight of your deep sleep, is the weight of sleep itself. Without it, the notion of sleep is emptied of meaning. You have left an indentation of exactly the size of your body in our bed, but your body is unavailable to substantiate its weight. Which is why I am lying here at four in the morning, sleepless.

I was working in A&E when the position at the care home came up. Which was a good thing because I would never have survived the emergency room. Although I remember the training well.

First, you must consider the damage. When the slatted light from the window softens the red glare of the lampshade and your side of the bed is greying, I know it's time to act. I lift my head and look around. Here is my sore neck. Here are my thighs, stiff and sticky with night sweat. There is your dressing gown on the back of the door, hanging like a bandage. The moccasins are missing; you left the hiking boots behind. You were in a hurry. In an emergency, leave behind anything that might weigh you down: bags, coat and other personal belongings. But why have you chosen the moccasins over the hiking boots?

I am utterly exhausted. I shut my eyes and it's the wrong thing to do, because as ever with closed eyes, my other senses are sharpened. It all comes back to me with the taste of last night's dinner: something with leek. I can't quite remember.

Take a deep breath. Tell me what happened.

I liked having dinner with you.

What you did is you collected the plates from dinner, took them to the kitchen, and waited for me to come through and wash them. Fish. Haddock. That's what I'd made. Yours in a cream sauce, mine steamed and cut into morsels. The plates were there on the side, sticky with fish and wet vegetables.

I ran the hot tap and took off the engagement ring. I put on the Marigolds instead.

Sometimes the body knows before the mind. Something in your tone, or how you began, by calling my name.

'Ruth.'

Water hit the hem of my right glove, scalding my wrist. I pulled my hand away.

'Neil,' I said.

My fingers throbbed inside the yellow gloves. I was distracted, interested in my own task. We weren't often apart from each other in the evenings and so I cultivated my small solitudes in mundane pockets of the day, retreating to a quiet corner of my mind when busy with something. So that when I was with you – *with* you – I could really be present.

Now I was busy.

'Ruth,' you said. 'There's something I need to talk to you about.'

The mind, you see? The truth is that, right then, I wasn't fully there. Only with difficulty can I trace back to those few moments before things fragmented.

I wondered if you were testing the skills you'd learnt in your mindful assertiveness class. Or if you'd found something else to be excited about, after the percussion box, plant cuttings, upholstery class and fossil collection. This current wholesome phase, at least, didn't make as much noise or take up as much space.

I made a sound to convey my engagement. You wanted more.

'Yes,' I said, finally, looking over my shoulder. 'What is it?'

'I've had an epiphany. I think.'

3

Here we go, I thought. I turned around and rested my bottom against the cupboard. Let the tap fill up the sink. Ready for your lecture. I put on my usual smile. I never learn. I'm seldom smug about my intuition, but when I am I always get it wrong.

I gave you a visible nod, so you knew to continue.

Your lips were a line. You needed my help and I was eager to offer it. That's how it worked for us.

'What is it?' I nudged.

'Nothing we haven't talked about before, to be honest.'

'So what is it? What's your revelation?'

'About love. Relationships. The idea of a couple, I guess.'

'The idea of a couple?'

'Let me speak first.'

'Oh, come on,' I said. 'We've talked about this, haven't we?'

I didn't get angry. And you didn't look angry either. I can tell when you're about to get angry. I turned off the tap.

'We have,' you said. 'I just said.'

'And we're not discussing the possibility of an open relationship again.'

'I'm not trying to discuss an open relationship.'

'That's good. Because we've discussed it enough times, I think.'

I looked at the white gold ring on the side, deliberately, so that you'd have to look at it too. When you did, I turned back to the sink, picked up a plate and began to scrub.

'It's different for me,' you said.

'Is it?' Your hand on my hip made me jump. I turned back around.

'Listen to me, babe,' you said. 'I'm serious about this.'

'You're always serious about everything,' I said. 'Until you get tired of it.'

'We're too good for this, Ruth.'

'Too good for what?'

'This conversation. I mean, look at us.'

'Us? We're fine. Aren't we?'

'Yes,' you said.

'Well then.'

Wherever this was going, I didn't like it. I had stuff to do, stuff to get done. I pushed you to the side and opened the drawer, pushed aside the candle stumps and the empty matchboxes. Found a tea towel, looked at you. You were quiet. You looked sad. I hate it when you look sad. I drew you into me with my elbows because my gloves were dirty and wet and I didn't want to ruin your shirt.

'What is it, baby?' I said. That note of desperation in my voice. I hadn't intended that. We were fine. Hadn't you just said so yourself? But the atmosphere in the kitchen had shifted. I clutched at your hips but your arms stayed put along the sides of your body. You rested your chin on the top of my head.

'Well, I'm just trying to say that . . . I've been thinking. You know what I'm like. That we all have this great love there inside of us.'

I held you a bit tighter and your hands rose to the bottom of my spine. I looked up. You were staring out of the window.

'I don't know, Ruth,' you said into the darkness of our garden. 'Don't you ever want to share it with more than one person?'

It's tough to patch together what happened after that.

My forehead becomes damp with the effort of remembering, and I wish I had a wet towel, the folded kind a loving parent might bring to a sick child.

5

Incoherent memories are a common reaction to trauma. Scraps of last night's conversation fly violently against the walls of my skull. A subdural haematoma is usually associated with traumatic brain injury. This is what it feels like. My head hurts badly. There are violet dots behind my eyes, lines of dialogue but no punctuation.

I think most of it took place in the kitchen. I broke the hug, pushed you away. I shouldn't have because you really went for it after that. I stood next to the sink and watched that familiar confidence fill your features. I'm sure I must have been nodding, because you didn't wait for me to catch up. And that's how it had worked for us, remember? You, in the driver's seat. Me, sitting next to you, tracing our trajectory with my finger on the map. Following your route. Except you weren't even letting me do that. You didn't seem to care if I came along.

Finally, you lined up the evidence. You went on and on and on and on. My patronizing attitude, your restlessness, my silence, the ways we tended towards and shrank away from each other, never quite meeting in the middle.

'That's just us,' I said. 'Isn't that what we're like?'

'Right, that's what we're like,' you said. 'It doesn't mean that it's right,' you said. 'Like two parallel lines,' you said.

'Wow,' I said. 'Are you serious?'

'Of course I'm fucking serious.'

'I don't understand why you're getting wound up,' I said, because right then I really didn't.

'Jesus Christ, Ruth. You know exactly what I'm getting at,' you said. 'I want to break up.'

I thought you were joking. I thought you were annoyed about something I'd done, wanted to get laid, probably

6

wanted to get laid more in general, had got something into your head. You were always getting something into your head. I remember my cheeks heating up, becoming intolerably hot. Did I raise my voice?

As an accountant you took pride in your end-of-year financial reports. Who knew you'd been keeping tabs on our private life, too? You were unsatisfied with your return on investment, as it were, so you were chucking me. Well, we hadn't exactly been focusing on team building, had we? When was the last time you'd taken me out for dinner? I did say that. My voice sounded nasal and pedantic, and I revelled in it, trusting my outrage to guide me as I talked, prodded you – another mistake.

I said to you, 'Go on. Tell me more about your notes on our relationship. You want a reward? For being so meticulous. You want a gold star?'

I slammed the palm of my hand against your heart. You stumbled backwards and I saw something in your eyes that I'd never seen before, and couldn't name.

I looked down and I remember noticing my hands and that I still had my rubber gloves on. My yellow arms looked stupid. I hated them. And then you hugged me and I stood deflated in your arms.

'Listen, Ruth,' you said. 'I don't mean to hurt you. I cannot bear to see you hurt.' And though I registered the official tone – its eeriness, its uncompressed, regular syllables – I let you continue.

There are bits that I can't remember: holes, where the fabric of our conversation is stretched so thin that I can see through to the other side. I can see last night's Ruth pulling her hair back into a too-tight ponytail; these same

7

strands, thick with sweat, glued to my temples, my cheeks, my top lip, as I wake up alone in our bed.

Home, marriage, kids. You thought there was more to life than just that. You weren't putting the blame on me. You were willing to take responsibility for your own actions. Throughout our relationship, you'd been the one responsible for both of us, and here you were, once again, doing just that, finally addressing all the fucked-up shit in it. You might as well take the blame for it all – really it was your fault, though purely for going along with things for so long. Hadn't you bought me a ring, taken me on holiday, produced a bottle of champagne at the restaurant, even got down on one knee in the restaurant car park? Why the car park? For privacy. You thought public marriage proposals were tacky. Didn't I? Of course I did.

Your face slackened with pity. Poor little Ruth. You stroked my forehead gently with your thumb. That's when I knew you were going to leave me.

And then I couldn't see straight. In my head I ran through the first-aid emergency checklist. I ticked all the boxes, over and over again in my frenzy, finishing and then starting again from the beginning: clammy skin, shallow breathing, tachycardia, hypothermia. I slumped against the dry goods cupboard. You were calculating the hours we'd spent decorating versus the times I didn't want to practise tantric sex. We didn't even own our own place yet. I mean, I wouldn't even try anal sex.

You were tired of waiting for your life to kick into motion.

That's when I started laughing.

'You're a fucking cunt,' I said. 'You're a fucking hypocrite cunt.'

Where did that come from? People say stuff they don't mean when they're angry.

I know now that it was the cue you'd been waiting for. I fell for it.

'If that's what you think about me, Ruth, it's fucking over.'

Things moved quickly after that. You were angry, wired, efficient. You pulled books off the shelves and slammed them into our laundry basket, like it was just a thing for carrying other things and not something that had held your clothes tangled with mine. I staggered after you as you moved through the house, your anger throbbing, turning surfaces inside out. You grabbed an armful of underwear, kept shouting that you knew it, you fucking knew it all along and what was the point in being reasonable with people like me, what was the point in even trying to explain when it was obvious I wasn't willing to understand. I only looked like I was. Nothing ever went in.

You dragged your suitcase from the bottom of the wardrobe. You opened it and I looked inside. I saw it was already half packed. The numbing epiphany that you'd been making arrangements, that you weren't acting on impulse but carrying out a plan.

When I managed to speak, I asked a stupid question.

'Have you met someone else?'

'You're ridiculous,' you shouted from the bathroom. 'Do you ever listen to a word I say?'

I found you in front of the mirror with the electric clippers.

'There's a mindfulness commune in Cornwall,' you said. 'Very selective. I've been accepted and I'm going tonight.'

'Tonight?' I said.

'God knows I could do with some peace of fucking mind.'

The sink filled up with your thin yellow hair.

That's the last clear memory. I lie very still and wait for the room to settle. I have imagined a life without you some-times. I did it absent-mindedly after a fight, when we'd made up but my throat was still clenched with resentment. Or when the cute guy at the supermarket rushed to dis-count the bouquets early because he knew how much I loved flowers, that I always bought myself a bunch on a Friday. You didn't like it. You said cut flowers made you think of death. It was just another one of those things you said. You said so many things all the time. A life without you always struck me as a life of empty quietness.

Yet emptiness is the opposite of what I am experiencing. It isn't an emotion exactly, rather a physical sensation: a tingling. I'm thinking about the parts of my body I never think about: the backs of my calves, the tips of my elbows, the shells of my ears, the interstices between my toes and fingers. I'm able to locate it in the middle of my chest – ventricular fibrillation – electricity travelling along the tiny wires of my nerve endings.

It jolts me up and I stand for a moment, stunned.

I start blindly towards the kitchen. With each slow step something of what is packed inside starts spilling out, like I'm punctured somewhere.

Go on, I tell myself. Go on, move, walk. So I walk.

I walk with my shoulder to the wall so that nothing can grab me in the semi-darkness but my arse hits the phone stand and I look at my hips, disappointed, because I have put on weight and my belly sticks out like I'm pregnant. A sharp pain folds me in two and my hands shoot to my back to soothe the period pain. I realize that your and my baby will never be born and I have to lean against the wall while white grief washes over me and I feel the oldest I have ever felt. I think of how often my patients ask for water and how many times I have poured it into a tea cup, cool from the tap, and held it to their lips. My dry mouth meets the edge of your CHOOSE LIFE mug and, as cold water trickles down my throat, the noise within me finally stops and I know what the problem is.

I have never been a person alone.

After ten years with Neil, I don't know how to do it. I place my hands flat on the counter, inhale, open my eyes. Familiar things. I see the engagement ring between the pile of dirty dishes and the heart-shaped post-its. And this week's shopping list, a neat round water mark on its top-right corner.

I pick it up and read the items one by one.

04/01/2016

6 eggs
sandwich bread
diet coke
tampons
apples
sugar
deo
cotton wool
pizza
whole chicken
spaghetti
soup
tomatoes
teabags
aftershave
white wine
prawns
olives
mobile top-up
strawberries
honey
moisturizer
dates
flowers
conditioner
single cream
pulses
steak (lean)
bleach
some kind of pudding

6 EGGS

Ruth
Now

The light is dim in our west-facing kitchen. I keep the curtains shut. I call the care home and say that I am sick and then I climb back into bed and take a sleeping pill. The sun doesn't go up for six whole days, six empty shells of days, nothing in them, just me either asleep or about to be.

In this dream you feed us spoonfuls of bright white cream. There is something wrong about its colour; too white, iridescent. That can't be right, I'm thinking in the dream. 'It's organic,' you say, lifting your thumb to show me the picture of a cow on the tub, sketched by a grown-up imitating the hand of a child.

After he leaves me, I take to sleeping on my side with a pillow held against my belly and I dream of babies. It's unclear which of the two acts has triggered the other: did I begin clutching the pillow because of my dreams or did the clutching bring about the dreaming? I am comfortable sleeping like this, so I see no reason why I shouldn't continue. I dream of baby girls, never baby boys.

In this dream I miss her first steps, but you tell me it happened in the park. It is not clear why I wasn't also in the park, nor do I have a clear image of what the park looks like or where it is located. You refer to it as if it is a familiar location that needs no further specification, and it is implied that we often go there together as a family. You tell me that she got up to chase a ball and off she went, like she'd been doing it for ever. Walking, unaided, almost running away from you. It was a red ball, you say, with white polka dots. As if knowing this particular piece of information will make me feel better about not having been there.

This is how, in sleeping, I pick up my first solitary habit: I either sleep too much or too little. Sleep comes to me in uncountable portions; it surprises me, knocks me out like a seasonal sickness with no early, recognizable symptoms. I'm not used to sleeping on my own. When I was very little I shared a bed with my mother, our dotted spines lined up against one another, like rodents sleeping under earth. Then, for a year, I slept alone in my college room. It was the year I almost starved myself to death.

In this dream we are driving through a car wash. It is the kind you pay for with tokens. Our daughter is strapped into the baby seat on the passenger side. She is facing me. The shower jet sprays on to the windows, shadows moving across her cheek like grey water. Her face is calm. There is a feeling of calm inside the car. In her right fist, when she unfurls it, is the triangular shard of an egg shell. I look closer and I realize the shard is a tooth and yet it is way too big for her mouth, way too sharp.

★

Neil and I would sleep in a flat knot, pressed against one another like flowers in a book. He'd face the other side of the bed and offer me his back. I'd cling to it, marsupial, matching my smaller toes with his. His body was always hot, as if he were running a fever. I'd push my face into the hollow of his shoulders and breathe the oxygen out, until I fell asleep drowsy with asphyxiation. Often, when I couldn't remember my dreams, I assumed we had dreamt about similar things and that reassured me.

In this dream she is sitting on the floor of my mother's old kitchen, chequerboard lino throwing her tiny body into sharp relief. Her right leg is at an angle that I can tell is rather strange for a toddler. I'm not sure why I approach her, maybe nothing to do with the leg, some kind of instinct or intuition, because she honestly doesn't look distressed, but when I get closer it becomes apparent that something is wrong. There is definitely something wrong with her legs. Her leg that is bent doesn't match her other leg. Something about its length. I'm inching closer. It seems that her right leg is a few centimetres longer. I drop down to my knees to check: definitely some length longer. My mouth opens into the shape of B-A for 'baby', but the sound hasn't quite come out when she looks up and says, perfectly eloquently, 'Don't worry, ma'am, it's just tomato sauce.' There is nothing on the black-and-white tiles.

These days, sleeping feels like a kind of drunkenness, like travelling by sea. I roll from one end of the bed to the other, never comfortable, never warm, not enough limbs to hold down the covers. Sometimes it feels like sailing in a tempest. The flat is full of noises; the darkness is windy outside my window; all the surfaces slope. I crawl my way up through soggy dreams, craving fresh air to stop the nausea.

17

My eyes fly open on the upper deck and I am back in our flat: it is still night-time and I'm scared. He always fell asleep before I did. I fell asleep listening to his steady breathing. Now I am awake at two in the morning because the shower is dripping and it's driving me fucking mad.

In this dream, she's dressed like a cartoon frog except her costume is like no other costume I've ever seen: the head is sturdy and heavy, the body rigid. She has to leap forward to move at all. It looks more like a large plastic frog has swallowed her whole than a costume. Her eyes sparkle darkly from the frog's engorged neck. They follow me around the room. 'Mummy, Mummy,' she gurgles as if she's speaking from deep under water. I push my thumb into her frog mouth and it goes inside without hitting resistance, deep into her hollow limitless skull.

On the sixth day I wake with a start, my face damp and throbbing. I kick the cushion on to the floor, push at the duvet. The phone is ringing in circles on top of the wooden dresser, its calling: 6:30! It's a new dawn. It's a Monday. And one of the worst: a Monday in January.

SANDWICH BREAD

Four Years Earlier

From: cumulonimbus@ymail.com
Sent: 13 January 2012 01:23
To: s.hino@thekitegroup.co.uk
Subject: Good Morning

Dear Sumiko,

I don't doubt that this email will come to you as a
surprise. You don't know who I am and certainly I can't
claim that I know you. Technically, we've never met,
never made eye contact, not even in the shallow way
you sometimes do in a city like this, during shared
coffee breaks and cigarette breaks, smiles on opposite
sides of a zebra crossing, or at the offering of a seat on
the bus . . . Though a bus is indeed where I first saw
you. What a lovely coincidence that it should be the
number forty-three, as I had just that day in my book
read about the numbers four and three and their
combination: four representing stability, three the

bearer of joy and free expression. I couldn't help but think this was a happy omen. You stepped in through the doors in your chalk-white coat, like a pale water lily, just about keeping afloat in a stream of grey overcoats. I thought you might be a vision of hope.

Sumiko (I hope you won't mind me calling you by your first name), let me apologize if I don't yet reveal myself. I am feeling quite shy, you know, Sumiko. And what good would it do you to know my name, when you have never seen me? Your name was the first thing I learnt about you, when your coat came open as you walked past me, revealing the name tag pinned on your heart. So imagine my surprise when I saw it bore the logo of my own company, and underneath, I realized you were wearing our in-house staff uniform. I must say the colour complements your eyes perfectly.

Let me tell you this. Your eyes, Sumiko. Your eyes are the reason I write to you. Each morning, as I come in the door you startle me with those eyes. I have to hurry past reception, because I cannot look into those eyes of molten steel. You probably think I'm just another one of those rude boys who don't bother talking to the new receptionist. So I thought I'd write to set the record straight. I'd love to talk to you, actually.

Your Cloud

From: cumulonimbus@ymail.com
Sent: 16 January 2012 00:56
To: s.hino@thekitegroup.co.uk
Subject: Re: Good Morning

Dear Sumiko,

I apologize in advance if you should feel that this
email follows really quite soon after my previous one.
The thing is, Sumiko, I would be a fool if I believed love
to be an exact science . . . and yet, and yet, I couldn't
get that infamous three-day rule out of my head. I
thought you might be biding your time, waiting to get in
touch today. The third fateful day, isn't it? But since the
day is pretty much over and I have not heard from you,
I thought I would check in just to make sure you've
picked up my message. If you have, and you're unsure
what to write, please don't worry so much. It doesn't
matter. I just want to get to know you better.

In the glimpses I've caught of you, you have always
struck me as one of those rare creatures who will think
twice or more before they choose to express a thought.
In the images I have of you, you rarely speak. Swiping
in or out of the doors of our building, sitting on a bench,
unwrapping your little square sandwich and lifting each
neat quarter to your sweet little mouth: you always
keep your eyes trained on the object you are holding.
Your little sandwich. I've never seen you linger outside
of work, smoking with colleagues. Though many times
I have seen you smoke alone, lighting your roll-up
laboriously with your back against the wall. Why do you

choose to smoke in such a windy spot? Sumiko, all I
wanted to say is you don't have to be scared. I want to
reassure you. You can talk to me.

Your Cloud

From: cumulonimbus@ymail.com
Sent: 21 January 2012 01:10
To: s.hino@thekitegroup.co.uk
Subject: Sorry

Dear Sumiko,

I have spent the past few days in a daze, sitting around,
daydreaming, imagining the different ways you might
have interpreted my words. I've been waiting and
hoping. I'm not kidding when I say I've been longing
for your reply with sighs uncharacteristic of this era.
(Actually, I am; I am kidding, I am being ridiculous.
I am making things up, because I am starting to feel
like an idiot.) I was so excited at having finally
summoned the courage to speak to you that I never
tried to read my own messages through your eyes.
Now that I have gone and done so I realize how terribly
naive I have been.

Sumiko, I am beginning to suspect that you might be
reading these messages as the ramblings of a
madman. Well, listen, I'd like to send you my sincerest
apologies. I want to reassure you that I only wanted to
get to know you better. It is true that your modest

beauty has touched me deeply, but please believe that I never intended for my admiration to make you uncomfortable. Don't let me bother you further: write back and I can explain.

Your Cloud

From: s.hino@thekitegroup.co.uk
Sent: 22 January 2012 10:22
To: n.pratchett@thekitegroup.co.uk
Subject: Phishing Warning

Dear Neil,

I have been updating our company-wide contact list and couldn't help noticing that the email address cumulonimbus@ymail.com is listed as your secondary contact in your profile entry. I would suggest looking into your security settings, as it appears that a number of spam emails have been generated from that account.

Best wishes,
Sumiko Hino

Administrative Assistant
The Kite Group
London W1 3HN
+44 208 648 9992

From: n.pratchett@thekitegroup.co.uk
Sent: 22 January 2012 11:06
To: s.hino@thekitegroup.co.uk
Subject: Re: Phishing Warning

Dear Sumiko,

Thanks for letting me know. I have now changed the password to my account. Will you please remove said spam address from my record? Thank you.

Best,
Neil Pratchett

Senior Accountant
The Kite Group
London W1 3HN
+44 208 648 9986

DIET COKE

Ruth
Now

Coping with loss.
There is no right or wrong way to grieve – everyone can
find a healthy way to deal with pain.

I know the cover off by heart. I know the name of the colour too – periwinkle: a muddy, bluish violet. I looked it up
on Wikipedia and discovered that it's named after a flower.
Everything about the care home is carefully calculated in
this way, pastel and artificial; soft conventions that hold
meaning beyond their official functions.

There are a number of reasons why the booklets exist, the
least useful of which is for preliminary reading, although
that is their official capacity. They live in a discreet corner of
the visitors' waiting room and we only hand them out when
a patient is looking particularly bad. If the relatives haven't
actively picked one up (often this happens spontaneously)

we fold one into their palm to snap them out of their denial. Get them used to the idea.

Normally, we've called the family in ahead of this moment. These 'difficult calls' summon a family to the patient's bedside. We give these calls to the voluntary nurses. 'Candy-stripers': our American boss, Dame Melissa Barnes – 'Call-Me-Melissa' – likes to call them by their vintage name. She once confessed to me she might consider enforcing white-and-red pinafores as a uniform for the volunteers. She thought it would be quaint. 'Of course,' I said. I find it infantilizing: an excellent way to keep them in their place. We give the difficult calls to the candy-stripers so that they grow a thick skin. That is also the only official reason.

Guess what? Telling people that their relative is going to die is an unpleasant and thankless task and it's a lie when people say that you never get used to it. In a private care home like ours, where palliative care starts at three thousand pounds a month, without counting meals or toiletries, not even a fucking minibar for when the family visit, you get used to it. This place is engineered for a single purpose: to administer the death of the rich in the most graceful, effortless manner.

We give the calls to the candy-stripers because we can't stand going through the motions again. The statements of sympathy are like magic spells: they lose their power after they've been repeated a certain number of times. You stop believing in them. And without sympathy, how can a professional nurse be expected to do her job properly? We need a break once in a while. The candy-stripers are volunteers: they don't mind dealing with the difficult calls.

They like to feel essential. Are we *sure* we want them to? It's a big responsibility after all.

Of course we're sure. We have a million other things to deal with. And we don't want to talk to the relatives, who sweep in only for the grand finale, having rejected the very same experience we curate, handed it over to paid staff, a less pressing matter in their busy lives. Do I ever want to have a heart-to-heart over the phone with horrible Miss Hancock, for instance? Prepare her for the death of her equally horrible father? Not in this lifetime.

The booklet also reduces the need for conversation. It provides families with the correct language for grief, a prescriptive emotional route. But we nurses are already well acquainted with that path. That's why it hadn't occurred to me to actually take a look beyond the periwinkle cover. That stuff is for beginners.

Today, during my lunch break the limp illustration of a lily called out to me from the rack. I was sitting behind my desk. I've been unable to eat for days and my stomach feels like it has shrunk to the size of a fist. Caffeinated drinks keep me going: there's the shadow of a migraine constantly lingering at eye level and a silver can constantly clenched in my hand.

Funny how some things become meaningful only when you are very, very sad. This lily has suddenly fulfilled its intended role as a clever, multi-layered metaphor for the end of life's natural cycle – gentle decay, sweet final death, the syrupy smell of funeral flowers. Isn't it funny how the deeper meaning of these things only manifests for those who already grasp it somehow, slipping unnoticed past those who don't? They pay people handsomely to come up with this sort of trick. Nice job, everyone.

On page one there is an introduction penned in a slanting, longhand font, conveying both intimacy and authority. It's hard to read, presumably because everyone knows doctors have terrible handwriting.

> Grief is most often associated with the loss of a loved one. However, someone who has suffered a subtler loss can still experience grief. You may experience grief on the occasion of the death of a beloved pet, retirement from your career, selling your family home, or the end of a relationship.

Mona waved as she came through the front door and past the reception desk. We call reception 'the Goldfish Bowl' because you are tragically visible inside it. There's nowhere to hide. The plants are offensively green, polymeric. I flattened the booklet on to the desk then slipped it into the pocket of my smock as she rounded the corner to the back door. I took the booklet home with me at the end of my shift.

TAMPONS

Fourteen Years Earlier

21:31, 09/02/2002
[ⓜⓡⓢ ⓣⓡⓐⓒⓔⓨ ⓟⓘⓣⓣ IS ONLINE]

`⋅‿⋅˙¯⋅‿⋅ɞʌɞy ᑭ♡ĪS♡Ͷˋ⋅‿⋅˙¯⋅‿⋅` says:

trace babe u there?

ⓜⓡⓢ ⓣⓡⓐⓒⓔⓨ ⓟⓘⓣⓣ says:

hiiiiiiii

ⓜⓡⓢ ⓣⓡⓐⓒⓔⓨ ⓟⓘⓣⓣ says:

fully done w maths for tonight

`⋅‿⋅˙¯⋅‿⋅ɞʌɞy ᑭ♡ĪS♡Ͷˋ⋅‿⋅˙¯⋅‿⋅` says:

girl

`⋅‿⋅˙¯⋅‿⋅ɞʌɞy ᑭ♡ĪS♡Ͷˋ⋅‿⋅˙¯⋅‿⋅` says:

literally just came out of rehearsals

ⓜⓡⓢ ⓣⓡⓐⓒⓔⓨ ⓟⓘⓣⓣ says:

wow thats late

`⋅‿⋅˙¯⋅‿⋅ɞʌɞy ᑭ♡ĪS♡Ͷˋ⋅‿⋅˙¯⋅‿⋅` says:

yup

`·._.·´¯`·._.·ʙʌʙʏ ᴘ♡ɪꜱ♡ʍ`·._.·´¯`·._.·` says:

miss was in a real mood tonite she wouldnt let us leave unless we finished the whole routine

`·._.·´¯`·._.·ʙʌʙʏ ᴘ♡ɪꜱ♡ʍ`·._.·´¯`·._.·` says:

no mistakes

ⓜⓡⓢ ⓣⓡⓐⓒⓔⓨ ⓟⓘⓣⓣ says:

jesus

ⓜⓡⓢ ⓣⓡⓐⓒⓔⓨ ⓟⓘⓣⓣ says:

that woman behaves like shes the royal ballet

`·._.·´¯`·._.·ʙʌʙʏ ᴘ♡ɪꜱ♡ʍ`·._.·´¯`·._.·` says:

ya well

ⓜⓡⓢ ⓣⓡⓐⓒⓔⓨ ⓟⓘⓣⓣ says:

shes gonna break u one day or another

`·._.·´¯`·._.·ʙʌʙʏ ᴘ♡ɪꜱ♡ʍ`·._.·´¯`·._.·` says:

it takes what it takes innit

`·._.·´¯`·._.·ʙʌʙʏ ᴘ♡ɪꜱ♡ʍ`·._.·´¯`·._.·` says:

so u get me

`·._.·´¯`·._.·ʙʌʙʏ ᴘ♡ɪꜱ♡ʍ`·._.·´¯`·._.·` says:

was hoping I could take a peek at yr homework tmw :P

ⓜⓡⓢ ⓣⓡⓐⓒⓔⓨ ⓟⓘⓣⓣ says:

ah yes

ⓜⓡⓢ ⓣⓡⓐⓒⓔⓨ ⓟⓘⓣⓣ says:

gna be carnage

`·._.·´¯`·._.·ʙʌʙʏ ᴘ♡ɪꜱ♡ʍ`·._.·´¯`·._.·` says:

rly?

`·._.·´¯`·._.·ʙʌʙʏ ᴘ♡ɪꜱ♡ʍ`·._.·´¯`·._.·` says:

cld u not work it out either

mⓡⓢ ⓣⓡⓐⓒⓔⓨ ⓟⓘⓣⓣ **says:**

not rly

mⓡⓢ ⓣⓡⓐⓒⓔⓨ ⓟⓘⓣⓣ **says:**

gave it a try

`._.¨¯··._.·฿∧฿Y P♡ĪS♡И`·._.·¨¯··._.· **says:**

can i take a look at it?

mⓡⓢ ⓣⓡⓐⓒⓔⓨ ⓟⓘⓣⓣ **says:**

do u ever like

mⓡⓢ ⓣⓡⓐⓒⓔⓨ ⓟⓘⓣⓣ **says:**

not take a look at it ;))

`._.¨¯··._.·฿∧฿Y P♡ĪS♡И`·._.·¨¯··._.· **says:**

thnx babe

mⓡⓢ ⓣⓡⓐⓒⓔⓨ ⓟⓘⓣⓣ **says:**

u know it <3

21:34, 09/02/2002

[ƒяαηκι ƒαямєя ωιℓℓ нανє нєя яєνєηgє ση sαιηт James IS ONLINE]

[ƒяαηκι ƒαямєя ωιℓℓ нανє нєя яєνєηgє ση sαιηт James HAS BEEN ADDED TO THE CONVERSATION]

ƒяαηκι ƒαямєя ωιℓℓ нανє нєя яєνєηgє ση sαιηт James **says:**

oi!

ƒяαηκι ƒαямєя ωιℓℓ нανє нєя яєνєηgє ση sαιηт James **says:**

u guys on here early

ƒяαηκι ƒαямєя ωιℓℓ нανє нєя яєνєηgє ση sαιηт James **says:**

whats up

`._.¨¯··._.·฿∧฿Y P♡ĪS♡И`·._.·¨¯··._.· **says:**

darling francesca

`·.ᵧᵧ·"‾··._·ßʌßУ Р♡ĪŚ♡И`·.ᵧᵧ·"‾··._·ᵧ says:

nothing rly

ⓜⓡⓢ ⓣⓡⓐⓒⓔⓨ ⓟⓘⓣⓣ says:

just homework

ƒяαηκι ƒαямєя ωιℓℓ нαⱴє нєя яєⱴєηgє ση ѕαιηт James says:

o god dont even

ƒяαηκι ƒαямєя ωιℓℓ нαⱴє нєя яєⱴєηgє ση ѕαιηт James says:

i was gonna ask if i could take a look tmw

ƒяαηκι ƒαямєя ωιℓℓ нαⱴє нєя яєⱴєηgє ση ѕαιηт James says:

T?

ⓜⓡⓢ ⓣⓡⓐⓒⓔⓨ ⓟⓘⓣⓣ says:

i mean sure

ⓜⓡⓢ ⓣⓡⓐⓒⓔⓨ ⓟⓘⓣⓣ says:

its not done but like

ƒяαηκι ƒαямєя ωιℓℓ нαⱴє нєя яєⱴєηgє ση ѕαιηт James says:

legend

ƒяαηκι ƒαямєя ωιℓℓ нαⱴє нєя яєⱴєηgє ση ѕαιηт James says:

literally have been sitting here so long I cant feel my butt

ƒяαηκι ƒαямєя ωιℓℓ нαⱴє нєя яєⱴєηgє ση ѕαιηт James says:

hows this shit even legal

`·.ᵧᵧ·"‾··._·ßʌßУ Р♡ĪŚ♡И`·.ᵧᵧ·"‾··._·ᵧ says:

ya

`·.ᵧᵧ·"‾··._·ßʌßУ Р♡ĪŚ♡И`·.ᵧᵧ·"‾··._·ᵧ says:

remind me who had the genius idea for all of us to take maths instead of science

ƒяαηκι ƒαямєя ωιℓℓ нαⱴє нєя яєⱴєηgє ση ѕαιηт James says:

whatever alanna

fяaηkι faяmeя wιll нave нeя яeveηge oη saιηt James says:

bet ud rather be slicing up frogs in science

fяaηkι faяmeя wιll нave нeя яeveηge oη saιηt James says:

cuz u were such a princess w options that was the only place we were ever ending up

fяaηkι faяmeя wιll нave нeя яeveηge oη saιηt James says:

honestly so fucked up

fяaηkι faяmeя wιll нave нeя яeveηge oη saιηt James says:

meat is murder man

ⓜⓡⓢ ⓣⓡⓐⓒⓔⓨ ⓟⓘⓣⓣ says:

they dont actually slice up frogs in science

ⓜⓡⓢ ⓣⓡⓐⓒⓔⓨ ⓟⓘⓣⓣ says:

ure aware of that franks?

`·.₍˒⎯¨⎺··.₍_·ßʌßʏ ♡̇Ī S♡И`·.₍˒⎯¨⎺··._· says:

ya franks they dont do that any more

`·.₍˒⎯¨⎺··.₍_·ßʌßʏ ♡̇Ī S♡И`·.₍˒⎯¨⎺··._· says:

also u stopped eating meat like 2 weeks ago

`·.₍˒⎯¨⎺··.₍_·ßʌßʏ ♡̇Ī S♡И`·.₍˒⎯¨⎺··._· says:

cuz u started hanging w that gross guy jack

fяaηkι faяmeя wιll нave нeя яeveηge oη saιηt James says:

his name is jake

fяaηkι faяmeя wιll нave нeя яeveηge oη saιηt James says:

and ill have you know

fяaηkι faяmeя wιll нave нeя яeveηge oη saιηt James says:

JAKE is a very good person to hang out w

fяaηkι faяmeя wιll нave нeя яeveηge oη saιηt James says:

if ur remotely interested in being cool that is

fʁaɲkɪ faʁmeʁ wɪll нave нeʁ ʁeveɲge σɲ saɪɲt James says:

lucky I got u

`⋅._„.⋅˝⁻⋅.._⋅ßʌßY P♡ΪS♡И`⋅._„.⋅˝⁻⋅.._⋅ says:

sure man

`⋅._„.⋅˝⁻⋅.._⋅ßʌßY P♡ΪS♡И`⋅._„.⋅˝⁻⋅.._⋅ says:

what u got is a c– in maths

fʁaɲkɪ faʁmeʁ wɪll нave нeʁ ʁeveɲge σɲ saɪɲt James says:

better a c– than a ★C+★

`⋅._„.⋅˝⁻⋅.._⋅ßʌßY P♡ΪS♡И`⋅._„.⋅˝⁻⋅.._⋅ says:

i do NOT have the clap this joke is getting tired franks

ⓜⓡⓢ ⓣⓡⓐⓒⓔⓨ ⓟⓘⓣⓣ says:

girls look ★im★ kinda tired tonight

fʁaɲkɪ faʁmeʁ wɪll нave нeʁ ʁeveɲge σɲ saɪɲt James says:

o are u now poor lamby

ⓜⓡⓢ ⓣⓡⓐⓒⓔⓨ ⓟⓘⓣⓣ says:

ya

ⓜⓡⓢ ⓣⓡⓐⓒⓔⓨ ⓟⓘⓣⓣ says:

u kno from actually doing the homework for all of us?

ⓜⓡⓢ ⓣⓡⓐⓒⓔⓨ ⓟⓘⓣⓣ says:

it's like being back in primary with u 2

fʁaɲkɪ faʁmeʁ wɪll нave нeʁ ʁeveɲge σɲ saɪɲt James says:

o ya sorry mum

fʁaɲkɪ faʁmeʁ wɪll нave нeʁ ʁeveɲge σɲ saɪɲt James says:

forgot u finally grew tits

fʁaɲkɪ faʁmeʁ wɪll нave нeʁ ʁeveɲge σɲ saɪɲt James says:

taken them for a test run with good old charles yet?

ⓜⓡⓢ ⓣⓡⓐⓒⓔⓨ ⓟⓘⓣⓣ says:

o shut up francesca

ⓜⓡⓢ ⓣⓡⓐⓒⓔⓨ ⓟⓘⓣⓣ says:

ur honestly the most obnoxious person i know

`·.„.·´¯`··._.·ßΛßY P♡īS♡И`·.„.·´¯`··._.· says:

franki

`·.„.·´¯`··._.·ßΛßY P♡īS♡И`·.„.·´¯`··._.· says:

come onnnnn

ƒяαηκι ƒαямєя ωιℓℓ нανє нєя яєνєηgє ση ѕαιηт Jαмєѕ says:

alriiiite

ƒяαηκι ƒαямєя ωιℓℓ нανє нєя яєνєηgє ση ѕαιηт Jαмєѕ says:

let me redeem myself

ⓜⓡⓢ ⓣⓡⓐⓒⓔⓨ ⓟⓘⓣⓣ says:

how

ƒяαηκι ƒαямєя ωιℓℓ нανє нєя яєνєηgє ση ѕαιηт Jαмєѕ says:

fear not my sweet lil nerd

ƒяαηκι ƒαямєя ωιℓℓ нανє нєя яєνєηgє ση ѕαιηт Jαмєѕ says:

for ur gal francesca is bringing THE GOSS

`·.„.·´¯`··._.·ßΛßY P♡īS♡И`·.„.·´¯`··._.· says:

XD XD XD

`·.„.·´¯`··._.·ßΛßY P♡īS♡И`·.„.·´¯`··._.· says:

finally something I can get on board with

`·.„.·´¯`··._.·ßΛßY P♡īS♡И`·.„.·´¯`··._.· says:

what is it

ƒяαηκι ƒαямєя ωιℓℓ нανє нєя яєνєηgє ση ѕαιηт Jαмєѕ says:

ummmm not much tbh

ƒяαηκι ƒαямєя ωιℓℓ нανє нєя яєνєηgє ση ѕαιηт Jαмєѕ says:

actually not worth talking about

ⓜⓡⓢ ⓣⓡⓐⓒⓔⓨ ⓟⓘⓣⓣ says:

jesus franki just tell us

fяаηкι faямєя ωιℓℓ нaνє нєя яєνєηgє ση saιηт James **says:**

XD XD XD

fяаηкι faямєя ωιℓℓ нaνє нєя яєνєηgє ση saιηт James **says:**

you rly are no fun tonight T

fяаηкι faямєя ωιℓℓ нaνє нєя яєνєηgє ση saιηт James **says:**

sooooooo

`·.¸„·˙¯·.¸__.·ßΛßY P♡ĪS♡И`·.¸„·˙¯·.¸_.·ˉ **says:**

omg spill it

fяаηкι faямєя ωιℓℓ нaνє нєя яєνєηgє ση saιηт James **says:**

ok so

fяаηкι faямєя ωιℓℓ нaνє нєя яєνєηgє ση saιηт James **says:**

u kno i have PE on tue

ⓜⓡⓢ ⓣⓡⓐⓒⓔⓨ ⓟⓘⓣⓣ **says:**

ya

ⓜⓡⓢ ⓣⓡⓐⓒⓔⓨ ⓟⓘⓣⓣ **says:**

so

fяаηкι faямєя ωιℓℓ нaνє нєя яєνєηgє ση saιηт James **says:**

so moobs let his pet sit out again today

`·.¸„·˙¯·.¸__.·ßΛßY P♡ĪS♡И`·.¸„·˙¯·.¸_.·ˉ **says:**

moobs?????

`·.¸„·˙¯·.¸__.·ßΛßY P♡ĪS♡И`·.¸„·˙¯·.¸_.·ˉ **says:**

moobs pet????????

`·.¸„·˙¯·.¸__.·ßΛßY P♡ĪS♡И`·.¸„·˙¯·.¸_.·ˉ **says:**

O_____O

fяаηкι faямєя ωιℓℓ нaνє нєя яєνєηgє ση saιηт James **says:**

weird rite?

`·.¸„·˙¯·.¸__.·ßΛßY P♡ĪS♡И`·.¸„·˙¯·.¸_.·ˉ **says:**

hold the fucking phone

`·._.·˙¯˙·._.·BΛBY P♡ĪS♡И·._.·˙¯˙·._.·` **says:**

O_____O

`·._.·˙¯˙·._.·BΛBY P♡ĪS♡И·._.·˙¯˙·._.·` **says:**

moobs has a PET??????

ⓜⓡⓢ ⓣⓡⓐⓒⓔⓨ ⓟⓘⓣⓣ **says:**

never in my life

ƒяαηκι ƒαямєя ωιℓℓ ʜανє ʜєя яєνєηɡє ση ѕαιηт James **says:**

yep

ƒяαηκι ƒαямєя ωιℓℓ ʜανє ʜєя яєνєηɡє ση ѕαιηт James **says:**

man is the definition of lack of personality

ⓜⓡⓢ ⓣⓡⓐⓒⓔⓨ ⓟⓘⓣⓣ **says:**

lack of personality doesnt require a definition

ⓜⓡⓢ ⓣⓡⓐⓒⓔⓨ ⓟⓘⓣⓣ **says:**

its already a definition

ƒяαηκι ƒαямєя ωιℓℓ ʜανє ʜєя яєνєηɡє ση ѕαιηт James **says:**

u kno what i mean tho

ƒяαηκι ƒαямєя ωιℓℓ ʜανє ʜєя яєνєηɡє ση ѕαιηт James **says:**

man doesn't look capable of keeping a pet fish alive

`·._.·˙¯˙·._.·BΛBY P♡ĪS♡И·._.·˙¯˙·._.·` **says:**

tru XD

`·._.·˙¯˙·._.·BΛBY P♡ĪS♡И·._.·˙¯˙·._.·` **says:**

it's a girl right?

`·._.·˙¯˙·._.·BΛBY P♡ĪS♡И·._.·˙¯˙·._.·` **says:**

dunno if I can take any more news for tonite

ƒяαηκι ƒαямєя ωιℓℓ ʜανє ʜєя яєνєηɡє ση ѕαιηт James **says:**

correct

`·._.·˙¯˙·._.·BΛBY P♡ĪS♡И·._.·˙¯˙·._.·` **says:**

ugh poor gal

`·._,.·´¯`·._.·BABY P♡IS♡N`·._,.·´¯`·._.·` says:

do I know her?

ƒяαηκι ƒαямєя ωιℓℓ нανє нєя яєνєηgє ση sαιηт James says:

its ruth beadle

APPLES

Ruth
Now

Back at the flat, I lock the door and stretch out on the rug, between the coffee table and the sofa. I like it here. It's a place I have chosen. It feels safer than sitting on my side of the sofa; from here there's no risk of looking at the other side.

I am reading in the booklet about the Kübler-Ross stages of grief. There are five bullet points:

- Denial
- Anger
- Bargaining
- Depression
- Acceptance

They don't sound like a completely foreign notion. I must've studied them in college. But the memory feels very distant, as if I'm reading through old handwritten notes and can barely recognize them as my own. I haven't thought about the stages in a very long time: when a death occurs in the care home, the emotional aftermath isn't our responsibility. There are other professionals for that. We need to call in the doctor, confirm the time of death, clean up the bed, get the room nice and ready for the next patient. Life must follow death efficiently. You put your emotions behind you. There is no time for grieving when you're on the job.

I stare at the paragraphs on the page, breaking down each word into its two-line definition. I study them, attempting the kind of calculations that Neil would make. What do the words mean? What do they want from me? Accountants have lizard brains. That's what he used to say about his workaholic colleagues. But he kept tabs on things too. On us, evidently: he somehow figured out that ten years was sufficient.

Here's what I think: it doesn't take two perfect halves to make up a whole. There are many ways to cut up an apple. Throughout our relationship, I'd engineered myself to occupy as little space as possible so that he could be as large as he liked. He was always prodding the world as if it were a piece of fruit, seeking out that soft, yielding spot. I figured out early on that in the unit of us I was much less than an equal half. Perhaps it suited me, it took off the pressure. When we still went out with friends, I would joke that I was Neil's OQ – his 'Other Quarter'. He always took it personally.

'We are one and the same, Ruth. There are no secrets: we are safe inside the same skin.'

I think of that and the part of me that remembers what it's like to be a part of something splinters at the thought like raw apple. I never liked to think of neat parts with us, because the part of me that wasn't him always seemed a little frightening. So I haven't devised an emergency plan for myself – all I have is a handful of truisms I've picked up somewhere: from people, from TV. 'It'll be OK eventually.' 'You are very brave.' 'You do you, girl.' Occasionally, I have said these things to others, although it was always hard to get the tone right.

Neil has been my only partner: my only long-term, proper partner. There weren't many others before him and what use would it be to think about them now? You may find that grieving, the booklet says, is like crawling into a deep black pit where there is room for grievance alone. On the rug, my body braces for the smack of absence but it doesn't connect with the impact. I continue reading. So far, I would say, I have done everything by the book.

At first, of course, I was desperate. I felt I'd been cleaved down the middle, the moist pulp of me suddenly exposed. I knew I couldn't be out in public. I took time off work; I said I was ill and in many ways I was, or at least I behaved like it. I didn't eat, wash my hair, change my clothes. It was a relief that it all came so naturally. I cried, or I slept, or I clawed the bedding crying until I fell asleep. It was a black wet sea of a week.

And then it was time to go back to the care home. It was as if someone had flicked the switch back on. I pulled myself together, as they say – or at least I held it together – precariously, because simply presenting myself to the world required my full attention. It was exhausting. For days after I went back to work, I'd find myself standing at the foot of a patient's bed, in the afternoon light, and for a moment the hurt would fasten itself to my bones, threatening to push me to my knees. Often, my arms felt too heavy to lift. I look up at them, stretched out above my head: this feels like a memory.

According to the booklet, I should now be slap bang in the middle of my anger phase. But I don't feel angry, not at all. Could I be skipping this stage altogether? It's hard to be angry with someone when the thing they have done isn't something that was intended to hurt you, but a good thing they felt they owed to themselves. (Doesn't he have a right to be happy?) Should I even be allowed to be angry under these particular circumstances? (I miss him.) The booklet doesn't specify. Doesn't he have a right to be somewhere else, doing something else, with someone else?

But it's been ten years. Ten years. Jesus Christ. Three thousand five hundred and fifty-something days being a part of someone else's equation. Ten years enabling Neil's constant need for change. On a day-to-day basis, the list of the things I did for him was practically infinite. Over the last six months only:

The time he felt the seeds of a sustainable future lay in the consumption of kale crisps and I was the one who brought the cabbages home to desiccate in batches in the oven with olive oil spray and sea salt, like it said on the website he'd bookmarked. The bottom layer stuck to the tray like wallpaper, and the top was too crisp, verging on burnt. Neil laughed and didn't even try one. I chucked the tray out without bothering to clean it. I began collecting vouchers for Planet Organic. I didn't give up on him. I was good. I know I was good. I am good at being good to others. I accept that everyone has complex desires.

The time he read that Bikram Yoga offered the only really effective path to true clarity. He yearned for a steam room. We had a box bedroom, where I stored my clothes and magazines. So I got rid of them, buying white cushions and jasmine candles that he said would induce a meditative state. That Saturday, I spent the afternoon in my underwear in our sealed-up flat, the heating and the oven raging. I actually steamed some linen rags on a fucking pot on the stove and wrapped them around his head to provide him with the appropriate degree of heat and humidity.

Anger: I hunt for rage in my brain. I thought I had it, just a minute ago. But it's hard to recover that spark, lying here, with my limbs weighing down the carpet. I remember it searing through my brain, a blind white shock like the pain of a bone fracture, on the night he left. And then it was gone. In the aftermath, I couldn't sustain it.

Perhaps because life has resumed. I have kept at it. Two weeks, then three. I listen to the submarine thudding of my day-to-day. I do nothing but go to work, come back from work. I keep to the same path around the house, the desensitized neutral areas: the corridor, the bathroom mat, the hard spaces in front of the soft furniture. Floating in the bath for an hour, my body not touching the sides, mooring myself at the rickety dressing table, handling the hairbrush, the body creams, dabbing on foundation thicker than normal. Everything that is him is still here. I've just taught myself to ignore it. The booklet seems to think that's wrong. I carry on reading.

As an example we will apply the five stages to a small traumatic event some of us might have experienced: The Broken Mobile Phone! It's 15:10 and you are awaiting a very important phone call at 15:15. It's an interview for your dream job. All of a sudden, the screen on your mobile phone freezes, becoming unresponsive.

1. DENIAL – You quickly try to restart your phone, several times, trying any combination of buttons, until you manage to switch it off and on again. When the screen turns black, however, it doesn't come back on. You try several other things, nothing works.

2. ANGER – 'F**k you, phone! I should have got an upgrade!' Did you just throw your phone against the wall? Now the screen is cracked. It looks like you've really broken it for good. 'I hate these useless smart-phones! Smartphones are the ruin of this world!'

3. BARGAINING – It's 15:12: Realizing that you're really about to miss your call, you beg your phone to start again, 'Oh please, phone, start again, please please please. I'll get you serviced, I'll even buy you a new cover!'

4. DEPRESSION – It's 15:16. They've probably already called by now. You won't be considered for the pos-ition you've been dreaming of. This is it: you have lost the opportunity of a lifetime, all because of a stupid mobile phone.

5. ACCEPTANCE – 'OK, the phone is dead.' You have missed your call. You'd better get online and email the company. But before you do that, you must make sure to calm down, so that you can clearly explain your tech-nical difficulties and get your interview rescheduled.

The example depicted here is deliberately trivial: 'a micro-example', which demonstrates only a small part of the process we all go through several times a day. Grieving can be triggered by the smallest things: a dead car battery, a favourite dish dropped off a menu, a house move, a break-up, the loss of a pet . . .

Yes, but it's not the same as a fucking mobile phone, is it? It's got fuck all to do with it. I'm not fifteen years of age. I give the booklet a shake, stretch my arms out again, over my head, holding it up high. The key to a healthy recovery, it says, is in restoring one's routine. Keeping busy helps: you should feel blessed if you're working a practical job. I do; there's always something that needs doing, someone in need of help. But what about the holes in the texture? What about the nights, for example? The dreams.

1. Do not blame yourself for the things that cause you grief: any sudden change may trigger the grieving process and this is out of your control.

2. Recovery takes the time it takes: of course, a broken mobile phone will have less of a lasting impact than a serious traumatic event, but grieving time is not quantifiable.

3. Not everybody goes through the phases in order: some subjects jump between phases or go through the same cycle several times.

4. You're allowed to grieve.

Recovery takes the time it takes: I still have trouble sleeping. I'm a restless sleeper – but it was always that way with me. Nights are difficult but some things will always be difficult. The booklet agrees. My arms are feeling sore, my spine aches from lying here. I grasp the side of the couch and pull myself to my feet.

I know I have to retake possession of the flat, but I don't know where to start. I'm here, standing, the booklet in my right hand. I shuffle on the spot, like a character in a shooter videogame, paused by the player who wants to take a piss or make a cup of tea. Last year, Neil developed a soft spot for these games. The more gruesome the better, which seemed incongruous with his newly adopted spiritual lifestyle. The looping noise when he paused them irritated me so much that I'd bring the mug to him before he asked. ('Pretty sure that's not Buddhist,' I remember saying. 'Every man must reconcile himself with his most basic instincts. That's what Buddhism is all about, actually.')

I look around. I scan each open door in our small flat. Woollen throws on the sofa, the wheatgrass on the windowsill already going dry. Deflated cushions on the floor, mottled with incense ash, spice bottles fighting for space on the rack. The juice-maker bulging obscene and root-like from the darkened kitchen, its shadow spilling on to the living room floorboards. I've been burning his candles constantly but the house still retains its stale air.

The acronym TEAR was devised by Harvard professor J. William Worden to provide grief professionals with a clear outline of the steps that must be undertaken as part of therapy work:

Grief professionals. Is that me? We're the ones giving the booklets out: the tender authority.

T = To accept the reality of the loss

E = Experience the pain of loss

A = Adjust to the new environment without the lost object

R = Reinvest in the new reality

(J. William Worden, 'Four Tasks of Mourning', *Grief Counselling and Grief Therapy*)

TEAR. What a stupid acronym. For some reason I'm thinking about evidence; I have to remove the evidence. And why do I feel guilty?

'The only way to stop feeling guilty about something is to make a start at it' is a thing my mother used to say to me as a child. She's right. I always feel better when I get to work. 'You are practical-minded' is another thing my mother used to say, and it's true. If I hadn't wound up a nurse I would've liked to be a painter and decorator or an engineer, maybe a potter. I like fixing things. I make myself useful. It's just that out of all the practical professions, being a nurse seemed the most practical at the time. I enjoy most chores.

Player one, you may now make your first move. I drop the booklet on to the coffee table and pick up the remote control. On TV three presenters, one in a suit, two in red dresses, are raising money for charity. They introduce several acts: a familiar format. I turn the volume right down but leave the picture on the screen. I pull the Hoover out of its den in the corridor, its muzzle dragging behind us, a reluctant green herbivore. I switch it on. We start in the middle of the room; it's easy. Together we are predatory; we seek fluff, suck it up. It's satisfying teamwork. We claw our way under the sofa. The drone fills my mind. When

I'm done, I lean the Hoover against the wall. On TV a plump teenager is spinning an impressive number of plates on sticks, balancing them on each flat surface of his body: the top of one foot, a bent knee, shoulders, the palms of his hands, his ginger head. Patches of red crawl up his neck from the effort. They are a deep crimson colour and look painful. The audience quietly cheers. The door to the kitchen is open.

The difficult cabinet is the one to the right. It's where the corpse is hidden. It contains Neil's body weight in grain. I look at the jigsaw of stacked goods: variously sized bags of quinoa, chia, sesame and giant cous cous fill the gaps between the rectangular granola, vialone nano, sushi rice, basmati, barley. Have you ever wondered why they make the characters in cereal ads so over-excitable? They're compensating: this isn't even real food. It's so beige. I drag the big baking pot out of the bottom cupboard – the witchy, red one with the handles that was too cumbersome to cook with even when two of us lived here. I rip the tops off all the bags and boxes, and pour the grain inside. When I am done the pot is full and the cupboard is empty. I look into the mouth of the pot at the seeds, the sprouts, the clusters: so many different ways to be a unit.

In the Goldfish Bowl, we keep two glass pots on the reception counter. The large one is filled with pink and yellow sweets, the smaller one with one-pound coins. For one pound a pop, the visitors can guess how many sweets are in the large pot. We want to raise a thousand pounds for elderly people in need. Melissa's idea.

Not our elderly people of course, who pay three times as much per month; other elderly people. The small pot is half full, the other to the brim and sealed shut. The sweets at the bottom have begun to calcify and melt into one another. When I am bored at my desk I look at them and try to figure out which ones still count as singles, which as an agglomeration. Only Mona knows the secret number. Tradition dictates that only the most senior nurse should know. I swirl a finger in the grain, feel the dry seeds attach themselves to my fingers. What else?

The laundry. I put on the laundry this morning. It now pushes its face against the glass of the washing machine. Hanging the laundry is the worst job. I hate it because there's no immediate reward. I still have to wait for the clothes to dry, then collect them, iron them; all activities in themselves more satisfying than the act of hanging the laundry.

I could've got round to buying a new basket when he took away the old one. But the first week I didn't feel like it. Replacing it seemed too much of a definitive gesture and I didn't want to make any definitive gestures then. What use would we have for two laundry baskets if he came back? Then after a few more days I guess the idea of the laundry basket had become a sensitive thing in itself, which brought me right back to the night of the incident, in the quasi-arbitrary way in which daffodils are a reminder of spring, cinnamon of Christmas. The violence he used in slamming his books inside it.

If I leave the laundry in the machine any longer, I'll have to wash it again tomorrow. I open the round door. With my arms full of clothes, it takes me two minutes to make it to the drying rack in the living room. First, I drop a sock. When I bend over to pick it up pants fall from the other side of the bundle. I lean to the side to retrieve them and the rest of the pile tumbles from my arms on to the floor.

This is a moment in which I could very well sit down and cry, but I don't. I keep things practical.

Player one, you may now make your next move. I breathe deeply and use my next life. I pick up the clothes. I resume the action.

The t-shirts go up easily, so do the vests, the shirts just need a quick shake. Pairing up socks is challenging. It requires some degree of attention but not my full attention. It belongs to the group of mid-level intellectual activities that are particularly tricky in this state, the kind of actions I've been trying to avoid. I can feel my mind beginning to think. I look over at the TV still running on mute. The talent show has ended, cutting seamlessly to a nature documentary. There are lions and cats filmed in slow motion as they jump – predators – but then the camera unexpectedly cuts to images of baby birds and ducklings, their down yellow and heartbreaking. There is something soft in my hands: one of Neil's cashmere socks. It was white and expensive. Now it's tiny and grey. Still soft.

Should I try to find the number for the commune? It is the middle of the night. Still, Neil hates mismatched socks, so he might be grateful. Or he might say it's just like me; I couldn't leave him alone for a minute. It's only been three weeks. Barely. Did he even take the other sock with him? And if he did, does it look anything like this burnt, solitary one? Did he condemn it to the same destiny? Or is the other sock hiding somewhere else in the flat? Have I lost it, dropped it somewhere I can't remember? Did I shrink it? Is it my fault? What would I say on the phone?

'Hello, I'd like to speak to Neil Pratchett.'

'What is your full name, madam, and what is the reason for your call?'

They would sound suspicious, like I was trying to get through to a prison ward. I bet they worry that calls from the external world will steer their disciples from their path. I would never do that. I respect his wishes. I have respect for us both.

'I'm just trying to return a sock.'

Maybe they too have rules about footwear, like prisons. No shoelaces, no steel toes, no leather. No leather for sure. Is cashmere even vegan? I'm sure I've read somewhere it's made by caterpillars. Insects are animals too. You should always feed sugared water to a troubled bee. Can an ant be called an ant, when it's on its own, or does it only ever exist as part of an anthill? A part of a whole. And this sock is so alone and so soft and is breaking my fucking heart in two. I throw it in the non-recyclable waste bin.

I'd like to live somewhere where socks, at least, come in couples.

That night, I sleep a dreamless sleep.

The next morning, at dawn, I lift the lid of the pot. I walk to work instead of taking public transport, my pockets heavy, my hands sunk deep inside. Every few steps I pull my fist out, unfold it rapidly. I leave a trail for the small birds of London. Quinoa, vialone and chia. Soon, the birds will eat up the seeds.

I'll have to find my own way back home.

SUGAR

Neil

The Night After the Break-up

For the first time in ten years I am living alone and I want clarity, which I could never achieve in Ruth's presence. But even as I lie here, on this MDF bed, not quite the commune in Cornwall, but a flat near my office, between the four bare walls of my new room, Ruth inhabits my mind. That is the place where she first took up lodgings. In the beginning, before I had even met her.

In the summer of 2005 I moved out of my mother's house again and got a job in a travel agency. It was the sort of place where everything was on display: the holiday deals in the window, the bottles of Perrier in the microfridges lined up beneath the main counter, the employees. Those were the years before everything moved online: Skyscanner had one paid employee, probably working out of some shithole student flat in Edinburgh; lastminute.com was cutting its losses by going into third-party acquisition; Airbnb was just a glint in the eye of some San Franciscan hippie entrepreneur. Good middle-class mothers still taught good little middle-class girls that sleeping on a stranger's couch was a sure way to get oneself in trouble, regardless of how many stars someone had on CouchSurfing. In those years, travel agencies still made a profit with a younger crowd.

To attract these people, though, agencies needed us: the travel agents. Bait for the corporate thrill-seeker, making it happen for the not-so-adventurous student travelling to Thailand on a shoestring. Sleek, young, well dressed (in a non-threatening way, of course), we sat at parallel desks facing the street, encouraged by the management, if not to straight up walk out front to engage customers in direct conversation, then surely to make the best of our good looks. Through the glass pane, we smiled at anyone who looked even vaguely in our direction. But though the window was regularly refurbished (verdant plastic palm leaves on a bed of real sand as a backdrop for the summer deals to exotic beach destinations, colourful cardboard reproductions of the Kremlin on a bed of polystyrene snow for the winter deals to European capitals) and my colleagues and I made a fine smiling army of mannequins, business was slow that particular summer. Crushingly slow. I spent most days greasing up my side parting by running my fingers through it, bored to death, gazing out of the window like a sulky teenager. Then, somewhat unexpectedly, though I had been walking past its gates for three months, the nursing college across the street reopened for the autumn term.

I remember the very first time I saw her, the day Ruth came into focus in my life. It is so strange that this was over a decade ago: I can feel how I felt for her then even though

I feel none of it now. Maybe she joined the college later in the academic year or maybe it took a while for me to pick her out of the swarm; Ruth is incredibly talented at blending in. It was in the middle of winter, close to Christmas. I watched her through the glitter frost on the glass pane: a little thing in a white smock and no coat. She wore a large scarf – a misshapen, handmade wrap – and kept her fingers knitted into the folds to fasten it at the chest. She looked cold, all pinks and blues and whites, and very small, like a winter flower. A late bloomer, I thought, and I laughed at my own joke. (I tried to keep myself in good spirits. No one I worked with had a sense of humour.) The girl swiped herself through the gates of the ugly grey block of student halls beside the university and then disappeared inside and that was it.

From then on I saw her exactly four times a day, all during work hours. Once in the morning on her way to lectures. Once around lunchtime, on her way back to her student halls. Once on her way into Tesco. Once on her way out from Tesco. The regularity of those outings immediately struck a chord. Here was this small, clueless thing ploughing through life, while all around her two hundred young nurses spent most of their time idling, sneaking out to smoke outside the school gates, applying make-up in hand-held mirrors while walking to the lecture hall, skipping seminars to hang out with boys behind the chemistry department.

She alone had a timetable to stave off the chaos. She went about her tasks definitively, easily, like she'd been doing this for years, even though she must only just have moved out of her parents' house. She looked so young. Yet her behaviour resonated with me like a shared fate:

week-a-page diaries and errands and long hours sitting behind desks with one key difference: what appeared to suit her nature so perfectly made me feel trapped.

I was making myself sick with the life I was living. There was no excitement whatsoever in it. But I did nothing to change it: I hated my life, yet I kept at it. There I was, too: obligatory lunch break at one for one unpaid hour exactly, eating a three-pound meal deal in my sticky leather chair, pinned behind my desk like a bug in a glass case. I despised my colleagues and I despised my life, but this wasn't because I despised myself. Quite the opposite: I knew my own value, which made me angry, but I didn't know what to do with this anger. I had nowhere to put it. I was prone to internal fits of rage, in which I envisioned myself, machete in hand, hacking through those stupid window decorations and into my fellow bots, as a collective punishment for our collective surrender. In my frustration, in my madness, the girl's serene compliance to her schedule reached out to me. It lit a spark of hope at a time when I needed it desperately. Her tightly regulated routine struck me as necessary: not a default response to lack of stimuli or a dull inner life, but a deliberate decision.

Survival: she had it down. She was born for it. It wasn't hard to imagine her as a small child, paying the same undivided attention to each action in her day, slotting wooden shapes into their correct places or directing a plastic spoon to her own mouth. As is the case, sometimes, with young children, she had the air of the expert about her, yet no pretension, and this was simply because she excelled at being normal. She was better at it than most members of human society. I could tell. Her normal life, unlike mine, unequivocally had meaning. She had, I realized, a long-term plan.

It took me days to work out how I felt. Then, one day, I finally got it. I was jealous. And a little aroused. The two feelings added up to one nauseatingly intense, physical sensation, which I eventually had to admit was desire.

I began keeping track of her movements. I quickly realized that her schedule never changed: 9 a.m., 2 p.m., 4 p.m., 4:30 p.m. Soon, my observations became more detailed as I grew hungry to discover more. She always wore the same scarf; a lucky charm, I assumed: a token of someone's affection – her mother's, I thought – that she'd packed to take to college. And later, as the weather grew harsher, a pale woollen coat joined the scarf, and yet she always kept her fingers interlocked in the thick cable pattern, even when there wasn't a wind. It seemed to me she was protecting herself from the world.

In the mornings, she carried a drawstring backpack, the kind you get free at summer camps or in a sports shop, a simple rectangle of fabric with rope straps that sawed into the fabric of her clothes at the armpits. In the afternoon, she carried a white netted shopping bag. This was well before environmental concerns became a fashionable conversational centrepiece; only old ladies carried reusable bags and no one in Tesco would have guilt-tripped you for not bringing your own. In any case, she did; religiously. Always a single, string bag hanging from the nook of her arm; she never seemed to need a big shop. She let the bag swing in an unselfconscious sort of way, like an old lady would. I liked that. She looked like she was reusing her bag because it made sense financially, or simply because it was less likely to split, or because her mother had told her so, and had done so herself before her, like her grandmother before that and so on and so forth through generations of small birdlike ladies shopping for groceries. I never got the impression that in carrying the bag she was making a statement. It was a practical object, a bag with nothing special about it. Except that it was see-through.

I wasn't able to make out the objects from my workplace. I shouldn't have had a clue. But she bought the same things every week. So day by day, week by week, helped by the fact that the small Tesco Metro where I myself bought lunch held a very limited selection of items, I began to piece together the life of this tiny apprentice nurse who lived across the road. I gained an intimate access to her private world. But I still don't know what took her so long in the shop every day. She was only getting a few things at a time.

On Mondays she bought a pint of milk (skimmed, I could tell by the red lid). She bought one on Wednesdays and Fridays too. Mondays, she also bought a dozen eggs, which would last for a week. Twice a week, on Tuesdays and Thursdays, she bought a large tub of fat-free yoghurt, supermarket own brand. And a small box of teabags, once a week. After a few weeks, greedy for more intimate details, I began looking for less frequent items. I was eager to spot something more specific, something that would help me access a deeper layer of her personality: shampoo, seasonal flowers, a frozen pizza as a reward after an exam, tampons. I knew from the shelves in Tesco, and from previous girl-friends, that there were different types for different flows. I was curious to know what hers was like: purple for light, yellow for normal, green for heavy. She never bought any, which was in a way reassuring, because it meant that she must buy them in bulk. To preserve her modesty, I supposed. It made sense to me, with what I knew of her. I liked

57

that she must have been planning for life's little inconveniences well in advance. She seemed to buy a lot of sugar: a 500g packet on Mondays, Wednesdays and Fridays. Tate & Lyle, granulated, the two-tone pack, white and light blue.

Once I had a sense of what made up her month-long plan of purchases, I began to draw connections between one item and another. At this point I was detailing her shopping on paper: it had proved too hard to connect the dots in my mind.

I guess I had some notion, even back then, only a few weeks in, that I was becoming a bit obsessed with this girl. But I couldn't help it. I was too bored. It was too addictive. I wasn't hurting anyone, was I?

The women around me, women I worked with, women I worked for, had started to look increasingly tired, the way of old cars, rather than people. They'd lost their sparkle. It'd been a long time since any female had piqued my interest even slightly. They all seemed so boring, so predictable. Stick a curious man in a room full of travel posters and he's bound to be travelling in his mind at the very least.

It seemed to me that rather than buying ready-to-eat foods she was purchasing ingredients. But what was she eating, exactly? Not much at all, I know that now. That wasn't the best year in Ruth's life. She doesn't like to talk about it. But back then it seemed to me like a wholesome way to shop, and I liked that, though I couldn't for the life of me figure out what the hell she was making with all those eggs and all that sugar. Baking cakes? But I never saw her purchase any kind of flour. I looked up some recipes online and thought it might be meringues, but could she be living off meringues? There was something charming about that idea. I pictured her whipping up clouds of raw egg whites and sugar, blending plain milkshakes: she survived uniquely on angel food. I thought that suited her. I pictured her eating under her desk in class or with her knees up on the fireproof chair in her student room, still wearing her short white smock. Or sprawled out on her bed in her white underwear. Always in white. No one wore their uniform on the way into college or for any longer than was strictly necessary, except for her. I always saw her dressed in white. The first thing the other nurses did, when lectures were over, was unbutton the smock in a single quick fire of snap buttons, ball it up, and stuff it down their backpacks. I began toying with the idea that maybe she had nothing else to wear, maybe she was very poor. Maybe, just maybe, she wasn't wearing anything else. I imagined how her skin hidden underneath must've matched her clothing. Do you get the picture now? She was so clean. So devoted. An angel.

I got away with writing my lists for about three months, and I thought I was being subtle, but eventually my colleagues noticed that something was going on. A girl called Aimee who sat at the next desk watched my every move. She was always trying to lure me to after-work drinks, pursuing me passive-aggressively with endless post-its and gifted soy lattes. I had renamed her 'the Itch' because of the psoriasis on her elbows, which tarnished her otherwise tanned arms. Other than that, there was nothing noteworthy about her, nothing much that registered as human. She had no sense of humour. She wasn't attractive, not even for the quick fuck she'd made clear she was very much available for. Perhaps fucking Aimee was exactly what I needed to do to stave off my obsession with the girl. Thing was, I didn't *want* to stave off my obsession and perhaps that was part of the problem.

I had been getting worse. Writing the lists had become frustrating, because her shopping never changed. And I couldn't think of any other way to get close to her. Reaching out in a conventional way was out of the question. It was too dangerous. I had been so tense for so long without being able to find a release. I was already way too involved. I worried I wouldn't be able to control myself if I stopped the girl in the street. The thought of just touching her arm to draw her attention made my heart throb painfully in my chest. I wanted to run out as she passed, grab her face in my hands and plant a kiss on her little plum of a mouth. Bite down on it. This feeling was alarming, yet it was the best part of my day. When she wasn't around I was so depressed that I could barely function. Often, while on the phone, I let the line go slack and only realized when I heard the continuous buzzing tone that the person on the other end had hung up on me. It was only a matter of time before the big boss called me in for a disciplinary meeting.

Mrs Hewlett was the agency manager. She was always well dressed, with a flair for polka-dot dresses. She had a mahogany-coloured bob and a flamboyant manicure that changed colour every week. She wasn't averse to giving employees, girls and boys alike, a friendly ruffle on the head when business was good. She and the decent pay were the main reasons I'd stayed in the job.

Mrs Hewlett spent most of her day buried in the back office. It was an uncanny sort of through-the-looking-glass realm, where everything about the agency was inverted: order into mess, friendly composure into complicit friendliness, frosted glass into moth-eaten upholstery scattered with biscuit crumbs. The first time I'd been in there, for my interview, I'd discovered a furry boiled sweet in the lining of the armchair.

I'd barely been in the office since, so imagine my surprise when, out of the blue, I received a call on the internal phone and had to weasel my way between the towers of Colourful Cruises and Wah-Wah-Waikiki, to sit down in front of Mrs Hewlett's desk. She suggested she'd called me in because she was concerned. I immediately fell for it, which goes to show, I suppose, how effective her strategy was. She asked me if I'd been OK lately.

She said, 'Neil, you got us so used to such great customer service, this agency really wouldn't be the same without you, and your enthusiasm, and charm, and warmth –' blah blah blah '– but you see, lately, Neil, I couldn't help but notice how your head seems to be somewhere else, and you've been acting somewhat out of character, and I'm worried, really worried that something might be up with you. Is everything OK at home? What's up, Neil? You know we're here for you, anything you need just talk to us. I know you love this job.'

Her kindness poured over me like molasses and I was quickly smothered by it. I couldn't open my mouth to say anything. I panicked. I didn't want to lose this job. But how could I explain to Mrs Hewlett that she couldn't fire me, because – and it was the only convincing reason I could summon, with an urgency that horrified me – 'How would I be able to see my girl?'

'I'm perfectly fine,' I blurted. I had to say something, anything to switch the subject, to make her like me again, to make sure she would never consider getting rid of me.

But what? 'I've been thinking . . . of taking you up on the European ushering job,' I said. 'I guess I needed some time to turn the idea over in my head. I didn't want to accept the job unless I knew I wasn't going to let you down.'

Mrs Hewlett gave me one of her wide smiles, her cheeks contracting, filling the sides of her mouth with flesh.

'Oh, but how delightful! Letting me down? Don't be silly! I'll get your name on the list.' And just like that I was off the hook.

The European Ushering Partnership was a new scheme that the agency had devised to boost sales. The idea was simple: we contacted universities across Europe and checked for summer vacancies in their student halls and residences. We then rented out the rooms in blocks and sublet them to our own travelling students for a higher fee, which still worked out cheaper by the week than most hostels. Everyone was happy: the universities were able to make revenue on rooms that would otherwise be unoccupied. The students got safe, serviced lodgings in a central location for a very reasonable price. And of course, we crammed up to three or four students in a single occupancy room on bunk beds that were easily removed at the end of the summer period and made the best profit.

There was one downside. One of us had to work on location at all times. We didn't trust them out there on their own. We helped the kids to settle in and made sure that check-in and check-out duties were performed efficiently. To begin with, everyone was enthusiastic: the month abroad was a nice change of scene that came with a healthy extratime salary bump. Soon, though, subscription rates started dropping: two years down the line Mrs Hewlett was nervous she wouldn't find any takers. No one discussed their experiences, but the general vibe strongly indicated that the job wasn't exactly all fun and no business. I kept a low profile when the subject came up, trying to give off a shy vibe, as if I was too inexperienced to take up such a responsibility. But I'd just *volunteered*.

Which meant I was going to spend a good chunk of my summer cleaning up freshers' vomit somewhere on the continent and I only had myself to blame.

Except, of course, I'm the luckiest motherfucker of all. Six days later, on a Saturday morning, as I was sitting there, sourly contemplating my future, a small blonde student, sweetly buck-toothed, all curves and freckles, came into the agency. I recognized her, vaguely, as one of the students from across the road, though she bore no relation to my girl.

This girl came up to my desk, both because it was the only one free – everyone else was proficiently engaged in phone calls and talking to customers – and also, I suspected, because she was wanting to talk to me specifically. She made eye contact with me as she came through the door. I asked her name. She said Alanna and giggled for no apparent reason. Aimee turned to look at me, phone nestled between her ear and her shoulder. Already I found Alanna a bit irritating. I dislike women who attract a lot of attention. You know girls that age, they're like rodents, they get excited about nothing. They have that franticness about them. They fall for people that don't even exist. Little critters. Nothing like *my* girl. Nothing to link this strawberry-blonde girl to my girl at all. This one was so common, so cheery, so eager to please. She opened her clean pink mouth

63

and said, 'I'm looking to book a student deal for a double room in Rome, two people, two weeks.'

You know when you just know? I just knew. Easy to say so now, knowing what happened later, but I really did know. I felt it in my bones. This happens to me sometimes – I'm quite perceptive. Maybe it was because she said it was for two people, and there was no one with her, or maybe it was that she kept repeating the number two (two weeks two people two weeks two people two weeks two people). And so I said, in a professional tone, that yes, there were some rooms still available in Rome, although not many, not many at all, better book sooner rather than later as they were going fast, and guess what, she was very lucky (I winked at her) to have yours truly as a travel guide.

Which I didn't know for sure. I hadn't been assigned a location yet. But when I saw her chipmunk face light up I sure as hell knew I'd square up to Mrs Hewlett if she tried to stop me from going. I'd fucking kill her to go. And: all roads lead to Rome. And: veni vidi vici. That made me laugh. I was so witty.

'Who are you sharing your room with, a friend or your partner?' I asked, which wasn't strictly necessary and actually quite inappropriate, but the girl didn't know that. I asked because I was allowed to: I could do anything then, I was in charge. It was my fucking office!

'A friend,' she said, and I knew, I just knew, I was sure of it.

And I was right because the next Monday my girl is sat at my desk filling in the relevant forms as her friend Alanna chews my fucking ear off about how her friend Tammy or Franny, whatever, had been to Rome before and took a photo with the centurions in front of the Colosseum and my heart is stuck right in my throat because all I want to do is to look at her, finally, watch *my* girl, up close, all the little things about her finally in perfect focus — her hands and her eyelashes and the pores on her nose — but instead I focus on projecting my best reliable smile because I didn't want to spoil it and I watch as my girl is quiet and her hands shake slightly as she writes out her name on the dotted line all in capital letters:

R–U–T–H–B–E–A–D–L–E

I sign my name on the line right below.

DEO

Fourteen Years Earlier

`˙·.„·˝¯··._.·ßΛßY P♡ĪS♡И·˙.„·˝¯··._.·` says:

beadle?

`˙·.„·˝¯··._.·ßΛßY P♡ĪS♡И·˙.„·˝¯··._.·` says:

who's beadle?

ғяαηκι ғαямєя ωιℓℓ нαⱴє нєя яєⱴєηgє ση sαιηт Ͻαмєs says:

ruth beadle

`˙·.„·˝¯··._.·ßΛßY P♡ĪS♡И·˙.„·˝¯··._.·` says:

which ruth is this?

`˙·.„·˝¯··._.·ßΛßY P♡ĪS♡И·˙.„·˝¯··._.·` says:

there's like 3 ruths in our year

`˙·.„·˝¯··._.·ßΛßY P♡ĪS♡И·˙.„·˝¯··._.·` says:

do u kno who she is trace?

ⓜⓡⓢ ⓣⓡⓐⓒⓔⓨ ⓟⓘⓣⓣ says:

the skinny one with the eyes

`˙·.„·˝¯··._.·ßΛßY P♡ĪS♡И·˙.„·˝¯··._.·` says:

the eyes?

mⓡⓢ ⓣⓡⓐⓒⓔⓨ ⓟⓘⓣⓣ says:

i don't really know her

mⓡⓢ ⓣⓡⓐⓒⓔⓨ ⓟⓘⓣⓣ says:

ya

mⓡⓢ ⓣⓡⓐⓒⓔⓨ ⓟⓘⓣⓣ says:

u know who i mean alanna?

`·.„.·¨¯·..„.·ßΛßY Ṗ♡ĪS♡И`·.„.·¨¯·..„.·ˈ says:

fck I dont think I do

ƒяαηкι ƒαямεя ωιℓℓ нανε нεя яεvεηgε ση sαιηт ꝺαмεs says:

yea man her eyes are fucking creepy

ƒяαηкι ƒαямεя ωιℓℓ нανε нεя яεvεηgε ση sαιηт ꝺαмεs says:

girl is a certified freak imho

`·.„.·¨¯·..„.·ßΛßY Ṗ♡ĪS♡И`·.„.·¨¯·..„.·ˈ says:

who's this ruth with the eyes tho?????

`·.„.·¨¯·..„.·ßΛßY Ṗ♡ĪS♡И`·.„.·¨¯·..„.·ˈ says:

I cant believe ive missed out on a certified freak :''''''(((((((((

mⓡⓢ ⓣⓡⓐⓒⓔⓨ ⓟⓘⓣⓣ says:

i mean i wouldn't say

ƒяαηкι ƒαямεя ωιℓℓ нανε нεя яεvεηgε ση sαιηт ꝺαмεs says:

if she aint a freak then idk who is

ƒяαηкι ƒαямεя ωιℓℓ нανε нεя яεvεηgε ση sαιηт ꝺαмεs says:

genuinely gives me the creeps

ƒяαηкι ƒαямεя ωιℓℓ нανε нεя яεvεηgε ση sαιηт ꝺαмεs says:

you noticed this T dont lie

67

`·._.·´¯`·._.·ßΛßY P♡ĪS♡И`·._.·´¯`·._.·` **says:**

okay 1 sec

`·._.·´¯`·._.·ßΛßY P♡ĪS♡И`·._.·´¯`·._.·` **says:**

lets get this straight

`·._.·´¯`·._.·ßΛßY P♡ĪS♡И`·._.·´¯`·._.·` **says:**

who *is* this girl

`·._.·´¯`·._.·ßΛßY P♡ĪS♡И`·._.·´¯`·._.·` **says:**

what does she look like

`·._.·´¯`·._.·ßΛßY P♡ĪS♡И`·._.·´¯`·._.·` **says:**

is she in the d&d club like

`·._.·´¯`·._.·ßΛßY P♡ĪS♡И`·._.·´¯`·._.·` **says:**

does she have terrible BO?

`·._.·´¯`·._.·ßΛßY P♡ĪS♡И`·._.·´¯`·._.·` **says:**

does she have a glass eye and a walking stick

`·._.·´¯`·._.·ßΛßY P♡ĪS♡И`·._.·´¯`·._.·` **says:**

XD XD

ⓜⓡⓢ ⓣⓡⓐⓒⓔⓨ ⓟⓘⓣⓣ **says:**

she's like

ⓜⓡⓢ ⓣⓡⓐⓒⓔⓨ ⓟⓘⓣⓣ **says:**

seriously non-descript lan

ⓜⓡⓢ ⓣⓡⓐⓒⓔⓨ ⓟⓘⓣⓣ **says:**

doesnt surprise me u dont remember

fяaηκι faямeя ωιℓℓ нaνe нeя яeνeηɡe oη saιηt ɹameꜱ **says:**

yeah super insignificant

`·._.·´¯`·._.·ßΛßY P♡ĪS♡И`·._.·´¯`·._.·` **says:**

makes sense for moobs

`·._.·´¯`·._.·ßΛßY P♡ĪS♡И`·._.·´¯`·._.·` **says:**

but how

˙·.¸.·´¯`·.¸.·ฺBΛβY P♡ĪS♡И´·.¸.·´¯`·.¸.· says:

how is she a certified freak?

˙·.¸.·´¯`·.¸.·ฺBΛβY P♡ĪS♡И´·.¸.·´¯`·.¸.· says:

lets not jump the gun thank u v much girls

˙·.¸.·´¯`·.¸.·ฺBΛβY P♡ĪS♡И´·.¸.·´¯`·.¸.· says:

u have to tick a few boxes to earn that status u kno? :P

ƒяαηκι ƒαямєя ωιℓℓ нαvє нєя яєvєηgє ση sαιηт ɿαмєs says:

ya

ƒяαηκι ƒαямєя ωιℓℓ нαvє нєя яєvєηgє ση sαιηт ɿαмєs says:

u kno sum people just look at you in a creepy way

ⓜⓡⓢ ⓣⓡⓐⓒⓔⓨ ⓟⓘⓣⓣ says:

ya

ⓜⓡⓢ ⓣⓡⓐⓒⓔⓨ ⓟⓘⓣⓣ says:

proper sociopath vibe

ⓜⓡⓢ ⓣⓡⓐⓒⓔⓨ ⓟⓘⓣⓣ says:

I agree

˙·.¸.·´¯`·.¸.·ฺBΛβY P♡ĪS♡И´·.¸.·´¯`·.¸.· says:

jesus

ƒяαηκι ƒαямєя ωιℓℓ нαvє нєя яєvєηgє ση sαιηт ɿαмєs says:

freaks me out like

ⓜⓡⓢ ⓣⓡⓐⓒⓔⓨ ⓟⓘⓣⓣ says:

like she's always thinking

ⓜⓡⓢ ⓣⓡⓐⓒⓔⓨ ⓟⓘⓣⓣ says:

or something

ƒяαηкι ƒаямея ωιℓℓ нανє нея яεvεηgε ση ѕαιηт ɹames says:

watchin u

мɾѕ тɾасеy ριττ says:

like she knows something you don't

мɾѕ тɾасеy ριττ says:

or something

˙·.¸¸.·´¯`·.¸.·ßΛßY Ṗ♡ĪṢ♡И`·.¸.·´¯`·.¸.· says:

eugh

ƒяαηкι ƒаямея ωιℓℓ нανє нея яεvεηgε ση ѕαιηт ɹames says:

plans ur murder

˙·.¸¸.·´¯`·.¸.·ßΛßY Ṗ♡ĪṢ♡И`·.¸.·´¯`·.¸.· says:

XD XD XD XD

ƒяαηкι ƒаямея ωιℓℓ нανє нея яεvεηgε ση ѕαιηт ɹames says:

so moobs lets her sit out all the time

ƒяαηкι ƒаямея ωιℓℓ нανє нея яεvεηgε ση ѕαιηт ɹames says:

5 weeks in a row now

˙·.¸¸.·´¯`·.¸.·ßΛßY Ṗ♡ĪṢ♡И`·.¸.·´¯`·.¸.· says:

wtffff seriously????????

мɾѕ тɾасеy ριττ says:

that's not like mr alpin?

˙·.¸¸.·´¯`·.¸.·ßΛßY Ṗ♡ĪṢ♡И`·.¸.·´¯`·.¸.· says:

maybe shes srsly sick or something

˙·.¸¸.·´¯`·.¸.·ßΛßY Ṗ♡ĪṢ♡И`·.¸.·´¯`·.¸.· says:

dont u think??

`·._,·´¯`·._·ßΛßY P♡ΪS♡И`·._,·´¯`·._·` **says:**

its not like moobs lets you off if it isnt something serious

`·._,·´¯`·._·ßΛßY P♡ΪS♡И`·._,·´¯`·._·` **says:**

never worked for me in the past did it

ⓜⓡⓢ ⓣⓡⓐⓒⓔⓨ ⓟⓘⓣⓣ **says:**

ya remember that time u asked to sit out bc u were going to the movies with alfie

`·._,·´¯`·._·ßΛßY P♡ΪS♡И`·._,·´¯`·._·` **says:**

omg trace don't even

`·._,·´¯`·._·ßΛßY P♡ΪS♡И`·._,·´¯`·._·` **says:**

that was an evening of absolute disaster

ꜰʀaηκι ꜰaямɛя ωιℓℓ нaⱴɛ нɛя яɛⱴɛηɢɛ ση saιηт ᴣaмɛs **says:**

dude

ꜰʀaηκι ꜰaямɛя ωιℓℓ нaⱴɛ нɛя яɛⱴɛηɢɛ ση saιηт ᴣaмɛs **says:**

unfair to blame it on moobs for chambers floppy willy

ꜰʀaηκι ꜰaямɛя ωιℓℓ нaⱴɛ нɛя яɛⱴɛηɢɛ ση saιηт ᴣaмɛs **says:**

imho

`·._,·´¯`·._·ßΛßY P♡ΪS♡И`·._,·´¯`·._·` **says:**

ya well maybe if i hadnt turned up stinking of lynx safari

`·._,·´¯`·._·ßΛßY P♡ΪS♡И`·._,·´¯`·._·` **says:**

from french showering the fuck out of my clothes after PE

`·._,·´¯`·._·ßΛßY P♡ΪS♡И`·._,·´¯`·._·` **says:**

his willy wouldn't have been so floppy

ғяаηκι ғаямєя ωιℓℓ наνє нєя яєνєηgє ση ѕаιηт ɔамєѕ **says:**

guess its one of those mysteries we will never have an answer for

ғяаηκι ғаямєя ωιℓℓ наνє нєя яєνєηgє ση ѕаιηт ɔамєѕ **says:**

tho i maintain no amount of macho bodyspray will turn a real man off the smell of pussy

˙·.„·¯¨˙¯¨·.„·ßΛßY P♡ĪS♡И·.„·¯¨˙¯¨·.„·˙ **says:**

franki ur real fucking gross u kno :D

ғяаηκι ғаямєя ωιℓℓ наνє нєя яєνєηgє ση ѕаιηт ɔамєѕ **says:**

maybe baby

ғяаηκι ғаямєя ωιℓℓ наνє нєя яєνєηgє ση ѕаιηт ɔамєѕ **says:**

but dont u kno I speak the truth

ⓜⓡⓢ ⓣⓡⓐⓒⓔⓨ ⓟⓘⓣⓣ **says:**

what i want to know is why mr alpin is suddenly making exceptions

ⓜⓡⓢ ⓣⓡⓐⓒⓔⓨ ⓟⓘⓣⓣ **says:**

its not fair

˙·.„·¯¨˙¯¨·.„·ßΛßY P♡ĪS♡И·.„·¯¨˙¯¨·.„·˙ **says:**

ya not fair!!

ⓜⓡⓢ ⓣⓡⓐⓒⓔⓨ ⓟⓘⓣⓣ **says:**

i had to play in the volleyball tournament that time

ⓜⓡⓢ ⓣⓡⓐⓒⓔⓨ ⓟⓘⓣⓣ **says:**

i kept saying I wasn't okay and then the next day i came down with mumps

ⓜⓡⓢ ⓣⓡⓐⓒⓔⓨ ⓟⓘⓣⓣ **says:**

remember that?

`·.˛·˝ ¯·._.·ʙʌʙʏ ᴘ♡ɪꜱ♡ɴ·.˛·˝ ¯·._.·` says:

u did!

`·.˛·˝ ¯·._.·ʙʌʙʏ ᴘ♡ɪꜱ♡ɴ·.˛·˝ ¯·._.·` says:

u looked like such an adorable little bunny

ⓜⓡⓢ ⓣⓡⓐⓒⓔⓨ ⓟⓘⓣⓣ says:

it was awful

ⓜⓡⓢ ⓣⓡⓐⓒⓔⓨ ⓟⓘⓣⓣ says:

me and charlie couldn't see each other for three whole weeks

ꜰяaηκɪ ꜰaямєя ωɪℓℓ нavє нєя яєvєηgє oη saɪηт ᴊaмєꜱ says:

that cos u bought that shit about him having to get his balls chopped off if he caught it

ⓜⓡⓢ ⓣⓡⓐⓒⓔⓨ ⓟⓘⓣⓣ says:

it's true though

ⓜⓡⓢ ⓣⓡⓐⓒⓔⓨ ⓟⓘⓣⓣ says:

mumps can affect fertility in a man

ꜰяaηκɪ ꜰaямєя ωɪℓℓ нavє нєя яєvєηgє oη saɪηт ᴊaмєꜱ says:

god forbid you may one day . . .

ꜰяaηκɪ ꜰaямєя ωɪℓℓ нavє нєя яєvєηgє oη saɪηт ᴊaмєꜱ says:

. . . .

ꜰяaηκɪ ꜰaямєя ωɪℓℓ нavє нєя яєvєηgє oη saɪηт ᴊaмєꜱ says:

whenever you're finally READY of course

ꜰяaηκɪ ꜰaямєя ωɪℓℓ нavє нєя яєvєηgє oη saɪηт ᴊaмєꜱ says:

XDDDDD

ⓜⓡⓢ ⓣⓡⓐⓒⓔⓨ ⓟⓘⓣⓣ **says:**

fuck off franki

`·.„·´¨`·._.·ßΛßY Ṗ♡ĪS♡И`·.„·´¨`·._.·´ **says:**

yeah franki •

`·.„·´¨`·._.·ßΛßY Ṗ♡ĪS♡И`·.„·´¨`·._.·´ **says:**

too much is too much

ƒяαηκι ƒαямєя ωιℓℓ нανє нєя яєνєηgє ση saιηt ʒaмєs **says:**

yeah all right

ƒяαηκι ƒαямєя ωιℓℓ нανє нєя яєνєηgє ση saιηt ʒaмєs **says:**

sorry dude

ƒяαηκι ƒαямєя ωιℓℓ нανє нєя яєνєηgє ση saιηt ʒaмєs **says:**

u know I love u

ƒяαηκι ƒαямєя ωιℓℓ нανє нєя яєνєηgє ση saιηt ʒaмєs **says:**

i have a lot of respect for my elders

`·.„·´¨`·._.·ßΛßY Ṗ♡ĪS♡И`·.„·´¨`·._.·´ **says:**

franki

ƒяαηκι ƒαямєя ωιℓℓ нανє нєя яєνєηgє ση saιηt ʒaмєs **says:**

u and charlie remind me of my mum and dad

ƒяαηκι ƒαямєя ωιℓℓ нανє нєя яєνєηgє ση saιηt ʒaмєs **says:**

married

ƒяαηκι ƒαямєя ωιℓℓ нανє нєя яєνєηgє ση saιηt ʒaмєs **says:**

no sex

ғяaηκι ғaямɛя ωιℓℓ нaⱱɛ нɛя яɛⱱɛηgɛ ση sαιηт ɔaмɛs says:

i wonder if charlie has a lover too

[ⓜⓡⓢ ⓣⓡⓐⓒⓔⓨ ⓟⓘⓣⓣ IS OFFLINE]

ғяaηκι ғaямɛя ωιℓℓ нaⱱɛ нɛя яɛⱱɛηgɛ ση sαιηт ɔaмɛs says:

fucking hell that girl can't take a joke

ғяaηκι ғaямɛя ωιℓℓ нaⱱɛ нɛя яɛⱱɛηgɛ ση sαιηт ɔмɛs says:

lan?

ғяaηκι ғaямɛя ωιℓℓ нaⱱɛ нɛя яɛⱱɛηgɛ ση sαιηт ɔaмɛs says:

so this girl

ғяaηκι ғaямɛя ωιℓℓ нaⱱɛ нɛя яɛⱱɛηgɛ ση sαιηт ɔaмɛs says:

ruth beadle

ғяaηκι ғaямɛя ωιℓℓ нaⱱɛ нɛя яɛⱱɛηgɛ ση sαιηт ɔaмɛs says:

she *stares*

ғяaηκι ғaямɛя ωιℓℓ нaⱱɛ нɛя яɛⱱɛηgɛ ση sαιηт ɔaмɛs says:

u kno?

[˙٠,·˙‾˙·٠_˙BᴧBY P♡ĪS♡И˙٠,·˙‾˙·٠_·˙ IS OFFLINE]

ғяaηκι ғaямɛя ωιℓℓ нaⱱɛ нɛя яɛⱱɛηgɛ ση sαιηт ɔaмɛs says:

seriously???

ғяanкı ғаямея wıll нave нея яevenge on saınt ɔames says:

girls??????

ғяanкı ғаямея wıll нave нея яevenge on saınt ɔames says:

SERIOUSLY

ғяanкı ғаямея wıll нave нея яevenge on saınt ɔames says:

jesus

COTTON WOOL

Ruth
Now

Alanna is leaning over the reception desk like a kitten ready to pounce. She hasn't changed into her uniform yet and her skinny buttocks jiggle in American Apparel jeggings. In front of her is a complicated house of greeting cards.

If you'd asked me, ten years ago – say eleven – who were the people I couldn't imagine living without, I'd have had trouble answering. Before I met Neil, nobody seemed destined to stick. I had always known that my school years wouldn't be the happiest of my life. Even as a young girl it seemed obvious to me that I wasn't destined to meet my real friends there. Girls who sat together on the first day of school stuck together throughout, despite the changing geography of the classroom and separations by teachers desperate to curb the giggling. I listened to Beth Wellbelove breathe heavily over her trigonometry exercises for five years. I told myself I was holding out for college, though I wasn't sure at that point if I was even going to college.

In a sense, my intuition was right: Neil and I met in the summer of my first year at nursing school, right after I'd finished my exams, though he had nothing to do with nursing school; he'd left school ten years earlier. After I met him I stopped worrying so much about making real friends. Perhaps I just wasn't built for friendship.

Throughout my life I've had the luxury of forgetting about Alanna several times. In the end, though, she always comes back, like a particularly pretty zombie or a deeply ingrained psychological trauma.

Our shifts haven't overlapped in a while. Not that I'd realized – I have enough on my plate – though on some level I must've been relieved. I have often wondered: did I commit a small crime during childhood that I can't remember? Have I accumulated so much bad karma that I must be punished with Alanna Hallett appearing at regular intervals throughout my life? She never sat next to me in primary school and, in college, she once told me she'd had enough of my depressing pigeon face and to get the fuck out of her life already. What have I done to deserve this?

I stand in the doorway, watching her slender, spandexed legs strain as she slides all the way forwards on to one elbow and angles her head to evaluate the stability of her construction. I drop my bag on the floor. Alanna is startled. Just like Bambi.

'Ruth! Jesus!'

'What's that?'

'Wait a second!' she says. 'I have big news.'

I stand to the side with my arms crossed, waiting for her to move so that I can finally reach my desk and sink into my chair. I haven't had a good night's sleep. I haven't for days. Not that I want to explain the break-up to her: I don't think I could handle her compassion. We have history. She might be the only person I have 'history' with who's left in my life, now that Neil's gone, which is depressing.

In any case, we've put the past behind us. These days we don't bring it up. Although it's not like she's given me a chance to forget: she looks exactly the same as she did at twenty, when she slept with him. Neil swears he didn't find her attractive back then. Of course, it's a lie. Because he did sleep with Alanna and I do know now that Neil is a liar.

Can you blame him? Who doesn't love pretty young girls? 'She's delicious,' Melissa said, when she gathered us to meet the new junior nurse. I remember Alanna appearing next to her like a six-year-old emerging from behind her mother's skirt.

'Helloooo,' she said cutely. I couldn't believe it was her. I thought I was rid of her when she dropped out of college.

Alanna flicks her white-blonde fringe out of her eyes and examines the house of cards again. The pointed tip of her tongue peeks out at the side of her mouth, as she stands on her toes – how tiny she is – and places one last card on top of the pile. The construction is uniformly pink, like the crop top she is wearing. She'll be bollocked for it by one of the senior nurses in three, two, one . . .

'Alanna, that top . . .' I begin but I stop mid-sentence.

She doesn't even turn around. I haven't seen her for over three weeks and now here she is, fully herself. Alanna, the whole package: big blue eyes, black eyelashes and that *killer smile*. Alanna always wraps her shapely little legs in tiny leggings. How she finds them is a mystery; she's only a size six and they're far too small. She must shop in the kids' section. Leggings are suitable work bottoms, but the added stretch thins out the fabric until they are practically transparent. Alanna leans in over the Goldfish Bowl counter when a male relative comes to visit, so that if he's tall enough he can glimpse where her thong slithers up her bum, disappearing under the hem of her smock.

Melissa thinks Alanna is delightful. 'I love her energy,' she says. 'So sprightly!' She runs the care home like it's a nativity play.

'That's it!' Alanna opens her arms, showgirly. 'I could've been an architect!'

Yes, I'm thinking, you could have, but for some reason you chose to be a fucking nurse in my care home instead.

'So what are these?' I say.

'I was wondering when you'd ask!' she says. 'You're literally the one person who doesn't know! But I wanted to tell you myself! Well, have a guess! What do you think!'

Alanna's sentences all end with an exclamation mark. It makes me feel like a toddler being quizzed by a nursery teacher. Which is another thing she could've done, but she chose not to do, so that she could plague my workplace instead. I look at the board and realize we're both on shift for the bedpans today.

'You're getting married!' I joke.

Turns out she really is.

Last night in my dream I was right here at work, at the care home. There was a birthday party being set up out on the back lawn. The bunting swung in the breeze. I wrote names on plastic cups, so that people could reuse them and none would go to waste. I knew that we only had just enough cups. I handed them to the guests: Mona, Alanna, those girls she hangs out with, Miss Phyllis, Don, Margaret and Comfort from the canteen, Call-Me-Melissa, Mr Chacko, Mrs O'Toole. Even gross Mr Hancock was wheeled out in his chair; he looked small and harmless out on the lawn. I handed him the last cup and he clutched it in his fist, the purple veins trembling.

I was all out of cups and my daughter was nowhere to be seen. I went round the group of gathered guests, increasingly frantic, tapping people on the shoulder and saying, 'I can't find my daughter, have you seen my daughter? Please, please, have you seen my daughter?'

'I wanted to get something a bit snazzy this time because otherwise it's literally just a layer of polish and what's the point of getting your nails done at the salon if you can do the same at home? Waste of money if you ask me!'

In the washing room, Alanna enlists me to help her put her latex gloves on. She lathers her hands with the antiseptic lotion. There's a ladybird sticker on every one of her fingernails, covered in a glossy layer of top coat.

'You never get used to it!' she says. 'This shit stinks!'

Well, yes. Quite literally.

'Bedpans coming in, hunny,' I mumble.

She ignores me. She's right to. What a pathetic attempt at sass. In my head, things always sound better than what comes out. Why try?

Alanna is excited because her boyfriend proposed. I almost feel like breaking into dramatic laughter when she tells me. Of course, this is unlike me: I'm no-drama. I guess we both turned out the way we were meant to. One break-up, one marriage. You win some, you lose some. Life moves on.

Alanna couldn't wait to tell me, but she didn't want to ring me while I was off, didn't want to bother me, and anyway, this is the kind of thing you have to tell someone in person.

'Am I excited for my old friend Alanna?' she asks. She

says she's been eagerly waiting for our paths to cross, but I'd been home from work, and then our shifts didn't match for a couple of weeks: 'Did I get some rest? Am I feeling better?'

You want to know how I'm doing? Well, I'm not doing that great. Remember our holiday to Rome? That was the last time I was doing this badly. Sure, it's where Neil and I met – the day I collapsed on the steps of St Peter's – so I think I was sitting in the tiled waiting room at the Catholic hospital while you fucked him. But I got the boy, didn't I? The man. Being with him blunted the edges, but I've remembered the kind of lucidity that comes from being completely empty. The body becomes more aware, develops sensitive tendrils. Look at us. Look at me now. You did the right thing in getting out early with Neil, Alanna. Why don't you share some of your wisdom? Do continue.

I say none of this.

She's still banging on about manicures.

'Anyway, it's worth saving up to get them done in gel! Shellac! What a world we live in! It's double the money but they last double the time!'

She holds out her hands, palms upturned, synthetic talons sticking up like phosphorescent branches. I snap the gloves on her. I pull a fresh pair out of the box for myself. I take my time.

She and this Paul bloke have been together eleven months. I'm supposed to have met him – 'Damn, girl, we never hang out any more these days' – she's sure she's mentioned him. This is huge news. This is way, way beyond the seven-month mark, which, as I know, is historically the problematic point for Alanna. Remember Michael in college?

I remember a creepy PhD student who worked part-time as a personal trainer.

Eleven whole months! A real achievement.

Most people suffer from the seven-year-itch: Alanna gets it seven months in. So what? Who am I to express this common-sense judgement that's clogging up my throat, dooming and despising such beautiful young love?

Eleven whole months of bliss! Already she feels like she's known him all her life.

Nonsense. Alanna doesn't understand the notion of duration. Perhaps because the process of aging doesn't seem to apply to her. When she has a new man, Alanna behaves like a loved-up schoolgirl, believes in the three-day rule of dating.

Jesus, I'm bitter. Alanna is happy. What's wrong with that? She's in love. It's unrelated to my situation. She doesn't even know Neil and I have broken up. Or does she?

I nearly lost my mind when she first started. I'd been happy at the care home and I couldn't believe I wasn't allowed to keep this one good thing. She'd given up nursing, hadn't she? So how did she wind up in the same place as me when I had worked so hard to get there?

Though she was small, she was so perfectly charming, so pretty, so full of life, that it soon felt like she took up all of the space. There was just so much of her. I had forgotten the way she did this, shifting the axis of attention in any given scenario so that it all revolved around her.

When she joined I relearnt her ways with fresh horror. Whenever Alanna was working with me, I felt cornered. She never had anything interesting to say, but she was always so relentless in saying something, all the time, that I lost my voice. I told myself it was my fault for not knowing how to raise it. I've never been a loud person, but in the years after I 'snatched Neil from her', her 'holiday boo' – this was a joke she once made to *loosen the tension* – I had found my feet. With her around, I lost my grip, turning inwards to compensate for the fact that I was seething. I couldn't believe that I was going through this for a third time.

Neil was delighted to discover that Alanna was back in my life. He fell victim to bouts of nostalgia in which he reminisced about his twenties. It didn't help that she was the last girl he'd slept with before we got together. I couldn't help but be petty. I said things like, 'It's great to see you're still thinking about her.' 'I was thinking of us, silly,' he said. 'About us getting together for the first time.' But he wasn't. He'd beg me to tell him more about Alanna, pinching my arm sometimes, which irritated me.

What had she been up to all those years? How could she pop back into my life like that? I'd tell Neil, 'Honestly, she is the kind of nightmare you never want to come across. She's still the same as you remember. Can you believe that? Total bimbo. She's useless. She won't learn. She is honestly a dog of a nurse. I don't think she's got the brain capacity.'

It amused him to hear me talking of someone like that. He thought it very out of character. 'God, you hate this girl so much!' He'd happily clap his hands, like my hatred wasn't a thing to be taken seriously, but a cute little birthmark he'd just noticed on my back.

In time I found ways to conceal my outrage. It wasn't professional so I told myself, 'Be the bigger person.' Sometimes repeating that sentence out loud to myself helped. I endeavoured to get to know Alanna better. Which was easy, as it would've been impossible to tune out her constant chattering anyway. She told me the story of her life, the years we'd spent apart, like some kind of fairy-tale that had reached its logical ending.

It was really quite ordinary stuff. Someone had offered her a modelling contract just before she started her second year at college and she'd gone for it. That was why she'd dropped out. I'd imagined some kind of tragedy. 'Hindsight is wisdom,' she says. 'I think I was running away from my own destiny.' The contract had been a bit of a hoax – not a bad one; she just wasn't making as much as she'd expected. But her confidence took a terrible blow and she became very depressed. She really wasn't coping. She overcompensated by attending too many castings, photo shoots that led to little more than nothing. It was exhausting. She cheered herself up with kiddy drugs, abusing her ADHD medication, staying up all night, frantically searching the internet for the right opportunity, which – she was sure – was out there for her. It got bad. 'At one point, I was behaving like a bit of an addict!' she chirps. Which is unsurprising, since she was; that's why she was sent to a rehabilitation centre.

At twenty-five she made a full recovery and re-enrolled in college, studying English Literature, just like Neil. She wanted to learn to express herself. She read Ian McEwan's *Atonement* – didn't just watch the film – and something clicked. It was an awakening of sorts. She felt so deeply about it that she wrote her dissertation on it. It was such a moving essay that it got her a job here – one of London's most exclusive eldercare facilities. She attached it to her application, and of course it struck a chord with Melissa.

Just the kind of sentimental tripe she would fall for. Never mind checking if the girl had any actual work experience.

'This is Alanna's true vocation,' said the reference letter.

Things had come full circle for her.

'You know when something's just meant to happen,' she said. She referred to the essay as one of her greatest achievements, occasionally as the 'turning point' in her life. Since then, she'd put her whole heart into nursing. She forwent her last summer holiday in order to take up voluntary work in a Brazilian hospital. It was a transformative experience and she'd come back more determined than ever, with her iPhone filled with colourful landscapes and cute parrots. I doubt they gave her any work to do; she probably stood in the way and took selfies. Because Alanna doesn't have a clue what real work looks like. She says she loves the care home because it makes her forget how fast the world moves and then she doesn't get tempted by the bad things. Well, that wouldn't be such a bad thing in itself if she could accomplish some of the basic tasks and make a valuable contribution. But Alanna lacks any kind of practical sense. She is way too excitable.

I smirk and move out of the way.

'You start washing and I'll dry,' I say.

'You're the boss, Ruthi!' she says.

I stand back as she tips the first bedpan into the sink. She is humming a tune. Alanna is getting married soon. She's happy.

Alanna – for the record – never wanted a husband. She's a free spirit. Haven't you seen her peace tattoo? It's on her ribs, just under the armpit; she'll lift up her shirt to show you. She got it a while back to celebrate her first year clean. It's a symbol of freedom. And yet here she is, four years later, acquiring a husband like it's nothing at all. Easy for some. No wonder: Alanna is disgustingly cute. Alanna is so tiny and sickly sweet, like jelly babies caught between the teeth. When I dream about her I wake up with a furry mouth, like I got drunk on vodka pops the night before.

'So this guy,' I say. 'Is he any good?'

In this dream we are kissing, nothing else, kneeling on a bed half undressed, and our hands are locked together into knots at the sides of our bodies. In my dreams there are no smells, but I remember thinking, upon waking, that her breath must've smelled of berries, the way no real girl's breath smells. In the dream I could feel her smooth stomach, her hairless skin frictionless against my pelvis.

Alanna commands henchwomen. She didn't have to go looking for them; they just appeared at her side, hired by management as a pair. They're even more useless than Alanna in terms of actual output. We call them the Lolitas, Las Lolitas sometimes; Mona came up with it. The two of them are near identical, perfectly groomed and prettier than any pet I've ever met. Cute pair of toy poodles, the Lolitas – one red, one black: ginger-haired Emmy with the freckles, and Bex with the cat-eye make-up and the jet-black geometrical bangs. This month, they're both real into yellow. We summon them when we're trying to seal a deal on a long-term in-patient because, like poodles, they amuse the rich ladies and shake their little fluffy tails for their husbands. Melissa obviously adores them. They are cute and harmless, although extremely annoying. And, like poodles, they are fiercely protective of their mistress. They look after pocket-sized Alanna with blind dedication.

Like them – more so – she is perfectly ownable, and sure enough, she has found her true master. Her new fiancé works in construction, as a contractor. Easy to remember, she giggles. According to Alanna, this means he signs contracts for buildings to be built and never does any physical work, although he does work out in the gym, she reassures me. She winks. This, she explains, tipped the scales towards marriage, because come on, if a man who decides whether buildings are fit to exist can't offer stability, then who the hell can? Neil was an accountant. 'Remember Neil, Alanna?' I want to say. Well, he liked even numbers and instruction booklets and meeting requirements and corporate health retreats. A sound, honest guy, yet not without his quirks: he was unafraid of looking at the wine card when all his mates were ordering pints. Who could've imagined he would behave like he did? This sensitive, clever man who sought the good pleasures in life: a glass of fruity white wine, and pimento olives, and having sex from behind. Alanna already knows that last bit. She saw through it all, years ago. Perhaps Alanna has always been wiser than me – certainly luckier. Perhaps she really has no need to worry that what happened to me could happen to her.

'I thought stability made you sick to your gut,' I say.

'Come on, Ruth,' she says. 'That's just a thing you say when you're young. I'm a woman now. Like you. I want the same things.' She gives me a serious look. She is *a woman*, though she acts like a girl. 'Do you think I would've survived the first month here with all these dying people if I was looking for excitement?' she says.

The sink gurgles.

I remember this. I was in the Bowl one morning. Alanna and the Lolitas were giggling and whispering. I knew it was about sex. I couldn't focus on my work. Then I heard Alanna say, 'Jesus Christ, don't you hate it when people talk about their relationship with their partner like they're hooked on life support or something?' It pissed me off how she phrased it.

I asked what was going on and the three of them laughed. One of the Lolitas grinned and said it was material unfit for a girl like me. The cheek of it. She meant *a woman* as 'settled' as me and it made me feel a million years old. It must've shown on my face because Alanna, sweet Alanna, with the bouncy ponytail and squeaky-clean soul said, 'Ruthi, it's just silly stuff. The girls are being silly. I'm just not looking for stability right now.'

The Lolitas quietened. She has that kind of authority over them.

I watch her exquisite profile as she tips out the bedpan.

'Where did you meet?' I say.

'He's a good guy, Ruth,' she says, inconsequentially. Had I asked? She looks right at me. I freeze.

'If he makes you happy,' I say.

'He will. And anyway, I think I'd like to have a party.'

Because of course she is having a party. A hen-do. I'm sure the Lolitas are over the moon.

'I've not told the girls about it yet,' she says, 'and that's the other thing.'

'What other thing?' I say.

'Well, we go back, don't we! We've been in this together, y'know? The shit and piss and all the rude bullshit we've got to put up with.' And it's true. We do put up with a lot of bullshit; people are sometimes rude, they do sometimes soil themselves, do die eventually.

She shakes her head like she's trying to remember a thought. 'Come on, Ruth. You're one of my oldest friends. You showed me the ropes. I would've been lost without you. You've always had my back, Ruth.'

What does she want? Why does she keep saying my name?

Her eyes are very blue.

Another time I watch her while she undresses out of her work clothes. I'm not sure this second dream is a dream.

Alanna with huge black pupils on her ninth or tenth day in the job; a new franticness about her, like a rodent, a spaced-out little bunny. I pulled her into the towel cupboard before anyone else could see her. She flattened herself against the back wall, looked up at me with her round, dark eyes.

'I am just so tired,' she said. 'I just wanted to make sure I could keep going.'

It was the most infuriating excuse she could've offered. I lost it.

'Everyone gets tired. You have to teach your body to get used to it,' I said, my mouth close to her ear, her Swarovski earring. I crushed her body against the bath towels, her tiny bones, tinier than mine. If I'd pressed down a little harder, I might have heard her spine crack. I felt her breathing hot against my neck.

The next day I found her at my desk, sober and conspiratorial. 'I owe you one, Ruth Beadle.' She pushed a bucket of Cadbury's Roses towards me. I told myself I wouldn't eat a single one. I left them next to the kettle in the kitchen for everyone else to share and then, when the tub was empty, I brought it back to my desk. I keep it there for paperclips and as a warning to Alanna. She has always behaved since then.

'Don't be silly,' I say. 'You were a very quick learner.'

'Listen, I wanted to ask you something,' she says.

'Of course I'll cover for you,' I say. I might be bitter, Alanna, but only a monster wouldn't cover for you on your wedding day.

'No, Ruth. What? You silly cow! I want you to be my maid of honour.' Her eyes are very large, very earnest, and I surprise myself by wanting her to mean it – wanting me, Ruth Beadle, her oldest friend, as her maid of honour.

But then the wariness hits. I check myself. I swallow. I remind myself that I'm the more experienced nurse. I keep it together.

'Are you kidding me?' I ask.

'Kidding you?'

'Rebecca and Emmeline will never forgive you.'

She sighs, 'Look, there was never going to be a way to get that right. You only have one maid of honour and there are two of them. They can be bridesmaids.'

'Surely that's not a good reason . . .'

'No. It's not. And the real reason is this isn't about Emmy and Bex. I want you.'

Alanna is quiet, eyes focused on the bedpan she's rinsing out, eyelashes pointing downwards, milky gloves squidging against steel, scrubbing away the invisible bacteria. Am I supposed to say something? She hasn't asked me a question. Anything I say now is tantamount to admitting I am keen on doing something I am not technically keen on doing. But the longer I am quiet, the deeper the notion sinks, like an oar in a puddle of murky water, dredging up detritus that I don't particularly want to look at.

Winning at life, isn't she? That's what everyone will say. Alanna is getting married. I'm single now. It hurts. The implications: no plus-one, terrible hair, only ate her starter, look at the old maid, look at her dance. Who even is she? Have some wedding cake.

'You can't be serious.' I try to make the question sound like a statement. I need to find a way to turn the invitation down and I need to do it quickly if I want to protect myself. Looking at her, so small and so pretty, you'd think she might need protection herself.

'Of course I'm serious,' she says. 'Look, this isn't the way you're supposed to react, Ruth.'

I've had the wrong reaction pretty much every time anything notable has happened in my life: I'm never going to get this one right. But I haven't said no, not yet. I take a deep breath.

Hypertrophic scars can appear while a serious burn is healing. The skin grows out too thickly, too fast, overcompensating for the damaged layers. It's impossible to know in advance whether the scar will resolve itself, in months or even years, and leave a rosy section of neat child skin, or if it'll stay dry, shiny and crumpled, like fresh papier mâché. You do everything you can to aid the healing process. You soak your cotton wool swab in disinfectant to clean around the surface of the burn daily. You wrap a compression bandage around it to keep it flat and then you do your best to forget that you are carrying an open wound on your body. You hope it doesn't get infected, that there are no complications. I've been trying.

Even though I can't help but drown in sleep. Even though I can't think of eating without feeling terrible. As if by restoring full proficiency, surviving correctly at this moment in time, I run the risk of being pulled further away from the future I thought was awaiting me. In which I am the woman at the altar. Instead, I am an actual bridesmaid, as Alanna and I hurtle towards the fulfilment of our respective destinies. Me, forever on the sidelines. Alanna, right here, waiting for me to say something.

I realize I haven't answered her.

She's waiting.

'Babe. I'm so sorry,' I say and I know from her face that I'm not supposed to react like this either. Why am I apologizing? 'Look, I'm just so honoured, so honoured, I don't even know what to say.'

'Say you'll do it,' she says. She holds out the wet bedpan. I wrap each of my hands into a pristine white towel.

The cotton is very soft on my skin. With my tourniquets I receive the first bedpan. I begin to dry it. I don't say anything.

'OK, listen: think about it,' she says. 'Shall we say one week. If I don't hear, I'll take it as a yes.' She smiles sweetly.

PIZZA

Nearly Ten Years Earlier

03/06/2006

Dear diary,

. . .

Cuz apparently that's a thing I do now, write in my
fucking diary. That's how exciting this year's been, I'm
literally just one step away from talking to myself out
loud. I can't wait to get away. That's the big news: we are
actually really leaving!

Rome baby! Two whole weeks!

Honestly until the end I thought Beadle would chicken
out which fuck me would've been SUCH a massive
let-down, given how hard it's been to convince her
to come in the first place. She'd convinced herself we had
to stick around school for 'summer term projects', can you
fucking believe??? We're not in drama school. What
would we even do? Take an egg home for ten days and

change its bandages daily? I showed her the term dates on the prospectus, where it clearly states that school is not on, like properly shut, dead, kaput, until September, but she looked at me with that weird bird face, like she hadn't heard a word I said. She's a nice girl really but sometimes I really wonder what her problem is.

So to clear any doubts and because the guy at the agency said we should book soon I asked Mike to tell her, since he's doing a PhD. Then of course I had to be nice to him for like a week to make up for it and he got super clingy. He's lucky there are no interesting guys on this course or I would've called the rape police on him a long time ago and then BYE BYE funded research post. But anyway he said to Beadle something like, Do you think any of us want to teach extra classes during the summer holidays? Academics are people too! Which is something he says at least once every time we hang out to remind me he's not so old after all. Actually all it does is remind me that I'm not sure they are. People, I mean. And he IS old. He only says that because he's behind with his PhD and feels bitter about it. I mean WHO. CARES. Mike is so boring.

Everything about nursing school is boring. What a waste. Honestly had I not maxed out not one but two card overdrafts (I know!!!) I would be out of here in a second. I'm not supposed to have a boring life. I miss dancing so fucking much sometimes it makes me want to cry. Still can't quite believe the girls ditched me like that. I always knew Trace would do well enough for Oxbridge but honestly Franki at Goldsmiths? What do they even do there? Bet all she does is take ketamine and glue her pubes to a canvas. She sent me a care package with these terrible taxidermy postcards, a dry red rose and an old copy of *Alice in Wonderland.* Is that supposed to be ART or something? She can be so gross. So now Beadle is as good as it gets for me, in terms of mates.

Rome! I would've rather gone somewhere a bit more lively, like Ibiza, or I don't know, Amsterdam. But I looked up prices for June and Spain costs crazy money cos it's already high season and Amsterdam is always high season ha ha. I can just picture myself getting stoned alone while Beadle swoons over the beautiful tulips, so maybe it's for the best we're not going there either. Rome'll have to do. I'm going to eat all of the ice cream and find myself a GLADIATOR for a boyfriend! That'll show Franks! She may be an artist now but I bet my left tit she's still boy crazy. Two whole weeks! Roma bambino!

Xoxo Ally

16/06/2006

OK, so, we're off tomorrow! For real!

I've managed to convince Beadle to stay over at mine tonight so that it'll be easier to get to the airport tomorrow. (Trace would say that I need her there to wake me up at 5 a.m. because I hold the World Record of Snooze Button Presses.) It's also good because it gives me an excuse to tell Mike not to come over tonight. He was all upset. I don't know WHAT he was thinking, that we were going to have a tearful goodbye? I'm only going away for two weeks. And then what? If he thinks we're staying together over the summer then he is even dumber than I thought. I'm not spending the rest of my life with a lab rat (even if he looks hot in a lab coat).

Thought Beadle and I could have a sleepover type thing. I was even going to get us Domino's. I thought it might be nice to eat together, to share something. I'd have paid. Can you believe? Beadle looked moderately excited when she turned up at the flat, which is huge news for her, she's always got that lost expression and I thought oh yay! But obviously as soon as I managed to put Mike off, Beadle informed me she was hitting the hay. At half nine. She's been asleep since then, which made me regret telling Mike not to come, because what am I going to do now. I'm all excited to leave with no one to talk to.

Xoxo A

WHOLE CHICKEN

Ruth
Now

I pick up the rotisserie chicken on my way. I go to Sainsbury's and not Tesco, though I've always considered myself more of a Tesco girl. Mother is a Sainsbury's girl, which is perhaps why I prefer Tesco. Or perhaps it's because there was one next to my student halls when I first lived alone. Either way, Sainsbury's is closer to my childhood home and so I buy the chicken there. I hold it in my arms and cover it with my scarf. It's windy and I like feeling its heat radiating through the layers of clothing, against my chest, breast against breast. I'm like a beggar holding her lovechild in her arms, a belated Christmas carol in late January, both of us trying to keep warm.

I've put the coleslaw in my handbag. I check that it hasn't spilled, before climbing the three steps to her door. It opens before I have a chance to knock. My mother and I thrive on punctuality: it's something that runs in the family, deeper than a habit, like our brown eyes, our straight backs, the way our lips chap and are sore throughout the winter months. Her dry mouth brushes against my cheek as she gives me a hug no longer than usual, holds me back by the shoulder to look at my face, takes a moment to gauge the right distance so her astigmatic eyes can focus. I don't like it when she isn't wearing glasses: the similarities surface in our faces and I don't like the feeling that she can read mine.

She is holding me the way all other mothers hold their grown children. There is nothing strange in her manner today and these measured gestures are a kindness she is paying me. She knows, of course, about the break-up. I called her to tell her two nights ago. I waited until I knew I was going to see her. I couldn't have foreseen the other thing, that happened only two days ago, and I don't want to talk about it. I don't need to ask her: I am sure that my mother was never a bridesmaid.

On the phone, she asked how long it had been since Neil and I 'parted ways'. I said four weeks and she said, 'Oh Ruth! Why didn't you mention it?' She is upset that I didn't call her earlier and so she won't ask me why he left me in person. If I hadn't waited to call, she would've had to find another reason not to ask, so my calling ahead and the delay in telling her are kindnesses that I am paying her.

We don't talk about these things in my family. We work together to avoid this kind of stressful conversation. Why dig it all up? Life is hard enough. My mother doesn't ask me about the break-up, but this doesn't mean that she doesn't care about the conditions regulating my life and how they have shifted over the last month. Quite the opposite. Her nonchalant manner is her way of conveying that she knows that I am strong and require no external support: she trusts me to be all right. Right now, my mother knows that it is crucial that the lacquer of our routine remain unaltered, even though there is no one here to witness our exchange. Our Sunday evening dinner is a family tradition. Sunday rotisserie chicken might not seem like a tradition that amounts to much in those families with more than two people – a favourite restaurant for big occasions, a set date for decorating the Christmas tree, or threefold Christmas gifts: something silly, something sweet and something to use in the bathroom – but they have seen us through my first period, my first exam, my first holiday abroad and its aftermath. They are going to see us through this and we are going to be just fine.

'Ruth,' my mother says, holding me by the shoulders.

She uses my name as punctuation, a full stop that ends this. I shut the door behind me and listen out for the neat click. Polishing the metal mechanisms around the house was my chore when I was little. My mother imagined it was a chore that would appeal to a child, so she assigned it to me at the age of five, as soon as I could be trusted not to pour the furniture polish into my mouth. When I left home the task reverted to her and even now all her doorknobs are shiny. Some people are capable of resuming full proficiency once they are left to fend for themselves. I hope that runs in the family too.

'So Ruth,' she says, as we slip past the American film-star portraits lining the walls of the hallway. I swing my hip to the side to avoid the long low table. She keeps twin Art Deco lamps at each end, a doily in between and a crystal dish of ancient sweets on the doily. Though narrow, the table is too large for this small corridor and the lamps rack up a substantial bill considering her modest, bread-and-butter lifestyle.

But their light is the glow you see through the half-moon window above the front door. It says, *If you lived here you'd be home now.*

In the kitchen we busy ourselves with dinner. We do this urgently because the chicken is already getting cold. We don't speak until the task is completed. We are removing the tinfoil, balling it up, binning it. We are sliding the chicken, whole, on to a serving plate. Pouring the coleslaw into two small shallow fish-shaped bowls, the ones we use for coleslaw, never fish. Putting the napkins out: squares of kitchen roll that we fold into triangles. What is the point of buying both kitchen roll and napkins? What is the point of buying both cotton wool pads and cotton wool balls? My mother and I are thrifty: we save money, time and space. We work as a team: no dishes, one carving knife. We sit before one another in opposite fold-out chairs. Two others remain against the wall, where they have left a grey smudge, dust accumulating between plaster and plastic until it turns into grease. Don't get me wrong: the house is well tended, in its well-used spaces. There is always so much to do, no need to go rooting around in dark corners. The kitchen surfaces are always pristine.

'Ruth,' my mother says.

'What can I say, mother,' I say. I raise my palms, upturned. I am vexed; I have to remind myself that there is no need to be. My mother looks at me with her bad eyes. I carry on. I tell her about the colony of moths that have settled into our bottom drawer, the one that housed Neil's winter jumpers, the one he has vacated. It's still empty. I don't need the extra space; I have nothing to fill it with. I withhold the meagre satisfaction of knowing that all the expensive jumpers he took with him will be full of holes by the spring. Baby moths are breeding invisibly in their woollen folds right at this very moment.

'Furry little turds,' I spit out. I feel my face contract into a mean little smile.

'Ruth,' my mother says. She doesn't like it when I speak like this. She waves at the chicken that sits in front of us, untouched.

'Sorry,' I say. 'The insects must've crawled up the back of the wardrobe, because all my singlets on the lowest shelf had holes in them too.'

At the signal – my mother's palm outstretched – we join our hands over the handle of the carving knife.

'So I had to go to Oxford Street in a hurry,' I tell my mother. 'Because of work the next day.'

She knows that it's freezing in the Bowl. She's bought me singlets every Christmas since I started there. It's her way of letting me know that she thinks of me as an adult – a sort of dowry, a motherly act she became attached to in my absence. I don't remember wearing vests as a child. My mother seems sad to learn that the new singlets she gave me at Christmas have been ruined. I shouldn't have told her. 'I went and bought some more immediately,' I try to reassure her. 'Shops close at ten p.m. in central London. I know. Crazy.' Together, we delve the knife into the chest of the chicken, just to the side of the breastbone. Like cutting a wedding cake, but clumsier, with the table between us. 'I knew that the queues would be long and the cold dreadful, but the big Primark is cheap and so it still seemed worth the trip.' A way to leave the house, something to do. I thought if I hurried perhaps I could still make it before rush hour.

'Primark,' says my mother – an admonition.

I shrug and then we flip the knife, left to right, left to right, to separate the two breast pouches, feeling the resistance of cooked muscle in the handle.

I had deluded myself. I'd had to miss the first tube because the carriage was packed and I was pushed to the back of the cluster of bodies by an aggressive man in a pinstripe suit. My mother wouldn't understand this and so there is no point in telling her: she has never lived or wanted to live in a big city. I got on the next train and spent most of the trip lodged between the door and the broad back of a tall teenager, my head locked at an angle so as to avoid touching him, my face still only an inch from the soft fold of his puppy-fat nape. His prickly ponytail swished across my cheek every time the train hiccupped to a halt. I stared at the underside of his jaw. It really bothers me when people don't squeeze spots that are ready for squeezing. Please squeeze those spots. In the tunnel at Camden Town we stopped for a long minute, the carriage lights flickering. People shuffled, then quietened. I could taste their impatience in the hot dark; the boy's Doritos sweat.

My mother and I dislodge the two sections of meat from the chicken's breast.

At Euston I got off the train to change to the Victoria line. I followed the light-blue line along the tunnel. Have you noticed that the Victoria line and the NHS are codified with the same shade of sanitary blue? But ask a professional in either field and they'll tell you that the premises aren't as clinically spotless as they'd have you believe. It's a cover-up. At our care home we don't do hospital colours or hospital furniture. All the furniture is real furniture, like in a real home.

When the doors swooshed open I clutched the overhead

bar with my hands and hurled my body inside. This carriage was also packed, thicker in the middle like an unpricked sausage. I rested my head on the pane next to the doors and stared into the empty space above the heads of the seated passengers. At the other end of the carriage an old lady with a shopping trolley had carved herself a rectangle of space inside the crowd. She was obviously a bus creature, who'd taken a chance and decided to enter this hostile world in which the elderly are considered a nuisance, an unacceptable presence. Why today?

No one was offering the old woman their seat; they frowned at the space in front of her, pretending not to see that she was struggling. Two further bodies could fit in there, three at a squeeze; certainly, we were all willing to squeeze in. The woman kept leaning against her trolley and it kept rolling away from her: off she went with it and when I thought she would hit the ground she'd pull it back and lean on it again. Swaying back and forth as if travelling on water. A man in a grey suit stood with his back to her and did a little skip every time the trolley hit his heels. The woman stared at me through the glass with her watery eyes. She pulled up her trolley and leant against it. I blew on to the pane to make her disappear.

'People don't like being around old people in London,' I say to my mother. My mother frowns. 'I guess that's good because it's how I make a living.'

'Ruth,' my mother says.

The chicken skin hangs loose from the carcass like an unbuttoned shirt. We lay each half of the breast on to one half of the napkins in front of us, then fold the other half over to rub off the grease.

'I got off at Oxford Circus. It was so busy that I just

couldn't bear changing trains again,' I say. It occurred to me that it was the station that Neil used (although he wouldn't be in work – would he? He wasn't even in London), perhaps that was why I wanted to get off there. As the train pulled into the station and I heard the announcement, I began to feel quite queasy. Still, I pushed my way out, elbows first through the crowd, weaselling in silence towards the mouth of the station. The descending crowd pushed down on me as I made my way up; halfway up the stairs I began to hear drums: some kind of demonstration outside. Someone repeatedly striking a bell. The noise irritated me; I gritted my teeth. It sounded like hail, or broken glass. I waded upstairs, my hand on the blue metal rail, white at the knuckles, identical ads ascending: CHUNKIER! CHUNKIER! CHUNKIER! McDonald's new CHUNKY dessert.

My hand missed the railing and then I was outside, frozen at the top of the stairs. There was a small mob ahead of me. They had signs: one said Free Hugs. I didn't see the others because stood in front of the sign was Neil. He had his back to me but there he was, his stubbly skull, his bald spot visible, the mandarin collar of his cheesecloth shirt. Was this the commune he'd been talking about? A suit jacket was slung across his shoulders, and he had a briefcase, as if he'd just come out of work. I picked out a woman, standing quite near him, striking a rhythm on a bottle with a wooden stick, bells around her wrists. Large and shabby and blonde, braless breasts hanging low. I wondered what her face looked like when she and Neil fucked. I imagined she'd have a very serene expression. I know what his looks like. Something rose in my chest and I pulled together the creases of my coat, knitted my fingers in my scarf as the cold pierced my throat. I couldn't stop looking at him.

'What are his new friends like, then?' says my mother.

'They don't believe in private property,' I say. We begin to shred the chicken breast into strips, distinct sections of fewer and fewer meat fibres.

'They never eat meat,' I say. I nod at the chicken. Technically, neither do we.

'Not even chicken?' my mother asks.

'Not even chicken,' I say.

We each take a new piece of kitchen roll from the pre-torn pile on the table. We set the used one to the side, the clean one in front. We arrange the chicken bunches on the new napkin in parallel lines. A tally.

'You're holding up the queue,' a woman said behind me. I stepped to the side and into the paperman. He shouted in my ear, 'Evening Standard,' and my mouth tasted sour. The football kit formation in the window of Nike Town stood like a firing squad. I took another step on to the foot of a different woman. There was a small commotion.

'I think he saw me,' I say.

Fingerpicking through our fish-shaped bowls, we pair the coleslaw with the chicken: one piece of cabbage, one piece of chicken, one piece of carrot, one piece of chicken, one piece of cabbage.

When Neil turned to face me, my breath collected in a pool at the bottom of my throat. He stared in my direction. Next to him, the blonde woman produced the unnerving noise. She didn't acknowledge him. Nor he her. They didn't know each other. So what was he doing there? He was staring right in my direction, towards where I stood at the mouth of the station. Why wasn't he doing anything? There were no hippie friends, no commune. He had lied about that too.

I did the only thing I could think of. I put my arm up and waved. Neil did the same. I stood, unblinking, with my arm up, as a child stumbled out of the exit, pushing past me, the back of his shiny bob charging through the crowd. Neil opened his arms to embrace the boy and as he swept him up into a hug I saw that the boy was a teenage girl, her short skirt riding up to expose the elasticated hem of her silver polka-dot hot pants, a flash of tanned leg flesh. Neil kissed her neck. Did he? He did. *He kissed her neck.* A black cab pulled up next to me. The driver yelled, 'Where can I take ya, love?' And everything came unstuck.

'Did you say hello?' my mother asks, pulling the last thin strip of chicken apart into two perfect halves.

She pairs it with a piece of cabbage, a piece of carrot.

'Too busy,' I say. 'Too many people.'

What I did was I stepped back and shook my head and put my hand away. The cabbie made a face, rolled up the window, drove off. I crossed the road diagonally: the traffic lights counted down, thirteen to zero, PEDESTRIANS CROSS NOW, the beeping, hammering at my temples. My feet moved quicker than the numbers, twice as quick, three times as quick. I dived into a United Colours of Benetton. The humidity struck me and the artificial light made my legs buckle. I pressed myself against the racks of monochrome coats. Two low rows of hangers parted to welcome me inside and I slipped between them, slid down until I reached the floor, sank into that hot place and sat there still, for a long time, as long as it took for me to stop crying.

We take a fresh napkin and fold it into a thick swab. We dab at the mayonnaise on the coleslaw until it's dry.

'Some things just take time, Ruth,' my mother says, as she unfolds a fresh napkin. She presses it on top of the food, and then she rolls both napkins into a ball. I do the same. I fold my hands over the kitchen paper and squeeze, feel the luke-warm heat of meat and cold vegetables crushing up inside.

'You know this,' she says.

'I sure do,' I say.

My mother rises from her chair. She stuffs her ball into the chest hole of the chicken. I stand up too. I push my nap-kins full of the chicken, the carrot, the cabbage in behind hers, push them deep inside the carcass. We're done. Nei-ther of us has eaten a thing. My mother carries the serving plate to the kitchen bin, steps on the pedal and lowers it carefully inside, like she's transporting a small child down a slide. She keeps her foot on the pedal to hold the lid open, so I can pour in the rest of the coleslaw.

'I got this jumper in Benetton,' I say.

She pinches at the fluffy red mohair.

'Looks nice,' she says.

'It was in the sales,' I say. 'I've been invited to a party.'

'That's nice,' my mother says.

The lid slams back.

SPAGHETTI

Three Months Earlier

cumulonimbus

Sent: 13/11/2015 – 01:06

Dear Lili,

This message will come to you, no doubt, as a surprise. You don't know who I am, and I should say now that, unfortunately, this shall remain so for a little while longer. I know, I know, I don't even have a profile picture, yet this is anything but one of those pathetic copy-and-paste jobs, that much I can promise you. The reason I ask you to wait before I reveal myself is simple: should I do it now there is still the possibility that you would take my efforts the wrong way, thinking me some kind of common man who only wishes to attract a pretty girl's attention. Which I guess I am, in a way. (There is no denying that you are a very beautiful woman.) But also . . . I like you. I do. I worry you might think I'm nothing special. So I guess I'm just trying to make sure you like me enough before I reveal my identity. I feel no shame in telling you this. I'm only being honest. Isn't that what all human beings want? To be liked. We know that the lasting impression of a person leaves its imprint on others within thirty seconds of first meeting. Life is ruthless, isn't it? Online dating allows us to entertain a little shyness, thank God, so I thought given the chance I would buy myself a little time. I ask you, please, will you allow me a little mystery before that first fatal handshake? Before we establish that first eye contact that I hope will be sustained between us for a very long time? In time, Lili, I promise I'll reveal all. For now, just trust me enough to read on.

So: I like you. You might be wondering, how do I know? Well you have a delightful profile picture, for starters. You look like a little pixie. So tiny, so perfectly chiselled, like a precious little bird. You have wonderful eyes, so deep and dark. Sorry I just had to tell you that. There's more. In saying this I am painfully aware that you might think I am already overstepping the mark. I have different friends with different opinions, but most of them agree that online dating is a way to meet new people – the etiquette says you should ignore the people you do know. You must get so much attention on this website, and God knows there are too many creeps in the world, so what are my chances, really? I wonder. But Lili, the button to click to write to you is right there, flashing, top right on the page. I only need to click on it to have a chance to talk to you – really *talk* to you, not on opposite sides of a counter. I may as well come clean now. I am a Fasta regular. Oh yeah, baby, can't get enough of that fresh spaghetti!

Sorry, you must hear that all day long from your customers. Why would you waste your precious time on a lengthy online conversation with someone you regularly ignore in real life? This is what I hope to demonstrate. Let me state my case.

I am, like many men, a man suffering from loneliness, lost in the stomach of this blind city. Most of us feel this way, but very few are willing to admit it. Let me begin with a broad statement: I'll say, then, that loneliness in London is the organic by-product of ambition. 95 per cent of men who come to the city to pursue a high-flying career are going to experience the acute symptoms of solitude within three years of their arrival. Of that 95 per cent, 50 per cent will settle for an OK job, a shit flatshare and a boring string of dates. They will begin to believe that the loneliness and frustration they experience every day is a given in life and never ask any questions. Fine: the human being is endlessly adaptable. 45 per cent will push themselves to their very limits in order to overcome loneliness. A third will go crazy, a third will succeed, a third will move away. The remaining 5 per cent are the kind of sociopaths who manage London's biggest firms. Mind you, I say all this with my tongue stuck firmly in my cheek: I know full well it's a bad idea not to crosscheck one's data, and I haven't been able to verify these percentages through a series of rigorous interviews, but trust me, had I attempted to, I would've had trouble squeezing the slightest hint of insecurity out of most men. I would've likely drawn a blank. Insecurity: that's really the problem for most of us. Whether us men like it, or not. I guess it doesn't rate so highly in compatibility charts on websites like this one. As a desirable trait, confidence is up there with height (a piece of crucial information I can give you is this: I am over six foot tall). I'm sure the proportion is more or less exact: what draws men like us to the city is what eventually undoes us, rots us to the core, transforms most of us into those tie-wearing, briefcase-wielding, dick-swinging twats you see filling up Farringdon pubs.

Apologies for my language. It's hard not to get carried away when I think about this stuff. You see what I'm getting at hopefully: I am a passionate man. Passion is historically connected with suffering, most of all in Christianity, but in many other religions less known in the West, too. Passion as well as ambition propels me, and this is why I have prospered, relatively speaking, surviving that critical three-year window. I have remained relatively sane. But rabies will eventually hit among the pick of the pack too, when your breed is rammed in a small enough cage, dog on top of dog. I worry that after ten years in the city it's begun to chip away at me too. I'm getting weary, Lili, which is why I write to you. I have known I wanted to meet you since the first time I saw you. I look at you every day, when I come in for lunch, but I have never had the guts to do anything about it. Asking the pretty waitress for her number is one of those things we, alienated new humans, seem to have forgotten how to do. This incapability (this condition of stillness) this is what I mean when I say my current life has begun to frighten me. When your lovely photograph appeared at the top of my screen I was frozen still. I felt in an instant I had a duty not to let my life slip by. It was the first time I'd had the courage to think those words so clearly. From the computer screen, I felt like you were looking right at me. So I wrote to you.

Your Cloud

SOUP

Ruth
Now

Life trundles on and I am keeping at it. March still feels a long way away, but I know better: spring will be here when we least expect it. Time to get started on a big clean. Like my mother, I keep the flat tidy in its well-worn corners. My flat, all mine. I cheer myself up: at least it is done, at least he's seeing someone else. This is final. I cannot contact him. I don't know where he's living and, after I saw him with that girl, I deleted his mobile number in horror. I don't regret it.

Where is he living? Certainly not in Cornwall. And certainly not with her, who looks young enough to be living at home. Probably in some bachelor bedsit with fittings chosen by others, where the bathroom mirror hangs so high that he can see his bald patch in full. I can picture the black mould growing in the cracks of his shower tiles. I, on the other hand, have a grown-up flat to tend to – a grown-up life. I lack none of the necessary skills for survival. I can do minor repairs, cure a variety of ailments. I have plenty of fresh water. I can cook soup.

Soup, I've decided, is safe. You don't have to bite into it and if you keep your eyes on the bowl you won't notice the level go down. I keep at it. This is the amended plan and I follow it religiously – I have come to believe that if I follow some arbitrary rules then salvation will follow. Though I am not sure what salvation entails, and I make up my own rules: I wake up each morning at 6:30 a.m., eat five spoonfuls of sugar and go to work.

In this dream we're holidaying somewhere exotic. There is soft, percussive music playing from beyond our open window. I am lying on the peach coverlet and you are holding my feet in your hands. You're trailing fluttering kisses along the sharp bone, where it juts out at the ankle. 'My baby my baby my baby my kitten my precious pearl my little baby girl,' you say. 'Mmmmmh,' you lick the length of my sole, staring right into my eyes. Your pupils are tiny in their white orbs. Your tongue is very cold. 'I love to eat baby girl's feet, baby girl's feet.'

One of Mrs O'Toole's granddaughters comes in to introduce her little girl to her great-grandmother. There is no chance that Mrs O'Toole or the baby will retain any memory of the encounter beyond this afternoon. The granddaughter will, though, and this is the point of the visit. Mrs O'Toole's arms get tired. She asks me if I can hold the baby for her and I sit very still, like I'm made of glass, and the baby is a live baby in a glass cradle that could shatter at any minute. When the mother gets back she picks the baby up from my arms. 'Don't want you to be late on your rounds,' she says. She smiles. Through the glazed bedroom window, I see her checking the baby thoroughly, tilting her backwards and forwards, as though inspecting a bicycle for scuffs or scratches. Well, you kids behave, off I go, back to my rounds.

This dream moves at an unexpected speed. Usually my dreams are slow and reflective, but this one looks like it's been filmed on a different camera and then it becomes clear that I am, indeed, being filmed. The film follows a morning in the life of two anthropomorphic animals, me and my companion. I'm both in front of the camera and behind it, and I can feel each part of my body simultaneously in both of those places. It is unclear in the dream to what extent the creatures are animals and to what extent humans; whether their evolutionary process has terminated or is still currently unfolding; whether we are shooting a nature documentary or a social commentary. This poses some issues. For instance, the camera kicks in as we are still sleeping in a pile. We are wearing no clothes and there is no bedding, but our bodies are covered with fur, some kind of down. In the dream I am considering with some difficulty whether the way we are sleeping means we are sleeping naked, whether I am infringing on any rights by filming this moment. I assess nudity in terms of the percentage of a body's surface that is uncovered by clothes or other garments − skin on show − and so it takes a while before it occurs to me that something that stems from the body is not clothing. I begin to find the intimacy of the scene unsettling. I should not be here, I think, yet I am. The camera fast-forwards as our conjoined bodies twitch in their sleep in the early hours of the morning. When the alarm goes off my companion pinches at the old-fashioned alarm clock blindly, with its finger and thumb, finally managing to depress the button with its left paw. We scatter to the kitchen, busy, fully proficient. I squat on my four legs to go through the motions of making breakfast.

I poach us two perfect eggs. We plate up and eat, our muzzles shoved together.

Call-Me-Melissa has come up with her seasonal project. It's her own New Year's resolution to give to charity, but of course, none of her subordinates are exempt from it. Care home staff and patients are invited to produce rag-and-cloth dolls, which are sold to wealthy women who like to furnish their houses in a 'shabby chic' style. This is only one of the many things that Melissa's charity does. The patients can choose whether to take part, but the staff aren't given an option. It takes me a whole night to make the doll for my contribution. I work with pieces of twine for the hair and use offcuts from the clothing that Neil has left behind. His running gear, for example: he phased it out when he started to wear natural fibres only. In his fitness phase, he'd insisted on wearing black hi-tech roll necks with luminous inserts along the stitching. He slunk out of the flat like a thief. Where was he going?

I sleep an hour and wake up at 6:30 a.m. with the alarm on my phone ringing.

In this dream his bald skull is lying before me. It is freshly shaved, for the first time in a while, the skin irritated along the grooves made by the electric razor. He's come back to bed. He's said sorry. All is good again. He's lying with his back to me. I cling to it and match my toes to his. I reach up my hand to stroke his face but find only a flat surface, smooth on all sides and dotted by the braille of his stubble.

The doll I produce looks like a miniature goth who might hang out in Camden. I email Melissa to tell her I am done and she immediately rings me back on my mobile, insisting I go to her house to drop it off, even though it's a Saturday. What she actually says is, 'Come over, sweetheart, I'll show you my collection.' I stifle a laugh; she sounds like an old pervert. And perhaps she is a little perverse, since she seems to be unable to restrain herself from showing off her wealth, her thorough happiness.

I fuss nervously over what shoes to wear to Melissa's house. Will my brown heels look dirty on her cream carpet? They do. The dolls are sitting in rows in the tall gilded cabinet. They look out of place, like adopted children, but perhaps that is the point and that is after all what the charity is about. Melissa is fretting; she asks me if I have a few minutes to listen as she practises her speech for tomorrow.

'A variety of representatives . . . from different sectors . . . will come to the conference,' she says. I agree to stand in as a representative. She hands me a cup of herbal tea. I want to go home. 'If you've ever thought of adopting a child . . .' she begins.

In this dream I am a young dog. I am running and I am blind with pain, blind with blood. My muzzle has been hit and I don't know where I'm running.

Mona's niece is pregnant again. Mona has many nieces and nephews, but this niece is known for having all the babies. This must be either her third or her fourth. To spice things up a little, she's documenting this new pregnancy closely.

'Fernanda is arty,' says Mona. 'Her husband Vasco is a photographer. He takes pictures of the bump.'

They update Mona on the progress once a week. In the photos, Fernanda is always wearing black, posing with her side to a white wall. The shadow of her belly grows like the phases of the moon.

'Why the black?' I ask Mona.

'After, they make a video,' she says, 'with the photos from every day.'

I google 'photos 9 months pregnant'. I am confronted by a list of stop-motion videos. I realize that Fernanda and her husband are not unique practitioners but are operating within a specific artistic niche. I trawl from link to link for a long time, well into the night. It is very nice in the flat at night, very quiet, peaceful. He is never coming back. I sleep two hours; wake up at 6:30 a.m., eat five spoonfuls of sugar.

In this dream I am leaning against a wall. A photographer whose face I cannot see – the heavy blanket of his old-fashioned camera is hiding his head – takes photo after photo of me against the white wall. Every time the shutter clicks, my shadow imprints itself on to the wall, remains there long after the flash has disappeared. The photographer holds up his left hand to signal 'stay still', as he takes the same photo, photo after photo. With each flash the shadow behind me grows larger, like gunpowder residue, like a dark halo the same shape as my body.

Alanna snatches Mona's reading glasses from her desk, positions them on the tip of her nose, turns to me and whispers in a nasal tone: 'After pregnancy, once they have stitched you back together, the position popularly known as "doggy-style" is the recommended position to perform penetrative sex. Says on Mumsnet.'

A nurses' in-joke: Mumsnet is full of terrible trash and the amateur medical advice is borderline criminal.

Alanna turns towards Mona, pushes the glasses up the bridge of her nose, shoots her an alarmed look. 'You might want to notify Fernanda.' Alanna doesn't smile, but that's part of the comedy of it: the professional voice, the butterfly spectacles. What she does is wink and that too is spot-on in character.

In this dream I am aware that Alanna suffers from a very rare although non-infectious disease and that, whether by shyness or illness, she cannot bear to be touched. In the dream we are trying to figure out a permanent solution to the issue. It seems several attempts to fix her have been made, with little success prior to this particular dream. The experts have given up. We are sat in her kitchen drawing diagrams in large notebooks, trying to come up with something that might cure her. As we discuss it, I experience the feeling that we are the only two people left in the world. I can't comfort her: touch triggers the illness. The dream is truncated: it ends before we reach a satisfying conclusion.

One evening I open my eyes in a dark room. I don't know what time it is and I don't know where I am. I don't remember falling asleep, but I obviously have. My temple hurts from resting on something hard. There's something hard in my throat. A hand pats my head gently. I have not moved at all so I can't be sure if I woke up to the touch of the hand or if the hand has been touching me all along or if the hand knows I am awake now and that is why it's touching me. It is a very solid, gentle, repetitive touch.

'We've all been there, darling. Don't you worry,' says Mrs O'Toole. 'It's much harder when it's your first. Then you get used to it.'

The thing about Mrs O'Toole is that she's so used to giving advice that she will attempt to do so even when she has no clue what she's talking about. Not knowing either, I thank her, because it feels good, for a moment, to be looked after.

TOMATOES

Nearly Ten Years Earlier

17/06/2006

We're here!

I've just finished unpacking. The guy at reception said the residence is half empty, so he gave us a free upgrade. So nice of him – he even remembered our names! This trip is finally looking up. Our new room is MASSIVE! Even Beadle looks a little bit pleased. She let me have the bed next to the window, which let's face it, is the best spot, all bright and sunny. I think monks or nuns owned this building back in the day because from my bed I can see the inner courtyard and it has a well in the middle like people used to live here. It's so weird to think these are student halls the rest of the year. Italian students have it pretty good! It's got a cool east London vibe. There's vintage stuff in here that's probably worth some serious bucks: a vintage aquamarine table and two huge twin wooden wardrobes stuffed full of prickly blankets in pastel colours like duck egg and baby pink and chick yellow. And the ceilings are hand-painted and in between the two beds there's a nook in the wall, with a ceramic statue of the Virgin Mary inside. Beadle said it freaks her out. Obviously. Is there anything in the world that doesn't freak her out? But I think it's so beautiful here, the garden in full bloom with peonies and hydrengaes (sp?).

★

Just chilling out in the halls of residence after dinner. Trying to digest some of this food before I can go to bed. The good news is: everything they say about Italy is true. I had a massive plate of pasta for four quid and the man called me 'blondie' and gave me limoncello on the house. Bad news: dining alone is NO FUN. I had to smoke a lot of cigarettes and pretend to be an American film star to feel OK about it. Beadle said she would join me at the restaurant but she never turned up. When I came back the light was already off though I could tell she had been to the shops, because there was a bag at the foot of her bed with some teabags or sugar in it, I don't know. Although maybe she brought it from home. She's totally the kind of person who brings teabags from home when she goes on holiday. My mum does.

Xoxo Ally

P.S. I didn't text Mike goodnight back. I can do this! I am an ADULT.

18/06/2006

Jesus Christ.

Just got back to our room and I'm fucking EXHAUSTED.
Totally worth it though! Today was SO GOOOOOOD.

Turns out Beadle had done her homework really well –
nothing strange about that, she always does her homework,
just I never had her down as an A student. Then again,
I don't know that much about her. She's a new friend.
I remember her from school, vaguely, but I never really
spoke to her much before college. Back then I had Trace
and Franki and I can't really remember who she used to
hang out with. Me and the girls were in our own little
world, which is why they sometimes said we were
cliquey but really what's wrong with enjoying each other's
company? Surely people are allowed to pick and choose
who their friends are. You don't have to be equally nice
or friendly to everyone. And let's be honest, nobody likes
everyone, and anyone who says they do is a big fat liar.
Anyway my friendship with Beadle today goes to show
I've grown out of that phase.

It's like this morning she woke up a new person. When
I opened my eyes she was already up, going through her
stuff. I asked her what she wanted to do and I expected her
to say the usual, 'Whatever you want to do, Alanna,'
which always pisses me off, like it's my responsibility to
make sure other people have a good time. To my surprise
she said a walk down to the Colosseum would be nice
to start with. She jumped in the shower and came out
twenty mins later wearing this yellow dress I've never seen

her wearing before. It really looked quite flattering on her! She has a nice figure?!! Beadle, my girl! I mean she's so awkward I don't think I ever thought of her as having a body. She could look good if she tried a little harder.

Turns out she had a proper itinerary. We went to the Colosseum and she explained that gladiators used to fight lions there and stuff, which was kind of cool because you could see the real place where they shot the movies. She can talk much better Italian than I can manage with my phrasebook. She said it's because she took Spanish and Latin in school and that Italian is not too hard to work out if you know a bit of those languages. Sort of a mix between the two. The girls and I all took French of course because French is sophisticated. I put Beadle's skills to the test to buy ice cream and it worked. SO THAT'S GOOD ENOUGH FOR ME.

Xoxo Ally

P.S. No word from M. Might he have finally got the hint?
P.P.S. Beadle still didn't come out for dinner.

23/06/2006

SORRY FOR RADIO SILENCE. I knew I would be shit at this. I'm trying!

But we've been doing so much over the last few days that whenever I'm home all I want to do is eat something and pass out. I genuinely have moments where I feel like I'm getting the flu I am THAT tired. So much for our relaxing holiday!

I don't know where Beadle finds the energy to do it all, especially as she never seems to eat any food. This morning I'd had enough of having to sneak behind her back and have dinner alone every evening, so I decided to confront her about it. She said something under her breath which I didn't fully catch, about a gluten allergy and keeping to a mostly vegan diet. It's nonsense. Franki went vegan for a while and I don't know many people who can put it away like that girl. Sometimes she would pretend she was drunker than she was just to attack some cheddar. Most girls are weird about eating and stuff. When I was fifteen sometimes I ate so much chocolate that I couldn't stop until I made myself really sick and I had to throw it all up. I stopped doing it after a while. This is something else. She makes excuses so she doesn't have to watch me eat, like I have a disgusting fetish or something. None of us wants to put on weight but there's no reason to be this bloody mental about it.

We've already seen all the main touristy bits of Rome and I know it's a big city but I kind of wish we could just have a retail therapy day or a day to sleep in or just wander around and relax. That would be part of the experience, wouldn't it?

A

24/06/2006

Saw the inside of the Pantheon for fifteen whole Italian euros and sorry but there is literally nothing in there, just a bunch of old stones. Bit bored of old stones at this point. Brought home a takeaway pizza to surprise Beadle instead of going to the restaurant. I thought we could have an early night. When I got in she wasn't there so I ate it all in the bath. I didn't even care that I was dripping tomato sauce everywhere in the water. It was disgusting – it looked like I'd been bleeding – but I sat in there anyway until it became cold. At some point, I heard the door open. Ruth was home. I only came out of the bathroom when I heard her get into bed and the click of her bedside lamp going off.

A

25/06/2006

Wasted a whole day on a trip to Ostia, just because the guidebook said it was 'worth the trip'. Ha ha ha. It's like Brighton with less piercing stores and no actual fun stuff to do. Haven't heard from Mike for like three days. Fuck that pea head. God I feel miserable.

A

28/06/2006

OK I'm actually done with this shit.

I honestly don't know how I thought coming out here with Beadle was a good idea. I should've known better. She's always been an obsessive little loser. She is like a sixty-year-old. We're like a sixty-year-old couple, making polite conversation, then turning in for the night at 9 p.m. WHAT IS MY FUCKING LIFE. Thank God there's no

Radio 4 here or we'd be catching up on *The Archers* like my granny. Two days before we go home and what does she do? She plans a trip to THE VATICAN. 'But the fresco in St Peter's is breath-taking. Look!' And she shows me her stupid *Lonely Planet* again. I don't give a fuck about the fucking fresco! And you can't see shit in those black-and-white pictures. 'Really, it's an INVALUABLE piece of history!' I don't give a fuck about the Pope either and the only time I enjoy looking at nuns is in horror movies when they get possessed and their heads start to spin. Beadle's too meek and I'm too nice and so she gets it her way, so maybe, really, she's too clever and I'm too stupid, I don't even know any more. All I know is I am done with her today. So I've stayed behind. Fuck venting in this notebook like I'm a schoolgirl, too. It's sunny outside, I'm going for a walk.

★

I just cannot believe it.

So much has happened in the last few hours that it's like a different person wrote the stuff I wrote this morning. I needed this so much. So, I go down to reception and that guy from the travel agency (the hot one) was sitting there on his laptop and there's no one else around. So I took the plunge and decided to speak to him. I made a joke, like, 'Can you believe a girl like me has been ditched for the Pope!' He looked up a bit alarmed so I lied because I didn't want to come across as a loser. I said my friend had family visiting so I was at a loose end and wanted to go on his tour: can you believe it, at this point I am fully willing to pay for this guy's time just to have someone to talk to. So fucking pathetic. So, at first he says tours are for groups, but I do a bit of sad eyes and he says, OK then, lemme take down your details. An exception because he thinks I'm a nice girl. And I notice he saves my number straight to his phone.

We leave the hotel and I could tell he was starting to relax and in a few minutes we were chatting like old friends, you know that special feeling – I felt properly comfortable around him, like I'd known him for ages. We get on the metro and we're sitting together, our knees are touching and stuff. Anyway I end up spilling the beans about Beadle and her funny behaviour. That she's always wanting to walk around twelve hours a day and never eats anything. I said I suspect she's surviving on condensed milk miniatures, because the other day I dropped a hairpin in the bathroom bin and found a bunch of empties at the bottom when I went to look for it. That made him laugh. He has a great laugh. It made me feel like I've been blowing it all out of proportion. It finally felt like being on holiday.

And anyway the long and the short of it is he's taking me for dinner tonight. Eat your heart out, Mike. Where is Beadle? Fuck me if I know. Fuck me if I care!

Xoxo Ally

30/06/2006

Diary dearest,

Back I am, with a deplorable little story from the other night. So the hotel guy? Me being me, I slept with him, obviously. It was pretty good sex. Franki was right to say that sex with a grown man is a completely different experience, so I texted her that, straight after. No reply. Probably high. After he went to take a shower, like grown-ups do after sex, you know? So I took out my phone and typed 'Goodnight, Mikey,' then I blocked Mike's number. I was done. He came back in a white towel and I thought he looked pretty hot. I was pretty pleased with myself. I took a shower straight after him, because he had taken one so I felt I should too. When I came out he was nowhere to be seen. I waited for an hour in his room reading through the messages saved on my phone, and when he wasn't back yet I thought I should leave, so I put on my clothes and went back to our room.

And guess what, Beadle is sitting up in bed, with these black eyes looking bigger than usual. It creeped the fuck out of me. I ask what's up and she pushes a fucking sugar sachet into my hand, with something written on it. A name and a number.

[NEIL: 07972839547]

He'd gone and given her his fucking number. While I was sitting in his bed, waiting for him to come back. Told her to ring him 'whenever she needs someone to talk to'.

I'd quite like to go home now.

TEABAGS

Ruth
Now

It's been over a week since I last spoke to Alanna, and just when I thought I'd imagined it all, the Lolitas ambush me. I am sitting at my desk and my tea has become blacker than I like it, when their signature high-pitched call sears through the hallway. So often, these days, I lose track of time. I squeeze the bag into the cup and toss it in the paper bin. The Lolitas scramble in. 'Ruth! Rise and shine, honeybee!'

It is too early. I am not prepared to be seen by others. This is why I come in an hour before my shift starts, to allow myself enough time to adjust. They scramble through the Bowl door, jangling and chiming, stretching their limbs, shaking their hair out of their hoods.

'You!' One Lolita points her finger at me. There are several diamond bands around it, probably fake but extremely sparkly. They make my eyes water. 'You're in charge of the hen-do!'

Am I? I'd hoped I had willed it away by ignoring it. When Alanna said she'd give me a week to decide what I wanted, a week felt like a very long time. And it does feel like she said it a very long time ago. Time is strange. I think I was awaiting direction or for her to change her mind. When she didn't come to find me after seven days had elapsed, I'd allowed myself to hope it might all be forgotten. Ruth Beadle organizing a party: chronicle of an announced tragedy.

I can count on the fingers of my hands the number of parties I've been invited to. With the same ease, I can recall the specific hue of each humiliation. I still have bad dreams.

As a child, you could've described me as shy, though I never quite got the hang of it. Other shy children were discounted from feeling bad about themselves. It was always the very pretty ones, whose cheeks glowed pink when they were asked a question in class. Alanna and I didn't cross paths until later, but it isn't hard to imagine her as one of those children. Unable to speak, they emitted eagerness from the tops of their cutely bowed heads. They wore soft woollen jumpers and tentatively offered their hands to the outgoing kids in the playground.

I was never that kind of shy. My shyness was impervious, with electric edges, like a ball of yarned nerves: sharp, throbbing, veined with inadequacy and unwillingness. Other children steered clear of me like I was a lame animal. In turn I began to feel like an animal myself: a feral, shaky thing that could make even adults uneasy. On my eleventh birthday I insisted I wanted to hold a party – a 'gathering', my mother called it. I collected recipes from old magazines and took the free paper home from the bus so that I could pore over the 'dinner-in-ten' section. I made my own canapés, decorated with pine nuts and olive segments. The kids didn't like them; olives and nuts were grown-up food. They lamented the lack of a face-painter. It was the first and last birthday I ever celebrated. I would never hold a gathering again.

Growing up, I might have found a way to turn my inwardness outward had I been willing to stick with the humiliation. Push myself. But I didn't want to – certainly not without any encouragement, and none was being offered. With time, people lose patience with shyness. They want to be rewarded for their time, turning callous when they see no improvement. The parties got worse. I would sit in a corner and refuse to play Spin the Bottle or whatever sticky game they were playing. But I would go because it felt worse not to. When I began to receive fewer and fewer invitations, I knew deep down that I had only myself to blame. Unable to disentangle my resentment from my awkwardness, I let my predicament conflate into a general feeling of malaise until I was unable to tell if I was right in hating them or they were right in hating me. I was too busy, at that point, hating myself for not trying harder. Finally, I made a resolution to tell people I hated my birthday. I wasn't the only teenager to say so, but I thought I was the only one whose wishes were never contravened. Nobody ever organized a surprise party for me.

Adulthood offered a chance to crystallize my adolescent resolve: I simply became a person who doesn't enjoy parties. That's Ruth Beadle. Everyone knows I'll be the first to leave the staff Christmas party, and the last one was no exception. I go because Call-Me-Melissa won't take no for an answer. She keeps an eye on me like you'd keep an eye on a child at dinner. I wash down her cardboard canapés with water and I stay sober until she is drunk enough that I can finally leave. I don't want Melissa to think I'm ungrateful.

I'll go to the staff Christmas parties because I have to, but for all other purposes I have developed a set of curt stock responses that I yield when I'm hard-pressed. 'I don't like the crowds.' 'I don't like the drinking.' 'I don't like the stink of smoke on my clothes the morning after.' Adults can sense when you're holding back from explaining a painful childhood memory; mostly they won't bother making it into an uncomfortable conversation. 'I was a bit of an outsider in school, I guess.' I leave a suggestive pause. Does she abseil at weekends and doesn't want to spoil her balance? they might think. Or is she into another kind of party – kink parties, perhaps, it's always the quiet ones, isn't it! – and doesn't want to waste a minute on a lesser occasion?

I don't know what people think I do in my spare time; most adults ask very few personal questions. So I guess my technique works well if you're the kind of person who is happy with letting others decide what you're all about. I am a private person, that much is known. It has its upsides in that mostly I am left alone. Or maybe I have been left alone for so long that I've become a private person. Neil said I was simply unwilling to make the effort. His workmates thought I was stuck-up. It reflected badly on him, although the fact that he's fucking a little girl will look even worse. I don't imagine he expects her to entertain Rory and Ian. Although, I wonder, would she fare better?

Now Alanna wants me to organize her hen-do. It's a surprise party apparently, although Alanna suggested it herself and will probably provide a list of potential dates. I don't like the word 'hen-do'. We are women, not chickens; but I can't come up with a better suggestion so I refer to it simply as 'the Party'. If it wasn't Alanna who'd asked me, I'd think this was all a cruel joke. But Alanna doesn't do cruel any more. Since finding out she's a born nurse, Alanna says she's resolved never to be mean to people for no reason. So it can't be a joke, can it? We are *women* after all, and not children.

I open my eyes to a feeling of warmth and the knowledge that it is very cold outside. Of course, I am still asleep and this is a dream. At first, in my dream, I cannot see clearly: all around me is a grainy, compressed darkness. It is a comforting feeling. When my eyes finally focus, I see that a woman is asleep in front of me. I am stood at the foot of her bed. She sleeps uncoiled, stretched out sloppily across the mattress. Thin light spills from the slatted window, slicing across her body like the spine of a striped animal. Her mouth is open and I want to push two fingers through her lips. I feel confident I could do so without waking her. I wait for the dream to kick into motion, but it doesn't: it stays as still as a picture. I look down at my hands and realize I am holding a tall glass of water, which suddenly feels very cold and impossibly heavy. 'Drink it!' I yell, and then I wake up.

When Alanna told them I was to be maid of honour, it took the Lolitas a couple of days to recover from not being chosen. Then their enthusiasm got the better of them: round they came, wagging their tails, begging to be involved with little yelps and leaps. So it seems that I'm not only in charge of a party, but also in charge of interns. The Lolitas have collated a list of possible guests from Alanna's Facebook friends. It includes female family members, friends from school and women who regularly feature on her timeline. This approach seems intrusive to me, but the Lolitas assure me that it was suggested by Alanna. Certainly, she seems concerned with her presence on social media: she has over a thousand friends on Facebook and has meticulously completed her profile information. It took the Lolitas a whole weekend to get the list ready. Like I say, there are many activities a person can choose to do in their spare time. Alanna can ask the Lolitas to do anything, and they'll promptly execute her request, like it's just the thing they've been waiting for. The wedding isn't even until June.

Still, she can't make them like me. They leave the list on my desk in a bright yellow plastic folder and scamper towards the laundry room. There is a sticker on the folder that says a tick equals 'compulsory' and a heart is a 'very close friend'. The folder looks thick. How many people can one woman form an emotional bond with? And, out of all of them, how is it possible that I have been chosen for this job?

The Lolitas reconvene at my chair. One of them perches on the armrest.

'So?' she says. 'What do you think?'

The Lolitas are in shock when the realization finally hits that, no, Alanna and I are not even friends on Facebook.

AFTERSHAVE

Three Months Earlier

kittenwithasledgehammer
Sent: 18/11/2015 – 03:11

dear claude (seems less creepy tho a bit like im talking to some old french dude but who knows, maybe you are one, anythings possible)

what can i say seems ridiculous i'm even getting back to your message in many ways. i didn't mention it to any of the boys at work even tho they set up the Kindred Spirit account for me and cant wait to marry me off to a good man. found it open in the tabs when i went to do the weekly paperwork on the work computer didnt i. they used this awful photo from the school yearbook, p sure they left it on deliberately, can u believe? i manage this shit! but often they forget. they wouldnt last two days in another establishment, goddammit i'm way too chill. imagine if i told them the only guy i finally decide to talk to is a total weirdo. they wouldn't drop it. you should leave a large tip for those boys next time, my creepy dear secret admirer. cuz i didnt delete the profile, simply changed the password and details. cuz you know i guess i am DESPERATE enough to meet someone nice to put up with the amount of weirdos on this piece of crap website. staggering. like you say. i mean it is funny bc in theory what is different about you, except your message is by far the craziest of the bunch? i mean you sound REALLY desperate for someone nice. maybe i like that. it makes me feel like i have nothing to lose lol. you're not gonna follow me around soho are you? actually if you wanted to stalk me full stop it makes no difference if i get back to your messages or not, you could just follow me when i come home from work. im not saying you should do that. pls don't do that.

all right, hamlet, the thing is I agree with you. something is rotten in london. i can relate. i often get lonely. at work, i am sad and distracted, and thats why i dont notice nice boys like you. assuming youre a boy, which i dont know. i dont know who you are so i cant say that i like you. im sorry. but i dont dislike you. let's keep talking.

cumulonimbus
Sent: 19/11/2015 – 00:54

Dear Lili,

Wow. Just wow. I'm about to sound incredibly silly since I obviously wrote expecting some kind of reply, otherwise I wouldn't have written at all, but now it has come I feel completely unprepared for it. It's just so *great* to hear from you, even beyond my own expectations. In the few days it took you to get back to me I have been thinking about the message I sent almost constantly, making myself sick with excitement and discouragement in turns. You know what's crazy? This rollercoaster of feelings (which started even before your reply came, if I'm honest) is the most I have felt in the last few years. Which has reinforced my belief that I have finally done the right thing in writing to you. Lili, I feel so alive right now. Thank you.

You spoke in your message about how hard it is to navigate dating and about feeling pressured by the expectations of others. I can really relate to what you are saying. Dating websites have long perplexed me and I only caved into them after long thought. I still have mixed feelings – though I accept that they have quickly become a pervasive tool for seeking new relationships (of many kinds, also). In no way do I mean to condemn any means that a human being might choose to employ to connect with other humans. But I *am* uneasy. It doesn't seem like a very holistic approach and I cannot cope with the predatory aspects. Much like yourself. I have an annoying junior partner who loves to corner me in the office kitchen to discuss our dating lives. I am sure that he – like your workmates – means well. Camaraderie: the process of bonding among males via sharing the edited, grandiose details of one's sexual endeavours. (Simple creatures, us men, aren't we? Well, some of us are.) He is young, inexperienced and new to the firm. Sharp, well dressed, always freshly shaven. He probably looks up to me as someone who might pass on some knowledge about the facts of life. I know I used to feel that way about my superiors and I can tell that not knowing half as much about me as I do about him frustrates him, puts him on edge. Still, he tries. He gets out his phone and shows me his Tinder matches: 'Fit bird, yeah?' he says. Something like that. Normally I would try to give him something back: I know he, too, just wants to be liked. But I find his manner unnerving – his persistence, also. I can't help but feel that he is using me to validate his own compulsion. And all these girls look the same to me, caked in tanning lotion, paralysed in their bikinis on tropical beaches. I used to work for a travel agency in my twenties and I hated it. That's what the photos make me think of. It's all very business-like: not unlike sourcing clients' profiles, like I do, or serving customers, like you. This isn't about that, is it? You and me, right? We've had enough of that.

Claudius (look him up, fascinating)

kittenwithasledgehammer
Sent: 19/11/2015 – 02:40

Dear Clay Who Began the Conquest of Britain (did my home-work, happy?)

maybe we'll settle for clay what do you think? by far least creepy nickname so far.

my dear clay how is it that you are both totally mad and also make complete sense to me? dangerous man to get involved with obviously. youre lucky i dont know better arent you? i think i did myself in by getting back to that first message so i guess worth keeping at it. thats a lie, im writing back cuz i want to. well done. youve successfully intrigued me. i wonder if ive even spoken to you in person this week. ive been trying to pay atten-tion, but theres no telling is there? you really are good at blending in despite being a complete weirdo. once i had a stalker who kept coming into my work and it was creepy bc he wasnt v good at stalking at all. i mean if youre stalking someone

139

pretty sure theyre not supposed to know. well this guy came in every day and bought the same thing each time – you know that teeny garlic bread basket we do? btw dont order that we bake it from frozen. literally no better than supermarket bread. you know the one tho? just because it was the cheapest item on the menu and clearly it wasnt his lunch because who the fuck is going to be full with one teeny garlic roll, and clearly it wasnt a snack or a side to something else he bought elsewhere, like idk a side salad, because he sat in store to eat it, a full hour between one and two, when we are at our busiest. taking up a whole table and just fucking *staring* you know? nibbling on that bread crust to make it last until the whole thing looked like a lump of baby food. *really* fucking creepy let me tell you. so in so far as regular customers go you cant be that creepy or i wouldve already called security on you like i eventually did on that guy. but creepy enough to tell me all this stuff in your messages, maybe i sold you your £9 lunch deal today and i don't even know it? why the cautionary tale? i dont know i guess i am wondering, why would you say you want to change your life and not take action? why dont you start by talking to me at work in person? talk to me, do something. maybe i do like you, you know, its just how can i be sure.

WHITE WINE

Ruth
Now

I gather the pile of unopened mail from the counter: letters, leaflets, a couple of slim parcels. I don't know who they're for; I haven't had the heart to look at the names on the address labels. They must be Neil's, or mine, of course; who else's? I take the mail and the folder from my bag and bring them to the coffee table. I sit down on the floor in front of the sofa with my legs crossed under the coffee table like I'm about to have dinner off it, which is another thing I've taken to doing. Is there anything sadder than eating dinner alone in the kitchen? Mostly, I snack in front of the TV, which isn't in itself less sad, but it at least makes dining on your own feel like less of an occasion, less of a reminder of everything that's changed. I arrange the letters on top of each other by decreasing size; the folder is the largest so it goes at the bottom. I push the pile to my left. One and a half months of letters is a lot of letters.

I begin opening them from the top of the pile. Most of

it is uneventful news. A couple of charity catalogues, a gift calendar from the bank, my nursing college's annual alumni brochure. A few takeaway menus. Mostly, it's bills in Neil's name. Neil owes money on the electricity bill, Neil owes money on the gas bill, Neil hasn't paid the last two months of our broadband and so unfortunately our internet has been disconnected, but could be restored immediately by simply calling an 0800 number, free of charge from any mobile on the same network. Neil is behind with the water payment that was owed in a single yearly instalment a month ago. Neil has been summoned to appear in court but does not have to attend so long as he agrees to pay council tax arrears and cover for court costs of up to sixty-five pounds. The bills aren't coming out of his account because I used his card reader and his savings card to transfer six months of our rent payments into my own private one. He was bound to forget something leaving in a hurry like that. I was among the pre-set payees so that was easy and after that his savings account was empty. He'd better make the best of his time with that girl; he might have to work a second job soon.

I reinsert each letter into its envelope and slide them to my right. I move on to the folder. Two hundred names. Two hundred. All women. I don't know a single one of them. I start with the names that belong to a different generation: Magdas, Debras, Marjories. I go through the list, axing all the old ladies. I'm quite enjoying it. I take a gulp from my writer's glass – I've had to crack open a bottle of Neil's organic wine – and hold my pen like a sword. I jot down some numbers on an envelope, tally marks, like in prison movies, for all the people in Alanna's life I absolutely won't be able to avoid meeting in person. The hearts and ticks add up to twenty-eight names. I go back to the beginning of the list. I take out the Francescas and Elizabeths and Bellas. I don't trust those names. On my third glass, I'm getting into a weird, jittery mood, not unlike excitement. I keep talking to myself in a voice that isn't my usual voice. Frankly, if this is going to be the coolest party, I can't go easy on the basic bitches. They're just going to kill the vibe. We don't want none of that. There is a Francesca Jammy Rodgers and I'm undecided about her for a while. I recognize the name but I can't place her. Her fictitious second name tickles me. 'Jammy.' Jammy like lucky? Was she one of those annoying girls who always won at everything? Well, not this time: she's a Francesca and my rules are strict. I mull it over for a while, chewing on the cap of my pen. There is a chubby yellow highlighter heart next to her name. Alanna would probably hate me if I forgot to invite one of her best friends. I guess I will make an exception and add her name to my list. I really don't mind doing this. Then the list is down to 120 so I allow myself a few minutes of me-time. It is the end of a long day, after all. I finish my third glass and dot on some eye cream.

I cross off a few more names: if I don't feel a strong connection or if I simply don't trust the way it sounds when said aloud. All the Eleanors and the Jessicas are gone. It is unlikely that, as maid of honour, I will be expected to make a speech or address all of the guests by their names individually, but I am taking no risks.

In this dream I am a child in the playground and I decide to stand on the swing instead of sitting, to be able to push myself higher and faster. It is the first time I have attempted this and, of course, I misjudge the swing and fall off. My right leg gets caught in one of

the chains and I hang there, crying, upside down, my hair dragging
in the mud beneath me. My mother does not make an appearance.
A large woman rushes over to help and scoops me up in her large
bosom. The white-and-red polka dots of her dress go out of focus
like squashed strawberries when she pushes my cheek against them.
'Poor little girl's leg,' the woman whispers, 'poor little baby foot.'

–187.

When I wake up on the floor the next day the number
flashes up at me from the piece of paper: dash – one – eight –
seven, like the emergency extension for a specific health
service or perhaps a specific sector of the police force. The
dash before it reminds me that this is a negative number.
Sadly, these people won't make it to Alanna's party. They
are the 187 people I have decided are not good enough for
Alanna. On a separate envelope there are thirteen names:
the chosen few. Budget issue, no hard feelings – sorry, girls.
I have a vague memory of triumphantly scrawling the number down and circling it many times with my highlighter. I
feel very hungover. I wipe my mouth with the back of my
hand. I still have a long way to go for the kind of intimate
party everyone has in mind, but right now I'm late for work.

PRAWNS

Three Months Earlier

cumulonimbus
Sent: 20/11/2015 – 00:03

Dear Lili,

It's so wonderful, each time, to hear back from you. I truly mean it. I was sorry, however, to hear about the guy at your work and I really would appreciate it if you'd make an effort not to conflate us. You are right, Lili, the world is full of weirdos. I am glad you managed to get him safely removed. But I have been nothing but honest with you: I genuinely cannot wait for us to meet, it's just that I need to bide my time until I am ready. Please be patient. Besides, that guy, what a moron, if you excuse my language. What's the point of queuing for Fasta if you're not going to order the prawn linguini? (There's a hint for you.) For bread rolls, I go to Tesco. And I never double carb, bloody hell, a man over thirty has to look after himself. (There's another hint. I wonder if it's enough for you to guess who I am or whether I remain in your eyes a more generic character than I'd like to admit.)

While we're at it let's talk about the menu choices in your particular establishment – and I am dying to know your opinion. It's not that I don't enjoy experimenting with food, for that would make me rather boring, but doesn't it ever grate on you, as an Italian, our peculiar British habit of inventing our own version of things? It's become a bit of a mania, hasn't it? We always have to make it *pop-up* or *fusion* or I don't know . . . a *molecular* version of a perfectly nice home-made dish . . . just to make up for the fact that we have no culinary tradition of our own. No one cares about authenticity these days. It seems so demeaning to your rich, nuanced food culture, which I learnt much about when I lived in Rome years ago. Don't worry, I do remember you 'manage that shit', as you so eloquently put it. But I also know that Fasta is a franchise, so I assume you have limited freedom in making executive choices with regards to the menu, let alone the décor. If only you managed the whole thing! I'd sign a petition to have Lili as CEO of Fasta in a heartbeat. Am I right in assuming you would have long shed the chequered tablecloths and those syphilitic basil shoots stuffed in mason jars? There is nothing about you that is caricature. And this is what I love about you: the simplicity of your southern beauty, your humble Mediterranean charm, with all the temper and wisdom of your own sun-beaten land. Lili, I know you want something more from me, but I'm not ready to reveal myself fully, not yet. What I can give you, right now, is a confession, which I hope you'll accept as a token of my good faith: I've been listening to the song you were named after endlessly, on repeat. I've found the Italian version on YouTube and it is so beautiful. I think I am falling *for you,* my charming girl, my little *Lili Marlene.*

Your Clay

kittenwithasledgehammer

Sent: 21/11/2015 – 19:40

knock knock

whos there?

no one bc youre a loser Lili and no one wants to hang out with you

not even the guy from the internet. ok listen its *fine* i can give you more time its not like i have a queue at my door, and its kinda okay if you keep on sweet talking me dont mind that *at all*. here i was thinking you were just some guy whod found a cute angle to ask for a pasta discount. turns out im some kind of mediterranean charm on a power trip who makes grown men listen to love songs on repeat. wow. idk dude real sorry to burst your bubble but lili stands for lillian, which is just as old fashioned as your average british grandma. also my dad's portuguese but ive not even met him. i grew up in lincolnshire with mum. but y'know what mate like i say its not too bad to be complimented. by all means do keep at it. ill tell you what else is good about you. all this talk of being true to yourself in a way is really helping. like it hits the spot. like i kinda thought this guy's spewing a lot of bullshit at first but then i keep coming back to it. ive reread your emails a bunch cuz its nice to have someone motivate you and say good things about you and your work. even if you take a million years to get to the point. even if most of the things you tell me arent even true, i appreciate you taking the time, man, and anyway im only 20. plenty of time to become a badass CEO bitch. cannot wait.

but really what i am trying to say is thank you for making me really think about this stuff because i don't reckon i was thinking about it very much before. and its nice that i am now. its not just that. i guess what im really trying to do here is ask you again, this time kindly, wouldnt it make sense for us to meet IRL? please and thank you. what are you afraid of? i mean im not stupid. ive figured out youre a lot older and stuff. high flying city job hey?!! giveaway, silly. im a millennial remember? they dont make them like you for our generation. its OK. ive dated older guys before. listen, there is nothing you should worry about. except maybe if youre one of those mid-thirties dudes who are like, patchy bald. why dont guys just shave it all off when it gets to that point? once i went out with this late-twenties dude who just wasn't gonna let go of the idea he still had a full head of hair and so he let the front bit grow as long as he possibly could and then he tied it all back into a teeny tiny ponytail on top of his head like a reverse comb-over. imagine when that fell apart during sex it was the saddest thing ever. so much for faking orgasms being a bad thing, i felt so bad i just had to give him something! no wonder i'm shit at dating.

another reason i am shit at dating is telling you about the guys i have fucked before we even meet up in person. i told you, you have nothing to worry about. you cant possibly do worse than that. come on babe, lets go on a bloody date.

OLIVES

Ruth
Now

The care home exists on two different planes, two intersecting maps, like a three-dimensional optical illusion. Staff and patients: blue lens you see one thing, red another. Our clients trawl the corridors like cruise liners, amenably, while all around them we are paddling busily, frantic with work.

It is 7 a.m. and Bex is running Mr Hancock's jute bathmats through the dryer. They make a horrible sound and I'm sure this isn't the way to do it, but unfortunately it's the only option this morning. We've been so focused on Alanna's party that we've forgotten that today is the first Sunday of the month: the preferred day for the less frequent visitors.

What if Miss Hancock turned up? We can't risk welcoming her with dirty bathmats.

Emmy, the redheaded Lolita, scampers into the laundry room.

She says to Bex, 'I see your boyfriend is expecting guests.'

'He's not my fucking boyfriend.' Bex turns, her elbow squeaking against the white plate of the dryer.

'Easy,' says Emmy. 'It's a joke.'

'Well then, you can take these up yourself.' Bex slams her palm on the dryer and strops out of the room.

'What's the matter, Emmeline?' I ask.

'Oh, nothing, you know. Mr Hancock planted a fat one on her.'

I am not exactly surprised. This isn't uncommon – some of the older men do get a bit handsy – but I have always had a strange feeling about Mr Hancock. Still, we all get old, sooner or later, don't we?

My first kiss happens in the back of a school bus. I'll never forget it. The boy is tall with round hips that I very much like. He is a well-liked, wholesome-looking boy with well-respected, stocky guy friends. He has beautiful brown eyes, round and soft, and the premature hint of a moustache lining his top lip. I'd never dare to think he might be interested in me.

The trip lasts a whole day. A picture of our class is taken in front of Big Ben, from the other side of the road so that the clock tower can be included in full. Kids crowd into the middle of the picture, like ants to a nest: around the edges, girls hold their fingers in peace signs, up high like majorettes, and behind them, boys hover rock horns over their heads. I am wearing a nylon pink top and keeping my back straight. The boy I like is to the far left, looking at me.

On the bus home, he passes me a note. It reaches me where I am sitting, travelling in between the rows of seats. He's sealed it with chewing gum and I pop it into my mouth without thinking. It is warm and a little salty.

In the note, he has written, 'Kiss?' Below he has drawn two
square boxes: one for yes and one for no.

I pull a biro from the bum bag around my waist.

Yes, I tick, quickly. Because I do want to kiss him. But what
does he mean? Does he mean right now, right here on the bus,
where everyone can see us? Not here, please, I whisper. But what
if this is the only opportunity he is going to give me?

I fold the note quickly, pass it back. I sit staring forwards, chew-
ing his gum. The laughter grows louder, row by row, as the note
finally reaches the back, where the boy is sitting with his friends.
There is a pause. Silence. I stand up, take a deep breath and turn
around to start making my way towards him.

I dream about this often.

'Those boys are forever terrorizing us,' says Miss Phyllis, as
I enter her room. She's relieved to see us nurses each day;
she's convinced that all the night porters belong to the
Soviet secret services.

Boys, boys, boys. Boys will be boys. At least that is true
of the boys I know, or have known in the last ten years.
There are the boys I see every day. I count them on the
fingers of one hand: my little finger for Donal, the porter,
who is a gross, Teddy Boy kind of hot; ring finger for
Timmy, the cleaner, bless his sweet, romantic soul, his
perfectly chiselled, curly beard; slimy Mr Hancock, who
would love to be added to my list of boys, though of course,
he doesn't quite cut it. Far too old. Index finger for Neil
and Neil and Neil. Although he was never a boy when I
was a girl, always a little older, knowing more, pointing me
in the right direction.

But I have seen the photographs of him as a boy and certainly I have witnessed the tantrums.

151

And who for the thumb?

Mrs O'Toole doesn't have a problem with boys: she likes the night porters. What she dislikes is when the pictures of her family are moved when we clean her room. Her photographs are her greatest pride. Mrs O'Toole's family is genetically atypical. At the back of the display, there are three larger frames with photos of her daughters; in front of them, six smaller frames with pictures of her granddaughters, and up on the wall, updated printouts of her baby great-granddaughter. A private, all-female pantheon. Her three daughters gave birth to couplets of perfect girls, and all the faces are perfectly balanced, stupefying multiples of sparkling brown eyes.

'Leave my angels alone.' She taps my wrist when I move the photographs to dust them. 'Look at them. Aren't they beautiful? We just don't know how to make them in my family, do we?'

She means boys. Boys aren't a problem in Mrs O'Toole's family. There just aren't any. And her girls are beautiful. She insists I bring over each of the photographs so she can kiss them on their etched lips, before I replace the frames on her dresser.

Lunchtime: the Lolitas roll Alanna into the Goldfish Bowl on an office chair. They have decorated her head with a garland of crimpled blue roll and it is my understanding this represents a crown, perhaps a halo? She looks even younger today. She looks like a child bride.

'God save our gracious Queen
Long live our noble Queen,' they sing.
A crown, then.

152

'How's the prep going?' Alanna is smiling, a little embarrassed. 'Sorry I'm late.'

The Lolitas are standing behind her. Alanna rolls her eyes. I feel like laughing.

The Lolitas have started singing again.

'*Send her victorious*
Happy and glorious
Long to reign over us
God save the Queen.'

'Don't you worry about a thing,' I say, pointing my thumb to my chest. 'I've got this.'

Alanna smiles. Looks happy.

After everyone has eaten, I go into the kitchen to prepare a small warm salad for myself. In a large bowl, I add one layer of spinach. I wilt it in the microwave for ten seconds. I take it out and add a few drops of vinegar, then another layer of spinach.

I can hear the Lolitas bickering in the Bowl.

'My place,' one Lolita says, 'has a living room. And yours doesn't. It's idiot-proof. We should do it at mine. We need a living room because we need space.'

'Hellooo?' I have noticed that the Lolitas often call out to one another in this way. 'We're getting ready to party, not play Twister! Everybody knows when you're getting ready it's bathroom space you need.'

'Hellooo? You wanna fit everyone in the bathroom? Where're you gonna put them? In the literal bath?'

I must say I'm impressed by the level of commitment they've invested in this project. I add one more layer of spinach to the bowl and put it in the microwave for ten seconds. They've been discussing the hen-do with the same dedication as little girls describing their imaginary ponies. I repeat the motions. A few drops of vinegar, one more layer, ten more seconds.

'Mine's pink.'

'Mine's pink with purple wings.'

'Mine's pink with purple wings and a silver horn.'

'Mine's pink with purple wings and a silver horn and gold glitter hooves.'

When I reach ten layers and the bowl is half full, I pour a few drops of vinegar on top and add five salted peanuts. I sit down to eat, listening to them, until it is time to go back to work.

If it's sunny and dry enough – which is rare, as spring isn't quite here yet – the inpatients receive their visits on the wooden decking at the back of the care home. A little fresh air is good for them. Mona and I wrap them tightly in coats and scarves and duvets, before moving them outside. We park their wheelchairs in discrete clusters around the garden heaters, and scatter stools between them for the relatives, a little coffee table for each cluster. Though our patients are rarely allowed to drink coffee. It isn't good for their old, weak hearts. It gives them trouble sleeping.

Still, the pretence holds and the elderly are in good spirits as the relatives start to arrive. Miss Hancock is a no-show, which is a relief, because it means her father isn't there to spoil a good day. This is a beautiful place, it must be said, with its Victorian glass-and-steel canopy and scenic steps descending into the back garden like a verdant, natural theatre. We've strung a necklace of fairy lights in the tree above the stone fountain at the back. In the evening we turn them on and, when there is a breeze, they flicker light into the bedrooms of the first-floor guests. The old people love it. The piano bar, Miss Phyllis calls it. 'Are we going down to the piano bar today?'

Nobody really comes to visit Miss Phyllis, but we take her out anyway, because she loves the open air. If there's time, I sit with her for a while, to keep her company. She tells me stories. Miss Phyllis once had her heart broken by a man. It was the only time she allowed that to happen to her. He was a police constable during the war, and she only ever refers to him as Constable, as if it were his given name, or as if remembering his real name might prove too much. Since then, she's 'saved herself', she says, thus preserving her capacity for romance. She is ninety, but it spills out of her, a transparent emotion. And while it may not seem obvious, a care home is a good place for romance. So much time to be spent daydreaming.

Miss Phyllis lifts her lashless eyes to the sun and says, 'A singer's heart is like the bluebird; it wants to fly.'

For the first year we are together, I am never beyond his reach. 'My angel girl,' he tells me. He's always touching me, following the edges of my body, with his fingers spread out across my collarbone or a thumb tracing the slope of a hip. 'Look at you.' His gestures when we are together are always a little larger than they ought to be, to accommodate me. He keeps me safe. In the pub, he draws me into him. He pulls out the chair at the restaurant. The crook of his arm designs a space for me on a packed train, on the sofa, in the bed next to him. 'Little bird,' he says, 'one day you'll learn to fly, but for now you're all mine.' I am happy when he says that. I give him my whole heart.

★

155

Policy dictates that we must lock our people in like children at 8 p.m., so the guests say their goodbyes early. There's a recent trend, I've noticed, in popular culture, concerning the hilarious adventures of senior citizens who've managed to escape the long arm of eldercare. Let me tell you: the outcome tends to be less entertaining than those airport paperbacks will have you believe. We prepare the patients for the night. Miss Phyllis looks dejected as I take her back to her room. Before the war, she was a cabaret singer. And during it they toured hospitals, keeping up the soldiers' morale. I know she longs to be out on the piano bar at night, in a sparkly gown, sitting on the wooden steps, holding a Martini, spearing a single olive on a toothpick. I pour her a mug of sweet tea instead and hold it out so she can rattle a teaspoon inside. Though her hands shake, she has a definitive air about her: she is quick and efficient in stirring the sugar. I put the mug down next to the press shot in which she is the second chorus girl from the left. She lifts a hand, points at the picture.

'That, my dear Ruth, was a wonderful party,' she says before closing her eyes.

Home: I open a new bottle, pour a glass of white wine, add three ice cubes: ice-cooler. The cubes clink against one another, making me self-conscious. My stomach rumbles. I open a can of pimento olives and I sit on the floor in front of the sofa. I skewer an olive; its red insides spill out. *A wonderful party.* I don't know where to start. I chew on the olive, the kick of the chilli making my gums itch. After two glasses, I feel quite drunk.

Sleep still doesn't come to me easily. Sometimes in the evening I lie on my back on the floor for so long that the nubs down my spine start to hurt. I watch the red chromo-somes on the clock display of the DVD player, as they change into the night. I think about things that make me upset.

He and I are taking a trip to the countryside to check out some cliffs. It's a weekend trip; his outdoor phase. We take trips every weekend that month. When we reach the site we walk halfway to the edge, then he drops to the ground, and I kneel next to him to ask what he is doing. Come here with me, he says, feel the ground with your underside, like this, like a lizard, and I do it as he does it next to me. On the top, we hold hands and look down and we do not fall.

I sit up, and reach for my phone. I tap on the Facebook app and search for Alanna's profile. I expand her timeline. The blue page unfolds into micro events: her whole life, all public, time sprawled out like a ribbon messily uncurled. I scroll all the way down. I realize I have missed out on most of it. Her little sister's birthday, the monstrous pink flowers from Paul on Valentine's Day, being upgraded to first class on the plane to New York for her twenty-fifth birthday. Some people I recognize from school, but I can't remember their names. This is unsurprising because I have spent the last ten years trying to forget the ten years before that. The Lolitas are a prominent presence, mainly because they chronicle Alanna's life themselves. There are several three-way selfies taken in the care home. None of me. Only one picture features us both: a festive shot from last year's party with Santa hats superimposed on to our heads. It makes me sad, like a pin has been dropped in time, at an arbitrary point, marking the fact that I have always been there, existing on the periphery of Alanna's life, but my presence was not worth documenting. Yet there I am, standing to the left of the group, with my specifically ugly body, bird legs, the tired slope of my shoulders. I am there.

I pick myself up and walk to the bedroom still holding my phone. I scroll further down: her graduation, her grandmother's ninetieth birthday, then she's nineteen, on holiday with her best friend. I make eye contact with 'Tracy Dunn'. Tracy stands in her bikini, one arm around Alanna's waist on a Marbella beach, and returns the stare. Familiar face. The original photo is old, a picture of a picture uploaded. In the right-hand corner Alanna's freckly thumb is visible, holding it. I scroll all the way down to the bottom, but her feed trickles out quickly, with fewer and fewer pictures, and sparse status updates in which she talks about herself in third person. 'Alanna Hallett is very happy today thanks to a very special person.' Alanna smiling in a picture in which she looks extremely young. I remember her looking like that. Her chipmunk grin as a girl. I'm still here – I have been here for her. She picked me. My body feels heavier, the phone is warm in my hand. My thumb slips, zooming into her picture, one blue eye blown out of proportion.

I fall asleep.

I have a strange dream. Alanna and I are performing giants with a joint act on the uneven bars. It is an important competition, perhaps the Olympic Games. It is obvious we both know the routine to a tee, to the point that we are both collaborating and competing, and this is what makes us such a strong team. We are spinning in opposite directions and I can only see flashes of her: her white thighs speeding past me as our outstretched bodies cross at the apex of the exercise, her fists white with talcum powder and the effort of holding the bar, white hairband, a halo of wet baby hair. When her baby-blue eyes fly open like a spring doll's, my hand misses the bar.

MOBILE TOP-UP

Nearly Ten Years Earlier

FROM: +44 797 2397555
01/07/06 — 10:34
hi handsome, so lovely
to meet u yesterday
this is my nr
catch ya on the flipside.
miss candy kane xoxo

TO: +44 797 2397555
01/07/06 — 16:41
who is this? is this ruth
beadle? if so, very lovely
to meet you, too! Sorry for the
late reply — was walking
the Germans, you know what
it's like. well no maybe you don't.
never mind, nice to hear from you
anyway, hi! X

FROM: +44 797 2397555
01/07/06 — 16:42
sorry who is this?

TO: +44 797 2397555
01/07/06 — 16:43
sorry my name is neil pratchett,
got a message from this
number? must've got the wrong
number, sorry

FROM: +44 797 2397555
01/07/06 — 16:45
wait, is this neil from
the hotel? how did u
get my number?

TO: +44 797 2397555
01/07/06 — 16:45
is this ruth beadle? i didn't
get your number you
just sent me a message!

FROM: RUTH BEADLE ???
01/07/06 — 16:46
this is ruth beadle, yes but
i didn't send you a message.

TO: RUTH BEADLE
01/07/06 — 16:50
'hi handsome, so lovely
to meet u yesterday
this is my nr
catch ya on the flipside.
miss candy kane xoxo'

FROM: RUTH BEADLE
01/07/06 — 16:52
u got that from my number
????? when?????

TO: RUTH BEADLE
01/07/06 — 16:55
i don't know, this morning?
i was working. not on
phone x

FROM: RUTH BEADLE
01/07/06 — 16:57
o i'm sorry
that would've been
alanna. my friend?

TO: RUTH BEADLE
01/07/06 — 16:59
your friend alanna? texting
from your phone? x

FROM: RUTH BEADLE
01/07/06 — 17:02
we were in airport
must've taken my
phone while I was
in the bathroom.

TO: RUTH BEADLE
01/07/06 — 17:05
why would she send me
a text from your phone?

TO: ALANNA ROME
01/07/06 — 17:06
hey did you text me
this morning? xx

ding dong!
whos there?
a text
message from
the love of your life
dickhead

FROM: RUTH BEADLE
01/07/06 — 17:12
i don't have a clue,
why would she?

TO: ALANNA ROME
01/07/06 — 17:12
i don't know what you're
talking about? did you guys
get home safe?

TO: RUTH BEADLE
01/07/06 — 17:14
why would she?

TO: RUTH BEADLE
01/07/06 — 17:16
why would she?

FROM: RUTH BEADLE
01/07/06 — 17:17
come on,
i know the story.
any girl would be
pissed off

TO: RUTH BEADLE
01/07/06 — 17:17
pissed off about what?

FROM: ALANNA ROME
01/07/06 — 17:21
got home all right
idk about safe
til I get tested tbh
yr a cunt u kno that

TO: ALANNA ROME
01/07/06 — 17:22
wow, what the fuck
is wrong with you?
we used a condom fyi
you were the one
who didn't want to

FROM: RUTH BEADLE
01/07/06 — 17:26
look, i'm staying out of this.
just saying what u did the
other day was not cool
u know

TO: RUTH BEADLE
01/07/06 — 17:28
what because i
gave you my number?
you can't kill
a man for that.

FROM: ALANNA ROME
01/07/06 — 17:29
just lemme ask u
one thing were u guys
fucking all along? that
the reason y I spent the
last 2 wks
alone like a dog?

TO: ALANNA ROME
01/07/06 — 17:30
i have no clue what you are
talking about

FROM: ALANNA ROME
01/07/06 — 17:31
i know you gave
her your number
twat

FROM: RUTH BEADLE
01/07/06 — 17:31
she saw the
sugar sachet
with your number
on it

TO: RUTH BEADLE
01/07/06 — 17:32
well if this is how

TO: RUTH BEADLE
01/07/06 — 17:32
sorry that was meant for
someone else. so she knows
i gave you my number
so what? i'm not
like married to her

FROM: RUTH BEADLE
01/07/06 — 17:33
so she was upset. I know
she was with u
that day she wasn't
in our room.

TO: ALANNA ROME
01/07/06 — 17:33
well if this is how we're
doing this I owe you
nothing you know?

TO: ALANNA ROME
01/07/06 — 17:33
what a little bitch

TO: RUTH BEADLE
01/07/06 — 17:35
sorry to repeat myself
that's hardly me
proposing to her

FROM: ALANNA ROME
01/07/06 — 17:35
get fucked
little shit
u and ur boring
little bitch

FROM: RUTH BEADLE
01/07/06 — 17:40
i don't mess with
my friends' dates

TO: RUTH BEADLE
01/07/06 — 17:41
hey we didn't date!
look that was just . . .
a fun thing between
consenting adults. a
holiday thing

FROM: RUTH BEADLE
01/07/06 — 17:44
well technically
u were in work
u were responsible
i think

FROM: RUTH BEADLE
01/07/06 — 17:45
she's my friend
I wouldn't
have got in touch

TO: RUTH BEADLE
01/07/06 — 17:46
well you're talking to me now
aren't you ;)

TO: RUTH BEADLE
01/07/06 — 18:05
ruth, are you still there?

TO: RUTH BEADLE
01/07/06 — 21:11
hi . . .
look, I'm really sorry.
i didn't mean to put you
in a weird spot i
was just being silly 1/3

167

what happened with
alanna was a so-called
holiday romance
she knows this but i
really want to get to 2/3

know you. for real.
i understand
if you don't want anything
to do with me at this point 3/3

TO: RUTH BEADLE
01/07/06 – 21:13
but if you change your
mind i'm here if only
for a chat. x

STRAWBERRIES

Ruth
Now

The Lolitas say that going out for cocktails is too simple. It wouldn't look like we'd made enough effort. The Lolitas really want to make it extra special for Alanna, the most special night ever. I suggest paintballing. I'm not quite sure what it entails, but it seems that cocktails and paintballing are the most popular options for this kind of event, and cocktails are definitely a nightmare waiting to happen. The Lolitas look at me and at each other with faces that don't exactly convey disgust but something quite similar.

'Now look,' they say. 'Everyone knows how this works: champagne cocktails, with strawberries or cherries or raspberries, whatever, for the girly girls. It doesn't really matter so long as it's berries. Jungle face paint and camo for the tomboys.' They giggle. 'Come on! Don't you know about this, Ruth? What type of girl do you think Alanna is, Ruth?'

They've started calling me by my name too, copying her. It grates.

I nod. Yes. A girly girl, I'm familiar with the notion of a girly girl. But a notion is one thing. It's quite another to understand the inner workings of girliness. I never have. Which is why the Lolitas are supposed to be helping me. If anyone knows what a girl is, on an instinctive level, then it's them. They are the experts. I go back to my spreadsheet and let them do their thing. They begin roaming the room, yapping ideas to one another from a distance. A mutual shriek marks a mutually exciting idea.

They reconvene at my office chair. They tell me about make-up sessions. Then about a trip to Ibiza that seems too costly. It has been tacitly established that I am in charge of the budget – an appropriate task that appropriately corners me in the role of the spoilsport. They suggest an *Alice in Wonderland* Mad Hatter's Tea Party, a sleazy-sounding spa retreat and an Ann Summers get-together that seems too risqué for the range of ages and people involved. They bark suggestions at me until I can feel my throat beginning to close up and I have to fix my eyes on the screen as my vision blurs, and all I can see is a stifling sea of pink under-tones, a bad feeling, a blown-out red nightmare ready to engulf our group, whatever we end up choosing.

Last night in my dream I was a strong swimmer, a member of an away delegation to a northern English beach, waiting to take part in some competitive outdoor swimming. I knew we were there for a marathon swim. It occurred to me that, despite being a semi-professional, I didn't know what marathon swimming entailed. I was surprised to find out it was raced in lanes. A large portion of the coast was sectioned off by long stretches of white-and-red plastic floating dividers, marking a mandatory swimming course. A larger yellow buoy with a petite red flag on top signalled the start of the race, a few metres out into the water. The swimmers didn't waste any time and waded into the sea. I began to swim after them, as we moved in a group towards the yellow buoy, the wobbling red stain. Because we were in the water, there was no way to mark a clear starting line, so there was no kick-off order: we all piled in at the mouth of the lane, and already I felt myself going under.

I nod. I nod again and inhale. Exhale.

'So, Ruth?'

I inhale again and for a few moments relish the authority to say yes or no, as the Lolitas grow restless at my ankles. I exhale. 'Fine.'

What do I care? It's obvious that I'm going to say yes to the least ludicrous, most affordable entertainment plan they come up with. I wipe my forehead with the back of my wrist: cold, wet. I know I've come too far to turn back. I hereby accept that this will be terrible whatever route we choose. I yield to it. 'Your pick, girls, and I'll see what we can do money-wise.' Great job, Ruth Beadle, you're the great mediator, the great judge, the expert nurse.

We're settling for a manicure plus mug-painting plus barman lesson. I keep looking at my screen, waiting for my breathing to settle, for them to finally leave me alone.

'Barwoman,' screech the Lolitas.

'Barman, OK,' I say. 'Same thing.'

'No, that's what it's called; it's the name of the course, "Man, I Feel Like a Barwoman". Get it?'

'Oh, OK, sure,' I say. I don't. 'Barwoman,' I say. They copy the activity code down on a post-it note.

I try to raise what seems like a fair point about the planned order for the day. Surely manicure before mug-painting is going to prove a hassle? What about leaving enough time in between to let the nail polish dry? I'm trying to remember what it was that Alanna said about manicures when we were washing the pans. What was it that was good? Gel or shellac? I should've listened. I voice another concern to the Lolitas. Surely both mug-painting and manicure would suffice for an exciting day out. There's no need to pick a third activity. Shall we just have drinks afterwards? I could duck out early, I'm thinking. I am just desperate to give enough input so that I feel like I've done my part.

'Do you know what? Mugs are lame, maybe,' a Lolita pipes up.

'Yeah, scrap that, we'll do mani and cocktails,' says the other.

'We can do champers pre-drinks in the salon!'

They high five.

They wheel me on my chair to their shared laptop. These girls are so well practised in collective tasks, in pushing friends in shopping trolleys in empty car parks. These girls know how to keep themselves entertained. They don't need a laptop for work, but one of them brings one in from home anyway, this thing they've covered in chubby Japanese stickers: yellow bears, white-and-pink cats, a sad-looking anthropomorphic egg. They watch videos on it, their pretty heads close together in the glow from the screen.

They want me to look at a photo of the bartending teacher. It is why we can't possibly miss out on the bartending course, I infer. They point at it urgently, like it's a mugshot. 'Is this the man who attacked you, miss?' 'Look, look!' they say. And I look. I concentrate on the black-and-white picture: his face a static composition of vertical and horizontal lines, his features meeting at ninety-degree angles in the centre of his face. A face of perpendiculars, perfectly designed: the strong brow crossing over the short nose, which runs along the middle of his face to meet the narrow lips, open in a wide, confident smile. Teeth strong, and regular like corn kernels; square jaw. His eyes incongruous; the kind you come across on boys twenty years younger, round and soft like those of a handsome young dog.

I paddled desperately, with both hands and feet, so that for a while I was so occupied that I didn't pay attention to the arm closing around my neck. I couldn't tell it apart from all the other limbs moving in the water. I was in a headlock. Then he pulled his elbow upwards and I was leashed, salt water pushing at my lips, my wet mouth parting.

'Stuart Brandon Pierce,' says the caption underneath. I blink. 'Purveyor of the finest drinks for the finest ladies.' The caption matches the smile but his eyes are speaking a different language, one I feel I understand, though not fully – a sort of tingling. Then the Lolitas go, 'Aaaaaand,' and they scroll down to a series of photos at the bottom of the web page. They take a moment to load; they are moving frames, GIFs of him whipping some pink stuff in a shaker, pouring it into a cocktail glass. The words 'FROZEN DAIQUIRI!!!!' flash intermittently across the last GIF. In the pictures, he is shirtless. The pixelated blur adds grace to his gestures. The Lolitas can no longer contain themselves. They do the girl equivalent of fist pumps and make the girl equivalent of bicep flexes. I roll my eyes and roll back to my desk.

'If it's less than five hundred,' I say, wiggling the mouse to wake up the monitor.

£299 for three hours. The Lolitas are triumphant.

★

In bed, washed and in clean new pyjamas, I switch off the bedside lamp and I think about him again. Stuart Brandon Pierce. I say his name in the darkness: three words, like a magic spell. I think of the GIFs on the web page: his swimmer hips, twisting right to left along with the shaker, right to left. A strawberry, tossed, flying in a perfect parable over his head and diving into a long-stemmed glass, again and again and again. His soft brown eyes coming into focus as the GIF zooms in and he holds out a FROZEN DAIQUIRI!!!! Pink cocktails for the ladies. How does one even get into that line of work? What kind of work does it qualify as and what are we even in for? I'm falling asleep. Strawberries, raspberries and cherries. I whisper his name again, Stuart Brandon Pierce, and as I do, my hand slides under the elastic of my underwear.

Flesh closes around my throat, rubber skin pulling my chin open, seawater in my mouth, as his knee snaps my spine backwards, as my body, released, floats downward, until it reaches the ocean's bottom.

HONEY

Nearly Ten Years Earlier

FROM: RUTH BEADLE
02/07/06 — 00:21
are u awake

> **TO: RUTH BEADLE**
> **02/07/06 — 00:23**
> hey

FROM: RUTH BEADLE
02/07/06 — 00:25
i wasn't sure ud be still
awake

> **TO: RUTH BEADLE**
> **02/07/06 — 00:26**
> i am now

FROM: RUTH BEADLE
02/07/06 − 00:26
sorry i didn't mean
to wake u
did I wake u?
i hope not

           TO: RUTH BEADLE
           02/07/06 − 00:29
           nah's cool
           what is it?

FROM: RUTH BEADLE
02/07/06 − 00:33
nothing u
said i could talk
to u

           TO: RUTH BEADLE
           02/07/06 − 00:34
           sure − i just didn't
           think in the middle
           of the night,
           it's almost 1
           out here

FROM: RUTH BEADLE
02/07/06 − 00:36
sure. sorry
just . . . why?

           TO: RUTH BEADLE
           02/07/06 − 00:37
           why what?

FROM: RUTH BEADLE
02/07/06 – 00:39
i was just thinking
u said u wanted
to get to know
me for real
why?

TO: RUTH BEADLE
02/07/06 – 00:40
what do you mean why?

FROM: RUTH BEADLE
02/07/06 – 00:42
like you slept w
alanna already
why me?

TO: RUTH BEADLE
02/07/06 – 00:48
because I like you,
and that's got nothing
to do with alanna
like I told you

TO: RUTH BEADLE
02/07/06 – 00:48
i liked you before
straightaway
when i met you

FROM: RUTH BEADLE
02/07/06 – 00:49
in the agency?

TO: RUTH BEADLE
02/07/06 — 00:49
i like you now

FROM: RUTH BEADLE
02/07/06 — 00:50
she was here before
just now
though

TO: RUTH BEADLE
02/07/06 — 00:52
i haven't spoken to
her since you guys
were in Rome,
ruth, please
believe me

FROM: RUTH BEADLE
02/07/06 — 00:54
she just came here
called me names
and said i'm YOUR
little bitch now and
that's what
u call me but 1/2

how
would she
know we talked
i haven't told her
unless u have 2/2

TO: RUTH BEADLE
02/07/06 — 00:56
and why would I do
something like that?

FROM: RUTH BEADLE
02/07/06 — 01:00
i don't know
for a laugh

                             TO: RUTH BEADLE
                             02/07/06 — 01:03
                     well she's making it up

                             TO: RUTH BEADLE
                             02/07/06 — 01:03
                          oh honey
                        i'm sorry but
what kind of sick twisted
person does that?

FROM: RUTH BEADLE
02/07/06 — 01:05
people do a lot of stuff
for a laugh
wouldn't be the first
or the last

                             TO: RUTH BEADLE
                             02/07/06 — 01:06
                    what, to laugh . . .
                      at you? baby . . .
                          i'm sorry

FROM: RUTH BEADLE
02/07/06 — 01:06
well yeah
i guess

TO: RUTH BEADLE
02/07/06 — 01:06
ruth what happened
with alanna?

FROM: RUTH BEADLE
02/07/06 — 01:10
nothing she just
sometimes
she makes me feel
like such a joke

FROM: RUTH BEADLE
02/07/06 — 01:11
it's ok

FROM: RUTH BEADLE
02/07/06 — 01:11
shes my friend

TO: RUTH BEADLE
02/07/06 — 01:11
what do you mean?

FROM: RUTH BEADLE
02/07/06 — 01:12
she said she told u
to leave me your number

TO: RUTH BEADLE
02/07/06 — 01:12
well you know that's not true.

FROM: RUTH BEADLE
02/07/06 — 01:13
but how do i know

FROM: RUTH BEADLE
02/07/06 – 01:13
she said u asked
her about me bc
u think i'm funny-looking

                              TO: RUTH BEADLE
                              02/07/06 – 01:14
                    it's true I asked about you.

FROM: RUTH BEADLE
02/07/06 – 01:15
she said u think
i'm like a little mouse

FROM: RUTH BEADLE
02/07/06 – 01:15
like u think
i'm funny-looking

                              TO: RUTH BEADLE
                              02/07/06 – 01:17
                              you're little
                    not like a mouse, maybe
                         like a little bird.
                         pretty little bird
                              a bluebird

                              TO: RUTH BEADLE
                              02/07/06 – 01:17
                              pretty

FROM: RUTH BEADLE
02/07/06 – 01:18
that's a really weird
thing to say

TO: RUTH BEADLE
02/07/06 — 01:20
a bluebird
you can hold in
the palm of your
hand, feel its heart

TO: RUTH BEADLE
02/07/06 — 01:21
bluebirds sing
beautifully
when they're
alone

FROM: RUTH BEADLE
02/07/06 — 01:21
that's even weirder

FROM: RUTH BEADLE
02/07/06 — 01:23
i can relate to that

TO: RUTH BEADLE
02/07/06 — 01:25
look, no kidding,
it's true, i asked alanna
about you

TO: RUTH BEADLE
02/07/06 — 01:25
if you need to know
the reason why I asked
alanna out is you

FROM: RUTH BEADLE
02/07/06 – 01:26
why should i believe that
you slept with her

> **TO: RUTH BEADLE**
> **02/07/06 – 01:30**
> for two weeks in Rome
> i'd seen you, i couldn't
> get you out of
> my head 1/2
>
> i was losing my mind 2/2

FROM: RUTH BEADLE
02/07/06 – 01:32
yeah right
u couldn't keep it
in your pants

> **TO: RUTH BEADLE**
> **02/07/06 – 01:35**
> look it isn't like that
> she came
> on to me

FROM: RUTH BEADLE
02/07/06 – 01:37
that's not what she said

> **TO: RUTH BEADLE**
> **02/07/06 – 01:40**
> she talks a bunch doesn't
> she, don't you wish
> she'd ever shut up?

TO: RUTH BEADLE
02/07/06 — 01:41
look I was just
in work and she
begged me
to take her out
she wanted to
have fun

FROM: RUTH BEADLE
02/07/06 — 01:42
she could've come out
with me in that case

TO: RUTH BEADLE
02/07/06 — 01:45
she said she was
bored, she wanted to
go out, get pissed
have fun

TO: RUTH BEADLE
02/07/06 — 01:46
i said tbh when
in Rome you should
make the best of it

FROM: RUTH BEADLE
02/07/06 — 01:48
. . . like sleep with you

TO: RUTH BEADLE
02/07/06 — 01:50
no silly. like go out
with you. i was trying
to convince her

i told her that.
but she made me 1/2

go to the shops she
said if i didn't she'd
give me a bad review
and so . . . 2/2

TO: RUTH BEADLE
02/07/06 — 01:51
she's not like you

FROM: RUTH BEADLE
02/07/06 — 01:52
u still didn't have to
have sex with her

TO: RUTH BEADLE
02/07/06 — 01:53
look we got drunk
she insisted
things escalated,
i made a mistake.

TO: RUTH BEADLE
02/07/06 — 01:54
it's happened to all of
us.

FROM: RUTH BEADLE
02/07/06 — 01:54
i guess

TO: RUTH BEADLE
02/07/06 — 01:54
look I really
really just want a
chance to explain this
in person?

FROM: RUTH BEADLE
02/07/06 — 01:55
y am I still talking to
u it's almost
2am

TO: RUTH BEADLE
02/07/06 — 01:56
yes, why?
makes you wonder

FROM: RUTH BEADLE
02/07/06 — 01:57
i just wanted to
figure stuff out
i guess

TO: RUTH BEADLE
02/07/06 — 01:58
you know now.
i told you what happened

TO: RUTH BEADLE
02/07/06 — 01:59
but you're still here

TO: RUTH BEADLE
02/07/06 — 02:05
are you still there?

FROM: RUTH BEADLE
02/07/06 — 02:06
yes

             TO: RUTH BEADLE
             02/07/06 — 02:07
             look, I am back
             in a week's time.
             do you want to
             meet up?

             TO: RUTH BEADLE
             02/07/06 — 02:10
             talk it thru in person?

FROM: RUTH BEADLE
02/07/06 — 02:15
i'm not sure what
that means but
ok

             TO: RUTH BEADLE
             02/07/06 — 02:15
             can I call you?

FROM: RUTH BEADLE
02/07/06 — 02:20
it's 2:30 in the morning

             TO: RUTH BEADLE
             02/07/06 — 02:22
             not now.
             when I'm back.

TO: RUTH BEADLE
02/07/06 — 02:22
i'll call you when I'm
back, OK?

FROM: RUTH BEADLE
02/07/06 — 02:25
ok

TO: RUTH BEADLE
02/07/06 — 02:26
no reason to hide OK?

TO: RUTH BEADLE
02/07/06 — 02:27
bluebird?

TO: RUTH BEADLE
02/07/06 — 02:28
blue?
i'm coming back soon and
i'm coming for you?

TO: RUTH BEADLE
02/07/06 — 02:30
OK?

FROM: RUTH BEADLE
02/07/06 — 07:15
ok

MOISTURIZER

Ruth
Now

What to wear? I need to think about what to wear, the Lolitas urge me. A shopping trip is imminent. In preparation I collate the data I've amassed on body types over the years. There are five standards: apple, pear, hourglass, inverted triangle, rectangle. Depending on your choice of secondary reading, you might identify further shapes: the diamond, the lean column, the Corinthian column, the stick man and the fuck doll. It seems reassuring to start with fruit types and basic geometric shapes.

To find out your body shape, stand naturally with your legs together and your arms away from your sides. Examine the area from your underarms, past your bust and ribcage, over your waist and hips, to the fullest part of your thighs. That's your shape.

In preparation for the big night, the Lolitas take me out to look for an outfit. They are hoping I might be persuaded to update my wardrobe. By now we have begun referring to the hen-do as 'the big night'. We leave work when it's still light outside. The March evening is bright and crisp. On the way to the shops I exchange a sorrowful look with a woman in a camel-hair coat, walking two small Chihua-huas. The dogs have diamanté collars, which choke them as the woman drags them by their leads. I am envious of their group dynamic.

When we reach the lingerie shop Bex turns to me. 'Are you ready?' she shrieks. I knew this would happen. In prep-aration, I was nil by mouth for forty-eight hours, with the exception of sweet tea. Yet as we cross the threshold I still feel my stomach turn inwards.

Apple pear rectangle hourglass inverted triangle. No one wants to kiss the spoilsport.

'OK, how do we do this?' I say, adopting a practical tone. The Lolitas look at me uncomprehendingly.

'What do you mean "how do we do this"?' they say.

They flick through the rows of bras at a mind-boggling speed.

'Come on, Ruth,' says Emmy. 'Don't you know your size?'

I hesitate. Bex nudges me to browse further along, and my arm darts out to pick up a cream bra with little cup-cakes embroidered on it.

Do you wear a larger size on your top half than your bottom? Have wider shoulders than hips? Have a straight ribcage? Then you're probably an inverted triangle. People will say you look like a swimmer on a good day or 'andro-gynous' on a bad day, which is intended to mean: you look like a man. You should wear straight lines, boat necks, muted colours. Why try?

When we've selected enough bras, the Lolitas push me

towards the changing rooms, where we are handed butterfly tokens in different colours according to the number of items we are taking in with us. The tokens are different pinkish hues, which seems quite impractical because it's hard to distinguish between them – as well as rather imprecise on a zoological level (pink butterflies are actually relatively rare). With a gentle shove, Emmy herds us down the corridor and it's just as well: I shouldn't try to entertain the concept of realism in a place like this. All the flat surfaces are reflective with glitter: I am blinded. I stumble to a changing room near the back and push through the thick velvet curtain. It is perfectly circular. I am standing in the middle of a minuscule opera theatre. Behind me, the crimson drape drops down to my feet, fringed with gold. The walls are papered with a continuous picture of theatre seats. A spotlight illuminates me from above. I hear the hiss of a hidden dispenser, vaporizing orange blossom fragrance. I lift my head. 'The world is your stage' is scrawled above my picture in the mirror. No pressure then.

No pressure to undress. I pull my sweater off, unbutton my shirt, slide my skirt down my legs. Take a deep breath. *Cutis anserine* is considered the medical name for goose bumps, but actually, it's a near-exact Latin translation, meaning 'goose skin'. An alternative medical term is 'horripilation'. Which is a terrible word. I pinch the cold, moist skin of my underarm. I lift my arms and look at my dry elbows. I should moisturize more often. I never do.

'Ruth, babe?' the Lolitas coo from beyond the changing room. 'How you getting on?'

I am wearing, I suppose, a red satin number. It does, I consider, cover my nipples. I rub my arm. It'll bruise.

'All right. I guess.'

191

There is a rustling and their little heads pop in from each side of the curtain, first the red hair, then the brunette. My arms cross over my chest as I back into the *trompe l'oeil*.

'Come on, let us see,' says Emmy.

'Fuck's sake, Emmeline. Stop torturing her,' says Bex. 'Oi, Ruth.' She nods in my direction.

'Yes.'

'You know what Miss Phyllis would say?'

'What would Miss Phyllis say?'

'Legs for days!'

'Let us see! Ruth!'

'Get the hell out of my changing room, you pair of per-verts!' I'm laughing.

I buy the bra and two sets of coordinated panties – identical bikini briefs. No, not the thong – no, a hundred per cent sure, thank you very much.

In this dream I am lying in a shallow pool of warm water, my elbows resting on the edge of the stone basin. It is a cool day and I am bathing out in the open, like a bird. Water, refracted, distorts my legs into inconsistent sticks, greying away under the surface. I am happy. I have always felt happier in water, I find myself thinking in the dream, though this is something I have never thought of while awake. I can't stop looking at my graceful legs. They look so long, so so long and then they turn to stone as I watch them.

Miss Phyllis wants to go down to the piano bar. I don't blame her. It's lovely weather this morning, but it's been raining all week and the decking is damp. We absolutely cannot let her out today. It takes nothing for them to get sick and it isn't worth it. She will forget she's even been and anyway, she'll want to go again tomorrow. It's nearly spring now and spring does strange things to Miss Phyllis. The bluebird in her heart just wants to get *out*. Something must have happened to her in spring. It makes her think of her only true love, the police constable who broke her heart. We don't talk about that, though sometimes, on a bright day, I have caught her muttering sweet things into the air, as if in conversation with someone. All afternoon she sits in the old armchair next to the bay window, looking out and refusing to move. We let her be for as long as we can but after an hour we need to move her. The chair isn't regulation, just decorative, and sitting in it for too long will hurt her back. Alanna kneels next to her to coax her into getting up. It doesn't work. Miss Phyllis refuses to move. She has fastened her fingers around the wooden knobs of the armrests and her veins bulge blue and painful.

'We have to try Mona,' Alanna whispers.

We call Mona on the interphone and when she comes she is holding the paper cup with Miss Phyllis's medication.

'Doesn't she take these a little later usually?' I ask.

'It's not like she knows what time it is.'

Miss Phyllis swallows the pills automatically. Most of them acquire it as a reflex: it's like feeding birds. When her head starts to lull to the side, Alanna and I pry her hands from the chair and escort her back to her room, holding her by an elbow each, like a lady to the dances. As we prepare her for sleep, quietly, she begins. I recognize the melody, she has sung this song before. It's a love song, and it was her *pièce de résistance*. All the soldiers loved it, on both sides. She always sang it last. But the words are not like I remember them; the lyrics are somewhat different, out of order, like a warped record playing.

★

All night Miss Phyllis is singing quietly in her room. She doesn't bother anyone but if you put your ear to the door you can hear it. Sometimes she pauses to take a sip from the mug on her night table. We think she will stop when the drugs wear off, but in fact she becomes a little louder, clearly enunciating,

Will you accept
This token of good faith
I'm falling for you
My Lili Marlene

DATES

Four Months Earlier

cumulonimbus
Sent: 22/11/2015 – 03:02

Lili,

Isn't it amusing that you made fun of me for using too many words to get to the point, and now I get to the end of your message and I find I have none. Except for one, the one that you ended with. I keep rereading that last word.

A date?

This is silly, I know, but the moment I saw the word written down I realized I'd never even allowed myself to fully entertain the thought that I should be so lucky. Simultaneously: that there is nothing else I want more in the world. Lili, I am afraid my condition has only got worse since I last wrote to you. I stopped listening to war songs, since you made fun of me, but now I feel a compulsion to copy down your name in a notebook, draw it out in chubby capitals like a schoolgirl would. I might be older than you, but I think of the two of us I am the excited schoolboy. I'm not even embarrassed to tell you this. But I hope you won't look down on me for this reason, thinking me juvenile.

i have rambled on again, haven't I? Forgive me, Lili. Let me reply to your question: of course. Of course I would love to go on a date with you.

God, I can't quite believe it. It's been so long since I last allowed myself to think about the world in a romantic fashion. The word 'date' itself seems so esoteric . . . almost mystical. Not merely a drink, or drinks, or the serious-sounding *coffee*. When I was a kid an older boy told me that the best way to trick a girl into thinking you're serious about her is to take her out for coffee on your first date, not drinks. Neither of us was old enough to drink alcohol then, and I am pretty sure we were both virgins, but in the years since I have thought about his advice often. He'd told me in hushed tones, right outside the headmaster's office, and so I have been thinking of *coffee* as the sentimental equivalent of a disciplinary meeting. No surprise it's been dull drinks with work colleagues and duller one-night stands for the most part of my life. Why am I telling you this?

. . . because a DATE, the soft potential of it, sickly sweet and self-contained in the word like in its fruit counterpart, compact and dry on the outside, but rich and melt-in-your-mouth once you bite into it . . . I'll stop rambling on. Shall we go on a date, Lili?

You pick where, let me treat you.

Clay

kittenwithasledgehammer

Sent: 23/11/2015 – 20:39

oh hey hello

woah intense, chill mate. Just when i thought you'd hit peak poet. were you high? in any case, progress! or as youd say We Shall Meet Up. what shall we do? typical you, now youve put a mega emo load on it. usually i can think of about six million things id like to have a sugar daddy pay for but now umm. mind. is. blank. i was going to suggest Drinks. god forbid lol. now idk, feel like you expect me to come up with some kind of leisure activity like some kind of TA organizing a school trip. shall we go to the zoo or like the aquarium? animals in captivity always seem to do the trick on dates. wonder if it's cuz seeing a large animal trapped in a small awkward space helps take your mind off the fact that's pretty much what first dates are like themselves. lol just kidding. listen so long as you dont take me for pasta im pretty much game for anything. oh and also no formal dresscode pls. last time i wore heels to a date the guy had to literally piggyback me home, which also meant i ended up sleeping with him bc i felt bad about it. o shit ive done it again havent i? im sorry.

shall we just say tuesday piccadilly under the statue of cupid? seems to fit your current vibe. no, but honestly, chill out. i promise i wont bail if you answer me this simple question: what is your actual name, clay?

cumulonimbus

Sent: 23/11/2015 – 21:05

My dearest Lili,

I have to be very brief as I am engaged right now, but I felt so elated when my phone vibrated (appropriately, I'd put it in my shirt pocket right against my heart). I got so excited I just couldn't wait to get back to you and had to do it straight away, for the irrational fear that your decision to meet me might somehow evaporate if I left it even just a few hours. I actually don't mind having to send you this quickly and in secret . . . I like the feel of it, like an eighteenth-century illicit love letter, penned on the back of official correspondence, a lipstick kiss hidden in the folded heart of a lady's napkin . . . Les liaisons dangereuses!

I'm running out of time and this is to say, simply, I cannot wait for tomorrow, my dearest dearest Lili. 6 p.m. I'll bring you a single red rose.

I just couldn't wait to tell you.

Yours,
Neil

kittenwithasledgehammer

Sent: 23/11/2015 – 21:20

hi NEIL

wow anti-climax

les liaisons dangerous?

didn't they do a movie about it with that chick from that 90s vampire show buffy in it? god ryan philippe is fit in it isn't he. but really all i used to watch it for was all that lesbian kissing. H-O-T

OK. COOL.

see you TOMORROW, weirdo.

Lili x

p.s. DONT BRING A ROSE. dont. cos that's just lame.

FLOWERS

Ruth
Now

Alanna has brought in a book. I've never seen her with a book before, though I know she keeps an old copy of a Paulo Coelho in her locker. It is a light-blue, slim book, with a picture of a man dressed in white on the cover. I recognized it at first glance because Neil also has a copy, or at least he used to. I gave it to Oxfam when I cleared out. I wonder if Alanna also thinks that Coelho is an 'enlightening writer'. I've never seen her take hers out of the locker so maybe she found it there.

The new book is thick; a hardback. It's called *The Flower Alphabet* and has a picture of a white man in a hat on the cover, bending over and holding out a bunch of red roses.

Alanna makes me a cup of tea, tells me to sit down. She says she wants us to read the book together. This makes me anxious. I've not read a book *with* someone since I was five years old and even then my mother had little patience for it. She'd rather put a film on for us to watch.

Will we read a paragraph each? Or does Alanna want me to read it to her? I don't mind showing her how to do things, but this seems a bridge too far.

She reveals, somewhat reassuringly, that the book is for research. It will help her to create a *mood board* for the wedding. She is dreamy and mysterious today; she smiles at the ceiling a lot.

'What's on her mind?' I wonder aloud.

'So much, my friend,' she sighs, 'so, so much.'

But, in short, she wants some help picking the flowers. It is traditional for the maid of honour to help the bride select flowers for the bouquet, the church decorations and the wedding tables.

'What about Emmy and Bex?' I ask.

'What about Emmy and Bex?' she says.

'Are you not going to ask them?'

'I don't want to ask Emmy and Bex.'

'But why?'

'They are busy right now. And they don't know a single thing about flowers.'

'Neither do I.'

'You're on your break. You're having a cup of tea. You're having a biscuit. Do you want a biscuit? Here, have mine. Relax! You're my maid of honour. You're supposed to help me with the flowers.'

'OK,' I say. 'But I genuinely have no clue where to start.'

I have noticed two things lately: I've been finding it easy to agree with her, yet easier still to speak my mind. I worry I am starting to trust her. And, although that's not a bad thing in itself, it makes me feel nervous. I'm not ready for it and it's not done me any good trusting people, not in the past.

'Look, Ruth,' she says. 'It's not as hard as it seems. Each flower, you see, has a meaning as well as a scent and a distinctive colour and shape. It seems complicated at first, but really I think it's quite easy to guess the meaning just by looking at the flower. Once you've guessed the meaning, even the scent will make more sense. I promise.' For a moment she looks incredibly serious.

'But isn't that what the book is for? To provide us with the correct information so we don't have to guess randomly?'

'The book has all the information we need, but what *is* the information we're looking for, exactly? The book doesn't know me; you do. Want to take a guess?' She flicks the book open. 'Come on; it's fun.'

Her cool hand locks around my wrist like a daisy chain. I don't remember her ever having touched me before, though I know this can't be true. I look at our joined hands. Alanna guides my fingers to the bottom of page seventy-seven, The Peony, and covers the description before I can read it.

'I promise it's not hard. We'll start easy.'

'Right,' I say.

'Right,' she says. 'What does this look like to you?'

'A peony?' I say lamely, reading the title at the top of the page.

'Jesus, Ruth. Come on, girl!' She gives my hand a little squeeze. 'Make an effort.'

'It's very pretty,' I say.

'It *is* pretty,' she says. 'And? What does it remind you of?'

'It looks like fabric. Like silk.'

'It does, doesn't it?'

'A bit like a tutu?'

'Well, ballet tutus are a bit – you know – fluffier.' Of

course, she took dance lessons as a teenager, I remember now. Her modelling career wasn't her only failure. She'd wanted to be a professional dancer in school, but then she did her knee in and had to quit. It was a minor scandal; it made the local papers, I think. Something to do with her ballet teacher, who'd been pushing students too hard and a whole host of injuries. I haven't thought about this in, how long? A memory flashes: I remember her pirouetting down the stairs of our hostel, in Rome, leaning against the railing. A white sundress and big round sixties sunglasses. 'This is a plié,' she'd said, bending low on her knees, her back straight. It was sunny and I remember I felt happy. It was the first day of our holiday. The memory is a small, good one. I smile at the thought of it. Alanna narrows her lips, looks at me seriously. 'Sturdier also. The tutus?' she says. 'More aerodynamic. They're work clothes, basically.'

'Of course you know everything about ballet,' I snap. Why try?

'No, but you're right, it looks a bit like a ballet skirt. Is that what you meant?' Her voice softens. 'I wore the kind you're thinking of, for training, and they look a bit like that, you are right. I wore it in the gym. I spent hours and hours there and the fabric was a little heavier, a little warmer. It was a comforting weight when I was there until late. And when I did the splits it would spread out and I felt a bit like a flower. A peony perhaps!' She claps her hands. 'Ruth! I told you you'd be good at this!' She flashes her little pointy canines. But she's just smiling.

'Do you miss dancing?' I ask.

'I miss it. But that's another story. For another day. I focus on the present these days.' She squeezes my hand on the book. She looks at me.

'Now, seriously,' she asks. 'What do you think the peony means?'

'Well, let's find out! What *does* the peony mean?' I try to pull my hand back but she holds my wrist in place, with gentle restrain.

'Take a guess?'

'I don't know what it means.'

'Think about it. It's not so much about what it means in general, but what it means to me. What would it mean to me, having peonies at my wedding?'

'To you?'

'From what I just said? About having to quit dancing? What do you think the peony means to Alanna?'

I don't understand. 'From what you said, I'm thinking – maybe, to Alanna –' I hesitate; it could be anything, so I say the first thing that pops into my mind '– a peony might mean working hard to achieve something she loves.' Her eyes are very blue. 'Something she loves very much.' She nods. 'It means determination,' I say. 'The determination to achieve something she loves.' Why are we speaking in the third person? Should I hold her hand in mine? She is nodding and smiling.

'Let's see,' she says. Alanna slides my hand gently off the book, releasing my wrist. My hand, where she held it, feels warmer than the rest of my body. I can still feel the ring of her fingers around my forearm. She reads out loud: 'Peonies promise good fortune. Watch them grow from small buds into strong, magnificent blooms and you'll see why peonies beautifully symbolize a long and happy marriage.' She claps her hands happily. 'Peonies are perfect! You're a genius, Ruth, I knew it!'

'Go for the fuchsia ones. They'll suit your skin tone,' I

say, in a nasal voice. What the fuck am I talking about? But there, I've said it. I do mean it. She will look incredibly beautiful. Alanna's eyes widen with surprise. She throws her arms around my neck and squeezes. I put mine around her waist and I squeeze too.

In this dream the water is blue and our heels are dipped in it. We have dropped most of our garments further up the beach. Our fingers are curled around each other's loosely in the sand. We wiggle our toes, tighten our hands together.

'Do you ever think,' you say, 'about the times you've been kissed for the first time? Not the first time you've ever been kissed – or not only that time. Each time you've been kissed for the first time.'

You look at me and I look at you and I can see that you are doing maths behind your eyes. This hurts my feelings.

I kick water on to your naked leg. You kick back with your shin against mine.

'You're peeling,' I say.

'You never answer me.'

Your head tumbles on to my naked shoulder.

In this dream we are lying together on towels on a roof terrace. The towels are much too small to hold our bodies; they are more like hand towels than beach towels. All the same, since we are not on a beach and there is no sand, we are fairly content. Our heels push into the hot grainy tarmac that covers the roof. It is getting warmer and I'm beginning to sweat. The country is Spain, maybe Italy. It is very early in the morning and perhaps we have stayed up all night. I am wearing tinted sunglasses and when I look at your arm through them, your skin is a burnt amber colour. I can make out the white hairs that fan out in circles around your shoulder bone. I look at the side of your face: from above, you could be looking right at the sky, but from here I know your eyes are shut. I roll my upper arm across the towel towards you so that the inner side now faces up. This way we are closer together by almost an inch. I walk my hand towards you sideways, like a crab, inch by inch, until my pinkie grazes the side of your sleeping hand. You don't stir, not even when the ends of the hairs on my arm are touching the ends of the hairs on your arm, static energy bringing us a few millimetres closer still. I am reassured and frustrated by your lack of reaction. I want more. I close my eyes and feign sleep. After a while I get bored and feign stretching in sleep. I roll over to your side and now my mouth rests against the heat of your shoulder. I can smell your sweat and its salty coating. The sea is very close, the sound of the waves is deafening. I lick your shoulder. You don't wake up, or if you do, you let me.

In this dream I am living in a very large mansion in the state of Florida and my husband is a very rich man. I, on the other hand, am the kind of wife who is never seen in public without heels. I lift a finger to my cheek and feel the powder of my make-up. I am curled up on the sofa with a chilled glass of white. I am vaguely aware that my husband is out with his yacht, but I am not perturbed by the idea. The trip has been arranged with a lot of notice and he has made thorough preparations. Despite his absence, or perhaps because of it, tonight I am throwing a cocktail party and all the ingredients are lined up on the long marble table in the hall, so it looks like it's happening soon. I am not fretting. I am having my nice, chilled glass of white in my nice sitting room. I look out of the bay window and realize there is a woman on the decking out back. I can see her from where I am sitting. She has a silk scarf around her head: it must be the sixties in the dream, or she has expensive sixties vintage taste. She is wearing big round sunglasses and holding *a large portable telephone to her ear. She twirls her headscarf between her index finger and thumb. The home telephone rings and I pick up its heavy Bakelite receiver. 'It's about your husband,' says the voice in my ear. I lift my eyes up and the woman is staring at me through the glass window. The light hits her sunglasses from behind, so I can see her dark eyes shining through the dark lenses. 'Never get your heart broken twice,' she says into the receiver and hangs up.*

The day after I dream the third dream is the day before the big night.

CONDITIONER

The Girls
Now

There are creatures that only come out at night: bats, mice and owls. They all have their own specific cry. And fur or down or feathers designed to disappear into the night.

In order to survive the hostile darkness, these animals have genetic mutations: evolution has conditioned them to adjust to their current predicament. Tonight, we'll paint our lips and lace up our waists and put gel pads in our shoes and fold soft pumps into our handbags. We will sing and we will dance in the footprints of those who came before us, orderly like wolves following a trail, placing a paw into exactly the mark left in the snow by the one in front. Our heels will skitter along prescribed routes. Hen-do as pastiche, a show reel: chick-flick, comedy, romance, damsel in distress, sexploit-ation, girl-on-girl, cuckold, female-friendly. Soft-bodied in the soft light, we are the girls and we are giving away our girl Alanna. It happens at night because it is secret and there is a right way to go about it that only we, the night creatures, know.

Her father will be in charge of the ritual. This is how it works: the priest will lift her hand in his and out of her father's and place it firmly into her husband's. Three men have outlined the conditions under which, swiftly, she will transition from a world in which a man bore responsibility for her wellbeing to a world in which she bears responsibility for a man. This exchange happens in broad daylight. The contract will be signed shortly after. Our girl Alanna. There is much more to her than meets the eye. It would take you years to know her properly. What makes daddy's little girl choose to find out about abjection? To choose to put her body on the line, to live in proximity of human decay? At heart, the girl's a born nurse: born to care for others. From rosy-cheeked childhood to changing old men's nappies: the end point of a parable of ballet competitions and bubblegum photo shoots and kiddy amphetamine addictions. The doctors prescribed the medication and then decided her excessive use of it was a sickness in itself and resolved to cure it. She struggled to see it that way in the beginning. Her body just felt very light.

Men love helping girls out of their trouble. Restoring their youthful glow is usually an endeavour easy to fund. Young girls have a propensity to gratitude. When a girl becomes attached, she will change her whole lifestyle for you. This is one way in which girls are unlike boys: they're willing to adjust their personality.

Alanna says that luckily, when you are really pretty, you don't ever have to do anything you don't want to do. She's lucky. She's beautiful. Anyway, she's all done with that kind of thing. We pass around a photo of Paul, this new man of hers. In the picture he is holding a whippet by its lead. It's supposed to be a cute shot, but the dog looks obscenely small next to his large body. It makes us uneasy. 'It's a miniature whippet, by the way,' she says when she sees us looking. As if that made the photograph less upsetting, that the dog would never grow out of its bony frame, like the man had. Our girl Alanna. Making excuses for the man she loves. Ain't she cute and don't we all make excuses? Isn't that what women do? Alanna and Paul, sitting in a tree, K-I-S-S-I-N-G.

Of course, we've reassured the groom that nothing bad is going to happen. We've provided a list of our movements, for safety purposes. The men have put in the effort for Paul: they've identical t-shirts to prove it. Professional partiers, branded like bulls with a number on the back and a nickname: COCK KNOCKER, BUTT TICKLER, AL COOLIC and PENIS PARMESAN (the oddball). They'll drink beer. They'll eat barbecued meats. Dark sauce will drip down their wrists like blood. Chuck us a bone, boys, we'll make it last. They're always hungry. They're a team. They write best men's speeches drunk in hotel rooms. They are always watching: TV, video-games, hen-do, pay-per-view, cowgirl, reverse cowgirl, reverse gangbang. The groom gave us a serious look. If the wife-to-be misbehaves, we promise, we'll tell on her. We wait until we're outside the building to start laughing.

History happened in the back rooms while we delayed our knitting: making and unmaking, the stuff of witches. We talked quietly. We trained our voices to speak so low that we could turn a thing into its opposite, making them still believe they're in control. We've learnt to talk softer when we intend to be misunderstood, so that sometimes men swap our words around for the opposite meaning, which is exactly what we wanted. We'll hold it against them in due time. We remember everything. We abide by the rules; we are clandestine. Tin phones threaded with wool: this hen-do. Perhaps the men suggested it but we planned it. They say a good soldier's strength isn't in winning all the battles, but in choosing the right ones. Although we didn't choose it, we know we must win this. It's Alanna's big night, we're going to have so much fun.

210

We chose the clothes in which to clad her: her armour. It is pink and white and gold, and the reason is the reason kings wore ermine for generations: garish and cruel and for special occasions. She is really pretty, and the pink is satin on her skin, and the white is silk, and the gold shines like real gold, so why should we have chosen differently? We've chosen her eyelashes: they have feathers on them and when she wrinkles her nose, they ruffle. She sits on the edge of the bathtub and swings her feet, fully a girl. We wing her eyeliner. We condition her split ends with a coconut mist. We paint her face. We take a long time, the time it takes. There is no one here to rush us. We drink fruit cocktails, which we set on the edge of the bathtub. 'Girls love sweet cocktails,' they say. Here in the bathroom it is safe to drink from a straw, bite on a strawberry; we could eat a banana whole, shove it right down our throats if we wanted. We touch her eyes, smooth out the primer. We sprinkle powder on to her eyelids. It makes her eyes sparkle. We shade in her bone structure and she acquires definition, coming into focus from the outside inwards. We say, 'Tilt your head up,' and she does. Baby girl. We work in a team, the all-girl team, in the top league of the overall league. We curl her hair in ringlets like a doll, then brush it all through to tousle them, and though the iron is hot, near her face, never once does she flinch. The last thing, of course, is to put the crown on her head. A crown, not a tiara. Gracious Alanna.

The very, very last thing is to slide the garter belt up her leg. This is a role that falls to me. It's like fitting Cinderella's shoe: it does, perfectly, and my heart flutters. 'Careful with the tights,' Alanna says. 'They are so delicate.' I am extremely careful.

Bex spearheads our party into the hall. She's blackened her beauty mark with eyeliner. It's slick on her left cheek, like a dot of caviar, like Marie Antoinette's.

Emmy braided her hair into a tight knot which looks like melted copper or coiled-up snakes. She's brushed red glitter into the creases of her hair-do, green glitter in the creases of her eyelids: the effect is Christmassy and somewhat patriotic, like she's representing a foreign country at Eurovision. She pulls it off with flair: her cheeks are sleek with powder, her eyes snake-like, too.

Mona has decided to change her name for the night. Tonight, she announced, she would like us girls to call her Jessica. So we will have a Jessica, after all of my efforts. She's wearing chunky heels and her round legs in shiny leggings look dangerous. She keeps her hands on her hips, fists balled up, don't-mess-with-me sexy. Her purse is full of tissues and Nurofen for tomorrow. Her cheekbones are high and round like thick apple slices. Her lipstick is wet-look. In the lift she pushes between us to check her backcomb in the mirror.

I am the last of the line as we leave the flat. I'm wearing a bodycon dress, like Catwoman, but with more thigh, and all my bones jut out, like I'm sketched out in pen. I've contoured my face: earthy shades filling in the hollows, translucent powder across the cheekbones, like slug trails in the light of the moon. I look beautiful. Around my neck is a locket of sentimental value and in the locket a picture of Miss Phyllis, who is alive, of course, and extremely miffed she couldn't make it. Earlier today she gave me the locket so she could go along, in a way. She said, 'Never lift your heels from the ground for too long when you're wearing high shoes because it'll only make your feet worse.' Grind down into the earth for balance. There was a festive air to the care home, like that on the dock when a ship sets sail. 'You girls have fun,' chorused the old women when we left. Mrs O'Toole raised one serious finger and pretended to think hard about something, so I bent over to offer my ear, into which she burst a peal of laughter. They waved goodbye from their chairs, which we'd arranged in the living room in a semicircle. Only that shrivelled root of a man, Mr Hancock, sulked in a corner. He could rot in hell for all we cared.

In the hallway Alanna pulled me into a corner. She popped the locket open, crushed a pink pill into it, against the black-and-white portrait.

'One night,' she whispered. She let the chain fall back between my breasts. Her breath smelt of berries. I held the necklace with the picture of Miss Phyllis between my fingers. We were together. Age is just a number and these were the things that were happening to me, on a night out, at thirty years of age.

Here I am, handing out cigarettes from a pack I have bought myself. Tonight we've all agreed to take up smoking. No one wants to be a spoilsport. Men do the real smoking, of course: they have special rooms laid out for this purpose, rooms we are never allowed in, gentlemen's clubs, with all the newspapers with all the important news and the leather furniture and the lack of noise, the noise of women shut outside finally, with those tall ashtrays you see in retro television series in which the overworked office clerk finally gets to fuck the office secretary. If she behaves, eventually, she'll have a career. There is hope for everyone in the free world!

A small cloud follows us as we light up, out of the door and into the street, where our eaux de cologne and celebrity fragrances begin to lose their battle with the atmosphere. We link our arms, taking over the width of the pavement. We're still smoking, so when one raises a hand to take a toke the whole chain shakes, like a vine heavy with fruit and flowers, the pendants jangling on our brace-lets. We take big puffs, hold the smoke in our cheeks, mimic blowbacks without touching lips, so as not to spoil our lipstick. It's our girl Alanna's big night so we've fitted her cigarette on a black-and-white mouthpiece. She's cutting circles before her, like an orchestra conductor, sashaying, left leg, right leg, heel first, click click, swan tonight, duckling tomorrow. But don't worry about tomorrow.

'We may be dead tomorrow,' says Mona.

Emmy and Bex turn around simultaneously, metallic superheroes in all that glitter and fake gold and they look old and sad for a moment, under this particular streetlight.

'Just me, it is possible, a bit before the rest of you girls,' Mona says. We all laugh. We aren't afraid of death. I shake my head, left and right. Tonight, death is only a notion. Look straight ahead. No tears, not tonight.

It's our girl Alanna's big night.

It's going to be fucking BRILLIANT. Our eyelashes are glued safely on both sides. We pushed them in with a cotton wool bud until we saw white, and then flashing stars and diamonds when we opened our eyes again. We helped each other out. The glue is holding. A girl's best friend never leaves her best girl alone. Our make-up stays on. Of course Alanna will still be our friend after she gets married. Let's worry about that tomorrow.

The others are meeting us at the venue later. So far the night is ours: we are the inner circle. It's us. We are the girls. We walk under the violet glowlights leading up to the entrance, skip the queue. 'Girls don't pay,' says the bouncer, and it suits us.

'We're fucking princesses! They should pay us!' says Emmy, and she really believes it.

'Well, she's the Queen.' Bex coyly stamps her cigarette and looks up at Alanna. We feel the bouncer's eyes follow us inside, as we spill through the padded door and it huffs shut behind us. Inside is a red and black and gold kind of bar, balanced between sleazy and smoky. No one can hurt us, so long as we stick together in the soft dark heat. We stand so close our cool arms brush against each *other. We don't need the cloakroom because none of us brought a coat. We didn't want it to get in the way. You thought a short walk in the spring chill would scare us? We can walk three miles to your house in the snow if we love you, six miles from your house if we're leaving you. We can do impulsive, crazy things sometimes. Be unpredictable. It's our night, remember? We break from our huddle. There is loud music playing, Mona is the first to lay her thick heel on the dancefloor – or actually, it's Jessica. I follow, I have always been Mona's best student, filling her shoes in her absence. I pull on the hand of our girl, Alanna, while Emmy and Bex cover her eyes from behind, one hand each, then uncover them when two beautiful boys, hair sleek like a raven's wing, not a day over twenty-seven, which is the age at which boys are ripest, square but gently rounded shoulders and lickable skin, escort us to the back of the room. They are so courteous. They may very well be fanning us with ostrich feathers.*

'Perhaps they should,' I say, and Bex winks at me.

See that girl strutting on in front of her, leading the way with steady grace? Who is she if not our Jessica?

'How very gentlemanly,' she says, when the boys each slide an arm into the crook of hers.

'Mona! Stop it! You could be their mother.' Emmy is laughing.

'It's Jessica,' says Mona in a husky voice that sounds like nobody's mother.

And Emmy keeps laughing, but this time she's in on the joke. And now she understands that Jessica is only gracing these boys with her attention because she knows there is nothing they can do to hurt her. These two boys, each exactly half her age: boys, only men at a stretch. It is a fictional stretch Mona is willing to consider tonight, because it's the big night, Alanna's big night. Jessica knows that these boys have been corn-fed to exert sex

215

appeal with no hint of a threat: a rare delicacy. And look at her side-butting one of them out of the way to pop herself up on the leatherette, sending for a drink immediately. 'I'd rather die of old age than of thirst and I ain't got that long left, boys,' she says.

When googling 'woman drinking' by far the most popular entry is 'woman drinking wine', probably for subliminal reasons tethering a woman's physique to the shape of the glass. Our girl Alanna has her crown on her head and each palm wrapped around a magnum of Prosecco. She does look mighty fine. Her rings sparkle.

Here we are: the girls. We've filled in a semicircle around her, and then Mona, or Jessica, in any case no boy's mother, pops the cork and pours. Of course it is pink wine, pinker in the low light that reflects off the red sofas.

Alanna takes a sip and sticks out her lips. 'Jeez, this Prosecco sucks, let's do cocktails!' We got you, Alanna, we got you, just you wait, just wait, baby girl. We raise our glasses and clink them. 'To our girl Alanna, on her big night.' Soon we're squabbling over the last half of the second bottle. When it's gone the boys return to the table, carrying a tall bottle of a liqueur they say they've invented. They call it The Cherry Punch, says the one holding a gold-plated Zippo. It's just a lighter. Why does it make him so smug? They exchange a look and it's not a hard task, all you have to do is pour some cherry pop. Hey! Over here? We're ready. It's our night! We were born ready. We forgive them when they put down the frozen shot glasses. We cheer! We're thirsty. The velvet liqueur pours out too slowly; we lick our lips. The other boy sets the shots aflame. We are parted from them momentarily by a wall of blue fire.

They blow the shots out and order us to drink them immediately. The hot syrup hits our throats with its balsamic edge and we

216

nearly cough, but hold back. Our eyes water. We are stronger than they want us to be. We laugh through our tears and at the end of it we all have big fucking smiles on our faces from the effort.

'That's why we call it a punch,' says one of the waiters.

'Get it?' says the other.

We burst out laughing and when they return with a new shot paddle we're still laughing about them.

'Oh,' says Alanna, voice soft like a kitten's belly. 'Is this another drink you invented?'

'Now, ladies,' says the taller boy, tallest by an inch perhaps, but we can only tell them apart because this one is consistently eager to talk. We can imagine them discussing the terms of this interaction beforehand: claiming the right to speak to the ladies first, for the simple reason that of the two he is tallest. These are simple creatures. 'Now, ladies,' the taller one says. 'This drink is called a Sasha Grey. Who knows who or what a Sasha Grey is? For a free shot!'

'I thought they were all free shots,' I observe.

'She means paid for,' clarifies Bex.

We're pretending not to know that Sasha Grey is a famous porn star. Emmy takes the bullet by pretending to fall for it. 'Let me guess, boys,' she says. 'Is it a cock-tail?' She clicks her tongue on the hard K. The boys are obviously elated. They begin to giggle.

Mona doesn't get it, though not for want of trying. She picks up on the sexual tension but blanks on the cultural reference. She doesn't care. She slides in with her elbows on the table, cowgirl-like. 'So, are you going to show us your Sasha?'

The boys lose their composure. They are howling with laughter. They'd roll on the floor like dogs if they had freedom to move in those lackey outfits.

'What?' snaps Mona, and her tone shuts them up.

217

Emmy pulls her in by the strap of her bra. 'Let me show you,'
she says. She pulls Mona into the crook of her arm and to the side
of the table. They huddle in the light from the touchscreen. Mona
gives a small genuine yelp and recoils from the device.

When her fingertips make contact with the sticky gloss on her
lips she composes herself. 'Oh my, dirty boys,' Mona or Jessica
whispers in an unmotherly rasp.

And the boys happily pour chocolate liqueur into the thick bot-
tom of the shot glass, and then another liqueur and then whipped
cream: truly a nasty, deranged concoction.

Really, we're starting to think that this is sub-par entertainment
and certainly it lacks class. We look at each other. When will this
pathetic excuse for a support act sing its swansong and make room
for the main party piece? The girls are unimpressed. We've paid
money for this. We down the shots. We get cream moustaches; isn't
that the point? We stare at them while we lick them off. And sure
enough it all becomes a bit too much for the two fancy mice, because
finally they excuse themselves and scurry away. Before they leave
they say, 'Are you ready for the soft touch of the World's Best
Mixologist? Cocktails for the ladies!'

SINGLE CREAM

Ruth
Now

What got into me?

The first thing I see is my wristwatch. At 2:53 in the morning I am holding tight on to the plastic bar fixed to the wall of the disabled toilet. This isn't the toilets in the club, which have blue neon lights and sticky surfaces – so that people can't do drugs in them, although I never know what exactly happens to drugs under blue lights – but the toilet out back, the one only staff use.

Stuart Brandon Pierce, the World's Best Mixologist, is fucking me from behind. I can feel his perfect abs pushing into the small of my back. Who takes their shirt off to have sex in a toilet? But then you would, wouldn't you, if you had abs like that. Maybe I took it off him myself. I can't remember, but I suppose I would've wanted to. Although wait. Was he wearing one? He was shirtless at one point in the evening – but I think I remember him wearing a hoodie when we stepped out of the building. My memories are all out of order since the Blue Volcano. That's the one he stirred into a tall-necked glass bottle, the sugar spoon plunging in and out of the Curaçao. Except now I have come to, and we are here and he is fucking me. A bright shard of pain cuts into my right temple and all the details in the room are hurting. I'm thinking of nothing but the practicalities of the act itself. I spread my legs a little to achieve better balance. One of the white tiles in front of me is cracked and the crevices have been filled in with whiter silicone. I can feel the latex of the condom chafing against my skin, which means he is wearing one. I'll be sore tomorrow, but it's better than the other option. Of course Stuart Brandon Pierce uses protection. On her second or third Brandy Alexander, Mona turned to me and whispered, 'Bloody hell, there's enough cream in this to kill one of our oldies.' Then, to him, she said, 'Boy, how are your sugar levels coping?' It was supposed to be an in-joke between us and not something he was expected to have an answer for or even enough context to figure it out, but he became very sombre. The man must have a serious customer service complex.

He looked Mona right in the eyes and said, 'I don't drink on the job.' He said he gets his blood washed once a month to get rid of the toxins. What did he call it? *Hemotherapy*. He tried to explain the medical process and then remembered he was talking to nurses.

'It sounds like unorthodox medical practice,' I said. The girls laughed.

Alanna pinched the side of my arse. 'Ruth! So sassy!'

This memory is quite clear. Then there are bits that I can't remember. Some holes. Some dancing. The feeling that Alanna was both proud of and irritated by my behaviour. It made her harder to approach, but not in a way that was altogether bad; a little like a thread tensing up between us.

I angle my neck uncomfortably to avoid my face rubbing against the tiles. I catch a glimpse of him, busying himself over me, a large bird tattoo twitching on his right pec, right under the collarbone. Is it a bird of paradise? A peacock? A phoenix? This is obviously a man who revels in simple visual signification, probably identifies with one of these birds or has at one point in his life identified strongly enough with it to get it tattooed on his body. He has his mouth wide open as if in a song, which frankly seems inappropriate, even to me, and I am the person this man is currently fucking. His eyes are shut tight, creased with those sexy smile lines. I remind myself once again: he's fucking *me*.

He utters a broken-up sequence of virile 'huhs' that sound suspiciously like porn. Animals don't emit that sound in nature. Would someone like him consume so much porn that he'd learn to mimic it? Doesn't he get laid all the time? Does he rehearse his sex cry in front of the mirror? I look at the crack in the tile and try to imagine him as a little boy, with braces on, dark hair he hadn't yet learned to straighten, olive skin turned yellow by the lack of sunlight, long before he discovered tanning salons, before the Pilates and the weightlifting and the therapeutic blood cleanses.

It's hard to think with him pounding me so hard from behind. The grunting never ceases, but now he adds something extra: a slap on my arse cheek. I hear the noise first, before I feel the sting. Again, I look sideways and see the underside of his arm flexing. It makes me think of the reclining armchairs we have at work, leather stretching with a creak as the foot stand snaps out of the bottom. Is his rhythm quickening? I think it is. I see the side of his calf muscle tensing. He leans in against me, his padded torso rubbing against the small of my back, my spine. His hands slide up and cup my breasts from below. Can he feel the exact sag of them, the weight, the stretch marks riding up the inner sides? He tries to reach my lips with his mouth, fails, settles for my right earlobe, and leaves a trail of saliva down the side of my jaw. His tongue is thick and rubbery. It rummages in my earhole, and then my ear pops, like when you've got water inside it. I tilt my head sharply to clear it. Which must startle him, because he stops mid-action. He freezes. Then he shouts:

'I'm about to come!'

His hands push against the walls either side of my head as he expels himself from my body so quickly I swear I can hear him pop out. He comes twitching, the plastic head of his penis contracting against my buttock. I feel a droplet of sweat make its way down the back of my thigh.

I turn around. I have tinnitus in the ear he's spoken into. I shake my head again, like a pony. I wipe my cheek with the back of my hand. I pull my bra back in place and roll my dress down. I inspect the backs of my legs. There is a rip in one knee of my hold-ups, but nothing noticeable, not in the dark of the club. How long were we in here? Where are the girls? Are they still going? When there's nothing else left for me to do, I look at him. Stuart Brandon Pierce. He has tied the condom in a knot and laid it on the side of the sink. He's leaning against the wall, his sweaty back forming a halo of condensation on the white tiles around his shoulders. He's buttoning up his formal trousers. His red braces hang loose about his hips.

'Why did you have to pull out like that?'

'I told you. I was about to come.'

'Well, so was I.' This isn't technically true, but I want him to feel as bad as I do.

He slides down the wall, with a light skidding sound, wet muscle on ceramic. He sits on the floor.

'I'm sorry,' he says.

'You were wearing a condom.'

'I . . . I feel like climaxing together is a bit too intense for a first date. It makes me feel . . . very naked.'

'You looked pretty naked for a first date.'

I shut the toilet lid and sit down on it. I swipe a hand across my face to push away the damp baby hair.

'Did you enjoy it, though?'

'Sure.' I look around for my heels.

Stuart is on the floor, motionless. His face a mask of disappointment. My perspective from up here makes the whole scene look quite pathetic.

'What's up?' I say.

'You know,' he says, bottom lip out. 'I just really wanted you girls to have a good night.' He looks like a beagle on a PETA flyer.

Before I know it I'm on the floor, too, taking him in my arms. I feel the sweat cooling on his back, the skin beginning to goosebump across the strong dorsal trapezius. He smells of mint and talcum powder. Holding him feels different from being fucked by him. It feels worse, in a way.

I'm not used to holding anyone who I'm not in love with. I only know how to do it tenderly. I don't want him to be sad, but his body feels different.

'Hey, look, look, of course I'm having a good time,' I whisper in his ear.

He wails softly and snuggles against me, burrowing into my hair. I can feel his lips brushing my neck, his hot breath, his five o'clock stubble, and three in the morning must be a barman's five o'clock. This tired and heavy body feels strangely familiar. It's nicely familiar to be holding a man. His breath becomes more regular and I become aware that his fingers have penetrated slightly under the hem of my dress and are moving upwards at an imperceptible pace with each of his breaths.

'I just wanted,' he murmurs, 'for you girls to have the best night ever.'

'I told you: we had a great time.'

'Are you, though?'

'I am.'

He pushes my soggy underwear to the side and begins touching me. I let out a sigh.

'Then tell me,' he says.

'What?' I say.

'You're having the best night ever.'

He is relentless. He must have been a popular boy in school or friends with popular boys. The only thing teenage boys will ever get right is that persistence pays off. Clearly this isn't the kind of man who gives up easily. Fail, fail again, fail better.

'I'm having the best night ever,' I say.

'Tell me again.'

'I'm having the best night ever.'

The repetitive movement continues, and it is pleasing. The inside of his arm against my cheek is cool, and smooth. I give up and I come.

He struts back to the table with his arm around my shoulders. I'm feeling utterly tired in that way you do after an orgasm when sleep overcomes you completely. The way that he holds me feels impersonal. He could be carrying a watermelon or a baguette under his arm. The lights are on. The girls have gone. The twin boys are stacking cocktail glasses. They look younger in this light. They look up at us.

'All right now, boys,' says Stuart Brandon Pierce. 'Who's the Best Mixologist in the World?'

He runs his thumb lightly across my arse. My heels feel heavy in my hand. The boys cheer and exchange high fives, low fives. I leave.

I pull the key out of the lock and shut the door to the flat behind me. I pause for a minute with my back against the door. I hook one big toe on the back of each foldable pump and slide them off my feet. I wiggle my toes. I double lock the door and find the packet of cigarettes in the bottom of my handbag. There is one left. I stick it in my mouth, my lips furry around the filter. I lock the door and leave the key in there because no one else needs to come back to this flat tonight.

No one's ever been allowed to smoke in this flat. I light up the cigarette. I feel sweaty and terrible and exhilarated. I feel exhausted. In the bathroom I sit on the toilet lid and unroll my hold-ups, squeezing the cigarette between my teeth, silicon glue squeaking against my thighs. I tie the hold-ups together and open my new laundry basket. I pull off my dress, panties and bra, add them to the basket too. I notice that it is half empty. I've been keeping on top of the laundry. I'm so much better at keeping on top of the laundry these days. I go to bed naked and unwashed.

I slip into a black sleep. There are no dreams, only a bright light I know I must follow, soaring white and fast and wild.

PULSES

Neil

The Night Before the Break-up

When I wake up, I can't remember it all, not straight away, but I recognize the fear, immediately. The same panic, black and gluey. The horror. The excitement. And I can't quite explain this, but a part of me almost welcomes it. In the darkness, I pick out the outline of Ruth's body next to mine. When she sleeps, sometimes it is hard not to admit it: things have been bad between us for a while. And this seals it.

The first time it happened I was fifteen and two months and one week. I still slept in my childhood bed. I'd bought a calendar to count down to my next birthday and I remember turning a page that day. I've always found it depressing that my birthday is in December, so close to Christmas. It's no way to party. As a kid I tried to keep it exciting by crossing off each day with a red marker pen, but by spring I'd always given up, grown deflated. Looking back, I realize that even then I thought of happiness as a distant thing, always out of reach. That's a lousy personality trait, isn't it? But big news: you don't get to choose your personality.

The 1994 calendar had cars on it. All my friends in school had ones with naked ladies, but a more risqué calendar would've upset my mother and I didn't feel like buying one, anyway. It wasn't that I lacked the guts to do it, but that I couldn't stand people looking down on me, not even back then. I fucking hate being laughed at. Why would I put myself through that ordeal at the newsagent?

That night, when I opened my eyes into the black room, the front lights of the Bugatti on my calendar sliced the wall across my bedroom, as it spun around itself in mad circles. The noises from the motorway, one mile down the road, spilled through the curtains like someone was turning the volume up and down. I couldn't move. I felt nauseous in a way that as an adult I have come to associate with a particularly bad hangover: vomit sloshing in the pit of my stomach. I looked up at the ceiling, hoping to find stillness there that matched my pinned body, but I found it was covered in neon signs, thick fluorescent gel travelling round in their glass tubes like a bloodstream. I considered that the liquid might really be blood and as soon as I formulated that thought I became sure that it really was.

I could hear the neon static crackling. I thought that I could see the heat from my body travelling upwards and condensing against the glass surface, as though the blood inside was impossibly cold. I heard the steam turn into water and drip back down on to the mattress holding my dead body. I don't remember how long I lay like that or when I slipped back into sleep.

When I woke up the room was filled with grey light. I tried to move an arm and it responded to the instruction. I was really awake. I ran my hands down my legs and arms. They were dry. The bed sheets stiff. I had been asleep for hours, and my sweat had congealed in a white patch. I looked at the ceiling: it was the same egg blue it had always been, washed out in the breaking light. The black Bugatti marked the month of March, its custom tyres aggressively pushing at the corner of the image. The whole room was quiet and I was hard.

The feeling of having lived through something dark wasn't unlike excitement. The visions became increasingly disturbing that year and even more so throughout my teens, more intricate too. From the age of fifteen to eighteen, the night paralysis kept coming back. I learnt how to recognize an attack, but it didn't make me any better at dealing with it. I didn't improve with time or with practice and it was all rather disruptive.

I'd barely paid attention to girls before. I remember this was a conscious choice; I was always very self-conscious. One of my mother's favourite memories was the one of the nosy neighbour next door asking me: 'Do you have a girl-friend?' I was three. I was playing with wooden cubes in the sandbox at the back of the garden. Without lifting my head, I responded, 'I am busy.' My mother liked to recall this memory as a sort of cautionary tale and brought it up often during my teens. So for a long time, since girls weren't spontaneously paying attention to me, and I was equally unwilling to go after them, I really did believe that I was destined to save myself for better things. Until the sleep paralysis started. At least, I think that's what it was. It made me feel restless. It was puberty, but it wasn't just that. It felt like a very specific need. A need I didn't have a name for, but which was a very strong one for sure.

The experience renewed itself each time, never losing its intensity. I jolted up from the blackout that returned me to myself after the paralysis, sitting stiffly in bed, my body throbbing with its own blood. I put myself under the steaming jet of the shower, scalding water lashing me across the back in wide red strokes. I knew with complete clarity what it was that I needed: I needed to push myself immediately into or through another being, crash into another body. It was a kind of hunger and I was so, so hungry. I was hungry for breaking into something, yes, but it was the act of breaking that mattered most. I needed to snap back into my own shape after my horror. I thought about this while I touched myself in the scorching hot water, punishing myself for my impure thoughts, though technically also indulging them.

At fifteen I no longer observed my mother's constellation of sins, but I still figured that wanting to hurt someone was a fucked-up thing to want, regardless of one's religious inclinations. I was too naive then, of course, to imagine that some people may wilfully seek to be hurt as a means to achieve pleasure. I thought that hurting would, well, hurt, and who wants that? So I crushed my urges, my chest pressed against the shower tiles, just in case my mother opened the door while I was in there.

Afterwards, I spent a long time cleaning myself.

I began to notice girls in a different way, much like other fifteen-year-old boys, I suppose, but for me it happened suddenly, after the hallucinations began. It was as though all the girls I knew had suddenly come into focus. I didn't initially connect the things that aroused me in my disordered sleep and the bodies of my classmates, because

230

what happened during the night didn't really belong to my waking life. My brain diverted my attention to localized detail. I don't remember the names of the girls in my school, but I remember liking the curve of an ankle that belonged to a girl who always wore frilly socks folded over her school shoes. I was fascinated by girls' joints. I liked their knees under tables, especially when they were eager to stop wearing tights in the spring, when it was still a little too cold and the skin on their legs turned purple and grainy. During the volleyball tournament, I watched girls fall to their knees for a save. I wanted to slip my index finger in the crook of the middle hitter's elbow – I have no memory of her face, but I remember she had long, sand-coloured limbs – and press the sinew under the skin until I held the rope of her muscle. I wanted to pull her to me, forcing her elbow on to my shoulder, her head against my chest so she would have to look up into my eyes. I liked watching girls when they put their hair up in ponytails, which at the time were very fashionable. I lay on my bed at night as the wallpaper swirled into night flowers, the black Bugatti humming angrily from its frame, and woke up feeling like I hadn't rested at all. I lost a stone in three months.

One night in June I opened my eyes to a figure in a top hat sitting at the edge of my bed. He began turning his head to face me, very slowly, and I felt extremely afraid. I could sense that the man was about to speak. I knew that what he had to say was extremely important and would bring about some kind of resolution. The feeling of dread increased as I waited to see his face and time stood still as the black fear clutched at my chest, and I waited, and waited, until I was sure my heart was about to give out, until I realized that there was no face, though the head kept slowly revolving on its hinge.

In the morning my chest stung like it'd been wound in barbed wire. My penis was so hard it hurt. I showered. I composed myself, put on my school uniform and took myself to the library to do some research. I have always liked to learn things: it is only once you've learnt everything about a subject that you can say you've truly mastered it.

There was no mention anywhere of sexual arousal occurring as a consequence of sleep paralysis, but I figured that if a correlation existed I wouldn't find it in the kind of books they kept in the school library. In any case, the fact that I had made the connection and now was seeking confirmation of it through secondary reading meant that my sexuality was already shaping itself from those lucid nightmares. Until then, I'd thought of sex in an abstract way and figured out in my head which positions would prove most efficient. It'd seemed to me that a lot about sex wasn't immediately obvious, but I didn't feel any rush to find out. Now, I had suddenly become impatient, my whole body feverish each morning. Whatever it was, sex needed to happen soon. The school term was almost over and I thought that this might be my last chance. It was time for me to take action.

I lost my virginity easily and to a girl called Roxy. She wasn't a virgin. I didn't care. It made things better. I knew that Roxy wasn't only sleeping with me. She slept with everyone – or that was what everyone said. It didn't matter so long as she would do it with me, which she dutifully did. All I had to do was ask. In bed she was disciplined, despite her experience, or maybe because of it. She was surprisingly pliable. She handed her body over as though she fancied stepping out of it and I could borrow it until she needed it back. When I roughed her up she went slack and pink, her white chocolate bob all scuffed, bottom lip out of axis, like a sweet posh horse. The third time we did it, she asked me to slap her, so I did what she wanted. The crack of my palm as it made contact with her cheek returned me to my body.

After that, the paralysis stopped completely. Three months of complete bliss. The next autumn, Roxy joined the young cadets. She died in Afghanistan a few years later. It made the national papers and when I read the obituary I smiled, thinking of her fondly. She'd never mentioned wanting to join the army during the brief time we had been together, but in my head it made perfect sense. You might say my sexual initiation was a paradigmatic experience. I will always be grateful to Roxy: she was a girl who put her body on the line. Just my type.

It happened again, many years later. 2007: the year my mother died. It was the night after the funeral and Ruth had come back to my childhood flat with me. That was the only time I would take her, because I sold the flat shortly afterwards, and shortly after that they turned the building into a bingo palace. The life of the city ticks on at its own pace.

Ruth and I had been together a year. Things were better, the best they'd ever been for me. I think that was the closest I've ever come to real happiness. She was my angel, my quintessential girl. It took me years of looking for the perfect girl, months of looking at her from a distance before I could call her mine. She drove me fucking crazy. The way there was always more room within her, like she had infinite depth.

The first time we made love I threw myself into her

completely, and she welcomed me, whole. I never felt the need to push things much further in bed, like I had with Roxy and the others. I didn't need to squeeze her or slap her or pull on her hair. With Ruth, these rituals of power felt obsolete. There was no doubt that she was all mine, my girlfriend: I'd never been so attracted to a girl before. Sometimes, when I watched her sleep, shut off from the world, her body felt like a substance heavier than water, a greenish-black oil, that exerted its own kind of gravity. I couldn't stop touching her. I was in love with all the textures of her body, the way her narrow bones were close to the surface. At night the presence of her small darkness was enough to ward off greater evils. Ruth was the medicine: my vaccine, my reminder of where the boundaries lay. With her by my side, I thought I'd never need to sink into that great black again, would never emerge wanting to kill something, if only a little bit.

I had never shared my childhood bed with anyone. My mother wouldn't allow it. The funeral had been a small affair but the paperwork afterwards took longer than expected and we both felt too tired to travel back home. We made the sensible decision to stay overnight and, though I had a bad feeling about it, I assumed this was normal. My mother had just died, after all. I didn't have it in me to move into the master bedroom where she had slept – I'd rarely been allowed in there as a child and I couldn't shake the feeling that I'd be doing something wrong by going in without asking. Even though there was now no one left to ask. Ruth mistook my hesitation for fresh grief and guided me by the hand to my old bedroom. She'd never been there before but she figured out the way. I followed her. The thing about my type of girl – and Ruth's *so* my type – is that

234

they can make you do anything they want you to. That night Ruth wanted me to fuck her and found a way to get what she wanted. She didn't ask; she just didn't leave me any choice. When I saw her in her white underwear, her slender frame white on my old floral bed cover, I had no choice but to have her.

We did it in the single bed with the flannel sheets rubbing my knees raw. I gave into her and felt her body flat against the mattress. I held her neck and she let her throat go slack like the stem of a flower. I pressed my fingers in until I found her pulse. I hated her then for what she was making me do. My mother had been dead forty-eight hours. But after it was over and I looked at her helpless face, so open and vulnerable, I felt myself warm to her again. She must've thought this was a way to make me feel better. Bless her. We fell asleep pressed against each other, like we do now, every night.

But when I awoke in my dead body, I couldn't find Ruth's small weight next to me. The bed had collapsed beneath us. I wanted to turn my head but my neck stuck. The sleep paralysis was back.

I looked up, moved my eyes from right to left. The room was painted a murky yellow, swirls of green around the edges, stretching, slowly, as I watched them, and meeting at the centre of the ceiling. Then the walls began to lose consistency, to wobble and melt, sliding down the swirls like stewed meat off a bone. They dropped off completely and I realized that the darker stripes were metal bars, held together by a circular railing at the top, like an aviary. The steel looked green against the sulphuric sky and I could hear the muttering, somewhere, of birds stirring. The more I listened, the more alien the noises sounded, and I began to think that these animals could only inhabit a world very different from ours. I understood then that my sleeping body must have travelled to a planet unfit for human beings, which explained the mustard-yellow sky outside the cage. In the distance, I spotted a pale moon, then another. This was wrong and I felt the panic rise like bile in my mouth. The humming escalated as the planet woke to a new day and my chest folded in on itself. I couldn't breathe.

I woke up, covered in sweat, really awake. I ran to the toilet, I had to get away from Ruth. I masturbated in the house of my dead mother. I cried with my forehead pressed against the tiles. I hate crying, so it offered no relief. My own tears filled me with a sodden kind of disgust. How could Ruth have let this happen? I thought that I could be completely safe with her. I felt alone in the world and I said to myself, eventually, you will find freedom in having no family at all. A man must learn to thrive in loneliness. These were the kinds of thoughts with which I comforted myself as a young man. I did have Ruth. But could I trust her completely, now she'd failed me when I'd needed her most?

Ten years together. Long enough to forgive and forget. Ruth is everything I like in a girl. There is a reason we've been together this long and it's not about choosing each other each day but about forgetting there is even a choice. In both good and bad ways, for better or worse, the things I find attractive in her are also the things that drive me absolutely mad. That's how love works. You can't pick and choose, can't have one without the other. And, anyway, the sleep paralysis didn't come back for a long time. I thought I might as well propose to her, in sickness and health, et cetera, et cetera. It made sense.

Sometimes I have needed a little distraction, felt the need again pulling me in a different direction. If you stick a curious man in two and a half rooms in north London, his mind is bound to wander, at least a little. I have never crossed a line. There were a couple of snogs at work parties – the joy of working in a company with over three hundred employees – but all were isolated episodes. Then when cybering got big, that kept me entertained for a while. Ruth always goes to bed so early. But after a while I got bored of typing, and live-camming with her there next door in the bedroom was out of the question. And so dating sites seemed a more satisfying way to tend to my urges. I really rarely met up with them. All I wanted was to talk, for them to talk to me, nothing perverted. I think to begin with my plan was to talk it all out of my system. I did for a bit. Then there were a few, no-strings-attached flings and a couple of coincidences: a girl who worked really close to my office and a nymphomaniac who practically stalked me. Once I developed a crush on the receptionist at work, but that didn't really go anywhere. A couple of times I couldn't say no, but I didn't pursue them. At night I still find myself pouring my heart into the inboxes of good-looking strangers from company websites or swiping through Tinder profiles within a five-mile radius until there are no more matches available. I'm just looking for some fucking appreciation, you know? I need to keep myself busy. And technology has made it easy. Who am I hurting?

What is the definition of betrayal? I am both interested in the chase *and* interested in Ruth. They are two different things. Ruth is my life. At night, on the internet, I wander lonely as a cloud, talking to other girls. I'm just playing, messing around. Sometimes I do meet up with them, not often. Sometimes I do like them. I've still got *eyes*. I would be dead if I didn't notice other women. There are a lot of attractive girls in the world: it's a game of statistics. Right now, for instance, I'm talking to a cheeky one. Her name's Lili, like the song. One thing doesn't preclude the other. I have tried to explain this to Ruth in the past, though I haven't bothered going into it for a while. She just pretends not to understand what I am saying. She knows full well what I mean, she just won't admit it. Whenever we are in a disagreement Ruth listens quietly without asking any questions until I lose track of what I am saying. She always chooses the path of least resistance. Sometimes I wonder if I haven't spent the best years of my life with her because she never let me get to the bottom of things. The things that I want, the things that I need to be happy, or closer to happy, or whatever a man like me is allowed to have. She knows me; she knows I feel restless. She knows I can't help it. She keeps me talking, so she doesn't have to listen. Her mind is made up: she wants things to stay the same way. She is happy with little, unambitious: our home, her work, our pithy existences. So long as she can keep me talking, we'll never get to it. Nothing will change. It's easy when some-one tells you how to be. But what about me?

Ten years together: 2006–16. When I write the dates down, one next to the other, they read like the epitaph of a child.

When I wake up, I can't remember it all, not straight away. But I recognize the fear, immediately. Her black shadow breathing, in the dark, next to me.

Something has happened overnight, I am sure of it. I can't remember seeing shapes, not clearly but I felt their closeness, the horror of their proximity raising the hair on my dead forearms. I sunk back under, smothered in sleep, then rose to the surface again.

I wake up panting like a dog. I look at my hands and recognize them as my hands. I can move them. I am awake, really awake. It is dawn and grey light floods our bedroom. I am soaked with sweat and my whole body hurts. No details, not yet, but I know they will come back to me. I can feel it in my body, beginning to tense up, bracing. There is another feeling; my spine tightens with a familiar excitement. I don't need to reach out to touch myself. I know I am sexually aroused.

Ruth is right there, next to me, right where she always is. One spindly arm folded over her head like a little wing. I watch her face, the side that is visible. Age hasn't blunted her features, but sharpened them, and she's even more bird-like now, which suits her, though I can't decide how I feel about it. I've always thought of Ruth as a bird but at first she was mostly a theory of one. At twenty-one she was very vague as a creature, her outline not quite so defined. I thought we would solidify together into a single shape, not separately. But I was wrong. She's hardened into a singular version of herself: these days she fully embodies her own spirit animal. It has become easier to pin Ruth down to one bird or another, though never a single species in particular. I've spotted a swallow's head as she exits the shower with wet hair all slicked back, a robin's proud chest when she is busy in the kitchen. *Bird watching*. I know this isn't a funny joke – even to me it sounds a little desperate – but the fact of her aging makes me uneasy. It's unnerving that it is there in plain view for everybody to see. She wouldn't have it this way, if she could help it. She's quite private. People think that change goes unnoticed in those with whom we share close quarters, but I don't agree. I don't notice it daily, but I'm certainly aware of it. It's not about the aging itself; I'm not so naive to think it isn't happening to me too. It's just that it suits some people better than others. What I liked about Ruth was that she used to be an intangible creature, an ethereal angel. These days, I wonder if I would find white marble under her bedclothes if she'd let me strip her naked. All smooth, with no openings: a statue of an angel.

Awake, I feel the space between our bodies and am relieved to find the wetness hasn't spread to her. She is fast asleep. But like a bird, Ruth can be woken by the smallest disruption. I stare at her profile in the low light from the curtains. I know that if I move she will dart her skinny arm towards me, in the anxious way she does, and ask, 'Are you OK, baby?' Or something like that. Something nice, concerned. She would want to take care of me, to get out of bed and change the bottom sheet, ring the doctor, take the morning off work. I'd have to explain what happened.

I'm always fucking expected to explain. I flip on to my side and get out of bed. I realize I am automatically heading to the shower. 'Are you OK, baby?' says Ruth, still half asleep. I don't respond. I shut the bathroom door behind me and lock it. In the shower I run the dial all the way to hot, just a notch under. I masturbate angrily under the jet.

When I am done, I take her hot-pink scrubbing glove from the soap dish and drag it roughly across my chest. It leaves a hot-pink scratch. I think about the incidence of my nocturnal disease: I know it spikes at times of great distress. My parents signed the divorce papers the year I turned fifteen. Whenever my father rang, which was always in the evenings, my mother would continue to do the dishes, her hands in Marigolds up to the elbow. I had to pick up. Then puberty. Whatever that was. Fucking hell. The time we had sex in my childhood bed and Ruth fell asleep after getting what she wanted. These episodes are easy to pin down, easy to analyse. What has happened this time? What is happening? Nothing's happening. And that's it. I can't stand it.

I stand in the shower and watch the water collect in the drain. A sliver of beige soap gets trapped in the metal and I bend over to retrieve it. My vision blurs for a moment. I steady myself against the wall. Like water, Ruth trickling into all things. She's drowning me. The details of the night terror are finally coming to the surface. I close my eyes and it all comes back to me.

My eyes open on to the blank ceiling. My head feels harnessed to the pillow and, at first, I think it must be the consequence of the two glasses of Pinot Grigio I had with my dinner. There's a hint of a migraine nudging at my temples. Then I realize that the straps hold firmly across my body. I see that the ceiling is shot across with small lights, like fireflies but electric, part of a larger body pulsating beneath me. More lights ascend, not like sparks from a fire in free upwards flight, but slowly, and I see that they are attached to tiny tendrils of coral, reaching around and above my body. I can hear these fingers creaking. They begin to close in on me as I lie on the bed, defenceless. I can't see Ruth next to me, but I know she is there. I know that this is her, a creature expanding. Then the light becomes so intense that all I can see is red, burning darkness, and I count the pace of my own breath, slower and slower, as I run out of air.

STEAK (LEAN)

Ruth
Now

I am half an hour late for work. I just couldn't get up this morning. The whole weekend is a blur. For the majority of it, I've been stuck in a sticky sleep, like a fly caught at the bottom of a honey jar. Granted, I am not a seasoned party girl, but I don't understand why I'm still feeling so bad two days later. I really can't remember the last time I had a hangover like this – sometimes a little headache, after three or four glasses of wine at home, but never with the added pressure of having to account for direct interaction with others. My mouth feels dry no matter how much water I drink and the stabbing pain behind my right eye is still there. I'm feeling a desperate kind of exhaustion. I have memories of the party but they are still unlinked. Little scenes with holes in the texture. The girls. Make-up. Frankenstein. Bex's hand on my knee. Her oval nails like black apple pips. *Malus domestica* is the Latin name for the apple. Shellac is the upmarket beauty parlour name for a manicure. Alanna's ear, as I struggled to push a diamanté stud into her lobe. 'Push harder! Go on! It really won't hurt.' Cream shots. Then more women joining us. Dancing. A woman I didn't know with lots of earrings, who grabbed me by the shoulders. 'This the maid of honour? Well, kill me now, I'm Franki! Remember me, Beadle?'

Alanna emitted a high-pitched noise, 'Oh my God, Francesca!'

'Jammy Rodgers?' I said, and I realized I was very drunk. Dancing. Alanna pinching me – on the hip, on the top of the hand, on the thigh – whenever she wanted attention. She didn't care that I bruise easily, though she'd figured it out quickly. Stuart Brandon Pierce. Then the car park as I waited for my taxi home. The fucking car park. Did I take a taxi? I cannot piece together the evening. It makes me feel irritable.

As always, getting to work, I am reminded that my lack of experience makes me vulnerable. I find the front door shut, which is confusing. I try it several times before realizing it is locked and trying my key. There is no one in the Bowl. I look at the rota on the wall: Alanna and the girls have taken the day off. I know we've been calling it the big night for months, but I honestly hadn't foreseen the kind of weekend that lasts until Monday. It hadn't occurred to me to check for any alterations in the rota. Anyone can put absences up there, but Mona or I have to OK them as we are the senior nurses. If no objections are raised by the end of the week, any absences are cleared. The girls knew there was no way we would OK this change but in the excitement, Mona and I forgot to check, which is what they must've hoped for. We are dramatically understaffed and I am half an hour late. This is incredibly irresponsible. So much for the girls sticking together. It's only Mona and me today, and unsurprisingly, she is nowhere to be seen. She must be halfway through the first-floor rounds and is probably really mad at me, though I am the one who has actually made it to work. I hurry to take my smock out of the locker and when I get back to the Bowl I see that the switchboard is going off. Room 214. I could ignore the switchboard code: I'm alone in the Bowl and the front door is unlocked. I really shouldn't leave reception unattended. But the switchboard is for emergencies. Which is precisely why he always rings the fucking bell.

Mr Hancock doesn't like me. This is strange, because while I'd hardly win a popularity contest out there, in here I am well liked. And yet he despises me. At least this is the impression I've always had. Anyway, it's OK, the feeling is mutual. I guess you could say we see through each other. Something about him makes me uneasy and I am convinced he senses it, feeds off it. We didn't expect him to last long, but he's been with us two years now and seems to be gathering strength as he gets older, like a dry-aged piece of steak, and despite the fact he is veined with rot. I think about Emmy saying that he tried to kiss Bex, that day we were in the laundry room. Mona says that all men get weird with age, when they aren't already weird before. Still, she knows how us girls feel about Mr Hancock and will cover for us if she's feeling kind. No such luck today and it's entirely my fault: I was in charge of this weekend, but I got distracted. I should've foreseen this. I hide my face in my hands and hope the light will stop flickering, but it only seems to flash more urgently. Because everything is an emergency for Mr Hancock.

But then what if it *is* an emergency? I'm already half an hour late. My head is fucking killing me. *Stop being a baby.* I grit my teeth. Be practical. It's easier to get this done than sitting around thinking up an excuse. I lock the front door and head for the lifts.

Mr Hancock's room is the largest in the care home, set apart from the others and at the end of the top-floor corridor. This arrangement was specifically requested and no one objected. If anything, we are grateful to be able to store him away from the others. We try to forget about him. Until he gets on the buzzer, that is. Which, yes, he does often, but am I being unfair? Other patients do this frequently, too: a glass of water, a cup of tea, feeling lonely and simply needing a chat. It's part of our job and a big reason why this job – this place – exists at all. In here, their needs have meaning and are a matter of urgency. Old people get lonely. Most have lost more loved ones than they have left. The heart deteriorates, in the same way as eyesight or hearing. What's wrong with me today? So I got laid for the first time since the break-up. That's no reason to get sentimental. It wasn't exactly romantic. Am I being sentimental? No. I think I am feeling morose. Everything seems so gloopy.

Mr Hancock's daughter had suggested 'a quiet, secluded room'. It was the first on a long list of privileges that were set in stone when he arrived, as if we'd been applying to have Mr Hancock stay with us as an esteemed guest and not the other way round. The special requirements are granted as a result of his daughter's generous disposition, which we enjoy in large quarterly instalments. Oh yes, she is a patron. She is a close friend of Call-Me-Melissa and just the kind of bitch Melissa would be friends with. She, tragically, is too busy to visit often: 'My apologies for being rather elusive.' I can't say we mind particularly.

I remember the day he arrived. I feel queasy thinking about it. Miss Hancock, a media big shot with appropriately auburn hair and little pointed heels, strode into the care home at lunchtime. In her right hand, she carried a stapled bunch of paper, fashioned into a sceptre. She unrolled it on my desk and began to stab her way through a bullet-point list.

'Miss Hancock,' she said, her manicured fingernail already on to item one, no time to waste. 'We spoke on the phone. Mind if we make this quick? I have a business lunch in Noho in forty and the traffic is just something else today.'

She flashed a little smile and I knew I didn't like her. Her lips twitched at the corners. Extreme Type A personality. I ran a list of popular antidepressants through my head: sertraline, citalopram, fluoxetine, paroxetine. Cocaine? A mix, probably. It's hard to tell at a glance. She wrinkled her nose. Definitely cocaine. She looked down at her list.

'Natural fibre pillows,' she said. She found my eyes again and nodded. A tinkle of her chandelier earrings. 'They're essential to aid my father's neck issues.'

'It's not unusual at that age,' I said. Another perfunctory tinkle as she once again raised her eyes to mine. I knew I'd fucked it already. 'Most of our oldies –' I giggled, because I giggle when I'm nervous, not a little nervous, but intensely nervous '– our patients. Most of our patients, they suffer from cervicalgia or cervical hernia. Neuropathic flare-ups are a frequent occurrence.'

Very good, medical language. She stared at me. I could feel Mona's eyes piercing my back. Sometimes she put me through little tests. This was one of them: I knew I was on my own. I had to act like a senior nurse. Mona's vote of confidence; she was trusting me to handle this.

'We provide top-quality ergonomic foam pillows to ensure maximum comfort. They are memory pillows. Do you know much about memory pillows?'

She looked at me as though I was talking about cushions hand-crafted by magical gnomes, and I wanted to shout in her face, 'They're all over fucking Groupon!' But, of course, why would a woman like this know about Groupon? A tinkle. Ice-cold eyes, no-smudge matte lipstick, brick-coloured.

She spoke. 'Yes. I would expect nothing less. As I'm practically bankrupting myself to pay for this place, I expect you to be able to provide the appropriate basic equipment. However, you understand that you need to make an exception for my father's particular condition? This brand –' her taupe fingernail tapped item one again and again until I had to break eye contact '– uses natural fibres that assist his posture during the night. Not only that: there are eucalyptus leaves embedded in the core of the pillow. To help him breathe – sleep better at night.'

Finally, Mona butted in, her matronly elbows sliding in next to mine. 'I'm sure we can arrange that, Miss Hancock.'

'Of course, I don't mind paying extra.'

'Not a problem.'

'Great.' A tinkle. Item two. 'Woollen blankets. I'm getting them sent over from Foxford. Lovely little mill in rural Ireland. Used to be run by nuns, you should look it up – fascinating story. They should be with you in the next couple of days. My father has a soft spot for the natural feeling of hand-loomed wool. There should be one folded at the foot of his bed at all times. I cannot emphasize this enough.'

'Our regulation duck feather duvets . . .' I began. Mona's clog pressed on to my toes, not hard enough to hurt, but hard enough to interrupt my sentence.

'No problem at all, Miss Hancock,' said Mona. She glared at me – my mother's glare. Mona has never met my mother but she manages to convey her so exactly that I'm not sure if it's my mother's glare I am thinking about when I think about my mother's glare, or Mona's. She was letting me know that I was about to cross a line. I stepped back and waited next to the switchboard as they reached the bottom of the list. Then I dialled the code for the porter's pager on the interphone. Donal arrived glistening with sweat, comb in pocket, iPod earbuds tightly screwed in, and I looked away so that I didn't have to see the frown on Miss Hancock's face.

The luggage came first. Four enormous trunks from the same brown-and-gold set. Monogrammed; but of course. The old man was wheeled in last. He looked at first like a bad cut of meat, muscular, livid and corrupted. His outsized forearms, grotesquely tanned, barely fitted into his chair. He held himself up with intimidating composure, given his age, like a Greek statue on its disintegrating plinth, legs crumbling under folded fleece. His thin white hair, at least, was consistent, plastered back over his skull. Shirtsleeves rolled up. Miss Hancock stood next to him and looked down.

'Yes, Daddy? It *is* nice, isn't it? You're going to have a really relaxing time here. It's the best in London.' She pecked him on the cheek.

The old man gazed back with milky eyes. He didn't look quite alive, which sent a shiver down my spine. I reminded myself to feel bad for him, dropped off like a suitcase at the airport. Mouth ajar, abandoned in the middle of a pile of expensive junk. With all that money, you could get staff to look after him round the clock in his own home, save having to move him at such an old age. You wouldn't even have to pretend you cared. One's own bed, own four walls, own trinkets and memories, are actual things that help an old person sleep better at night. One fewer soul for us to look after. *I cannot recommend enough that you look after your father at home.* But I didn't say anything, because the truth of the matter is, without people like her, we'd all be out of our jobs. It is better here, after all, with people who are paid to care – and such good pay that it is easy to count your blessings and start to believe it is more than simply a job. A vocation for empathy. I couldn't say I was feeling at my most empathetic right then. Miss Hancock stared at me, the incompetent nurse. Thankfully, Mona slipped out of the Bowl and took the wheelchair by the handles. She pushed Mr Hancock up the disabled ramp, parking him between the potted palm and the reconditioned Victorian lift.

'Well, I really have to run now!' said Miss Hancock, 'I'm just so awfully busy today. Thank you everyone. I'll call in a bit later to check everything is going smoothly.'

A tinkle, as she swivelled on her heels.

'Bye, Daddy!' She made for the sliding doors, swinging her car keys on her little finger. She halted with a jerk. 'One last thing. The cotton ones are in the second smallest trunk.' Confused, I glanced at Mona, by the lift, but she returned a blank stare. 'The pads, for Christ's sake! Do I have to spell it out for you? Incontinence pads, I believe you call them!'

The doors swished shut behind her. Suddenly everything was quiet. Mr Hancock hadn't spoken a word. My throat closed up. Despite all that money, he just looked like another poor old man. Mona turned the chair around and slid in behind him to pull it into the lift. I forced myself to look down at him. The old man locked his pale eyes on mine. Slowly, he ran his tongue across his top lip, so slowly I thought I must've imagined it.

I can hear Mr Hancock's voice as I walk towards room 214; faintly, not because his voice is faint, given his age, but because I am still far away. I am taking my time. If something happened to him now, I could say I had been on my way. But nothing is happening. He is just having a sing-along. Timmy comes out of room 205 wheeling the broom trolley. He rolls his eyes at me, *he's doing it again*, then scuttles off towards the lift. Timmy is twenty-three and the star of Christmas karaoke.

'Isn't he adorable?' said Melissa after his performance of Cher's 'Believe', with that peculiar balance of affection and condescension towards the less fortunate that comes from old money. Well, charming Timmy has no time to deal with Mr Hancock's terrible performance. I don't blame him. I don't want to deal with it either. I wait for him to disappear into the lift. I pause at the door marked 214 with my hand on the knob. I suck a big breath in and breathe out through my mouth. My nose feels sticky, plugged up. My face hurts. My poor head. This must be my punishment for getting distracted.

Dusty Springfield. 'Wishin' and Hopin''. Mr Hancock's favourite song. Before each verse you can hear the phlegm collecting at the bottom of his throat. I push the door open. The singing stops.

Mr Hancock is lying in his bed at an angle. He's wearing a white vest with thin straps, so that his large limp muscles are exposed. One of his arms is hooked on to the head-board; the other, stretched out, is punctured by the IV drip, its twitching blue vein pulsing through his jaundiced tan. When did they put him back on liquids? Has he been getting worse? I've lost track. I don't care. He looks uncon-scious, but I know better than that. One of his knees is bent, the other relaxed along the side of the bed, like an underwear model. A memory from Saturday night congeals in my head: Stuart Brandon Pierce stubs out my cigarette on a brick out back, taps my glass. 'Drink up, that's a good girl,' he says. His dumbstruck face as he looks up at me from the toilet floor. I shake my head to get rid of it. A yellow pool has collected between Mr Hancock's legs. There's piss on the bed sheet. It's filthy.

He snaps his head upright and opens his eyes. He stares at me and puckers his reptile lips. I notice he isn't wearing his lower dentures and so his upper teeth look too large, too many.

'Right, Mr Hancock!' I clap my hands and the sound sends a sharp pain through my right eye socket. 'You called.'

He is looking at me. His mouth and neck are barely moving. The voice exits his throat like a ventriloquist's dummy. *Did you show him that you cared?* Is that how the song goes? *Did you show him that you cared, Ruth?* Did he just say my name? He can't have. My head feels like it's about to explode. *Did I do the things he liked to do?*

'What happened here, Mr Hancock?' I say. I opt for the caring, babying tone that can snap our most difficult patients out of their mood. I don't feel very caring. I feel like throwing up. I decide to keep things straightforward. 'I think we need to get your bedding changed, don't we?'

I make towards the window, towards where his wheelchair is parked. I roll the chair next to his bed and slip the brakes on with my foot. He starts singing again, delivering each line with precision, a nauseating balance between sugar and decay. 'We love Dusty Springfield, don't we, Mr Hancock? But how about we get you nice and clean now—'

He slams a hand on the bedside table. A stack of paper cups falls to the floor and jiggles to a standstill on the turquoise lino. For a moment, nothing happens and I don't know what to do. I'm paralysed, a rabbit in the headlights. *Did you show him that you cared just for him?* Everything is so still for a moment, paused in the room. *I hate him.* We stare each other down. His head snaps towards me, his half-empty mouth wide open and hissing. I hear his neck clicking as he inches closer, nape rolling against the metal of the headboard. I withdraw. My elbow hits the IV stand and it pulls away from the bed, rolling towards the wall. The plastic tube tenses up.

'Mr Hancock,' I say. 'I'm going to change your bedding now.'

His head is hanging to one side of the headboard, like a doll's. He is unresponsive. He often slips in and out of consciousness but it's hard to tell exactly when. It's one of the official reasons why he requires constant medical surveillance. And also, might I add, one of the reasons why you should never trust him.

My elbow hurts.

I repeat myself. I am sure he is listening.

'Mr Hancock, I'm going to put you in your wheelchair now. So I can change your bedding.'

There is no reply. After a few seconds it seems safe enough for me to begin protocol. I am keeping it practical.

I find the box of latex gloves in the cabinet. I pull out a pair and slip them on. I remove the top bed sheet from the foot of the bed and shove that fucking blanket to the side. *We get them sent over from rural Ireland.* What a fucking nuisance. And look at what good your cotton pads have done. The urine is beginning to dry and I have to peel the top sheet off his calves. It offers a faint resistance but I keep at it, pulling firmly until the organic glue of piss and sweat comes loose and separates from his legs. There is no reaction. I ball the bed sheet up and toss it on the floor at the foot of the bed.

'Mr Hancock?' I say. He is unresponsive. His eyes are empty and fixed. How long, I wonder, until they will positively, permanently look like this? It's hard to tell, but he is pretty old. I rebuke myself. You don't wish death upon someone, anyone, no matter how horrible they might be. You just don't do that. What kind of sick nurse are you? Guilt pushes me closer to him, to his face, to take a closer look. I can hear his steady breathing scratching at his throat. His mouth gives off the odour of uncooked bread, breeding yeast. It makes me retch. I straighten my back and look down at him.

'Mr Hancock? I'm lifting you up now,' I say.

I follow the procedure I was taught in nursing school. I slide one of my arms under his legs, the other under his back. I lift his legs and shift them to the side, until they dangle off the edge. He is silent and compliant like a bag of old rags, and I can feel a trickle of empathy flowing back into me, warming me like a hot alcoholic drink. This is my job and I am good at it. My head hurts but I have got this. Mona will forgive me for being so late and everything that happened on Saturday will be forgotten. I will never go to another party again. I didn't expect it to happen this way – having sex with someone else, after all these years. And I guess, objectively, it could've been worse. You certainly couldn't fault the man for his looks. As Miss Phyllis would say, 'What a looker!' So why do I feel so fucking strange about it? Why can't I stop thinking about Alanna? I lift Mr Hancock's torso with my other arm. Then I push on the back of his shoulders to sling his arms around my neck, careful not to dislodge the IV drip sunk into the thickest vein. I hold him steadily around the waist.

'Come on then, Mr Hancock.'

And then he lashes out. His arms grip my neck. He squeezes. Like a hug, the kind of hug that you're forced to bow into. Then tighter. Too tight. I want to push him – away from my body – but that would be bad nursing practice. I could break one of his ribs. It would take so little to break one. If only I could shove him. *I hate you.* I try to pull my head back, but it's locked in his hold. I breathe in the expensive musk fragrance that we are paid to dab behind his ears. The yeasty smell that spills from his mouth, the hidden, rotting flesh of his throat. I submit to the hug. If I stay still perhaps he'll release me. He doesn't. I feel my cheeks heating up. It's hard to breathe against his leathery neck. I struggle for air against his shoulder, struggle gently, so as not to harm him, my eyes shut in concentration. The world narrows as I begin to run out of air. Incongruously, a National Geographic documentary appears in my mind. A python is suffocating a small dog then swallowing it whole, its little paws useless, spinning like paddles. Then the self-defence tutorials I watch late at night when I'm drunk in my flat. The girls that scream their war cry. They raise their arms, their legs. A little girl's silver polka-dot tights. Alanna's garter sliding up her thigh. Alanna has over a thousand Facebook friends. A friend in need is a friend indeed. Alanna in large round sunglasses, pirouetting down the stairwell at St Peter's in Rome, and I am watching her, from where I have fallen, where I am lying on my back on the bottom step, my face tilted up to the sun, blood flowing on the white marble stairs, geranium-red. Plié, tendu, pas de bourrée. It's not you, it's me, will you ever forgive me? Do you ever listen to a single word I say? Stuart Brandon Pierce slaps my arse over and over: 'That's a good girl, that's a good girl, that's a good girl.' Neil's hand on my throat.

Mr Hancock doesn't budge. I'm light-headed. My vision blackens. I cannot breathe. My hands can't find a grip on his hairless shoulder. I choke. He has tucked himself into my shoulder and he turns his head until his lips are on my neck. I can feel the smooth edge of his upper denture rubbing against my skin, the plastic teeth on real human tissue. The dentist pushing wax to the back of my throat. My knees on the bathroom floor, nylon ripping. I shiver. I choke. I'm choking.

'Ruthie Ruthie Ruthie.' His dry lips graze my neck, old skin on new skin. 'Wishing and hoping . . . Thinking all the time, but no faith in yourself. Have you?' In his headlock, I am perfectly still. I think he is going to eat me. He whispers into my ear. 'I wouldn't fuck a girl like you these days, let alone when I was your age.' The meat of his torso pushes into my open mouth.

I jerk back and the tap of his IV drip hits the floor. The stand rolls away and crashes against the tiled wall. Blood spurts out of his arm like the needle pulled the whole vein along with it. He flops back on to the bed. His head hits the headboard and his arms go limp. Did he really have me in a headlock a moment ago? I am perfectly still standing next to the bed. He is unconscious. His discoloured eyes are staring at the ceiling. I turn to look away from him. My clog squeaks in a puddle of saline solution.

It takes an effort to walk and not run, and I make it. I compose myself. I straighten my smock. *The tap of his IV drip hitting the floor.* Take the lift. Ting, stand, ting. Walk not run the three steps down to the Bowl. Mona is back behind the desk. She looks up sternly, then her expression changes.

'Are you OK, Ruth?'

'I'm breaking for lunch now,' I say. It is ten in the morning. I am panting.

She stares at me through the glass pane.

'It's my elbow,' I say. 'I've hurt my elbow.'

Mona doesn't say anything. I am nearly out of the door when I turn to take a look through the thick glass of reception. All the lights on the switchboard are off.

BLEACH

Ruth
Now

6:30 p.m.! It's Monday! It is customary for the staff of the care home to hold a small function when we lose a long-term patient. Sudden deaths aren't usual, more often there is plenty of time to make the essential preparations. Most of them die at home. At the eleventh hour, conscientious relatives will finally consider reintroducing a patient to their original household. Unfortunately, death in old age is as much of a gamble as it is throughout life. We keep our patients monitored where we can – anything short of wire-tapping their rooms – to keep the family informed. We can't record the images in their room; privacy comes first in private structures like ours. So sometimes we miss the exact moment of their passing. It's nobody's fault.

We'd started the morning round early, just before nine. There were only two of us so we had had to take on a whole floor each. No, this is not our usual practice. Our girl Alanna, yeah, the little blonde one – you see – is getting married soon. This weekend was her hen-do. Oh yes, we go back. We were in school together. I'm going to be her best girl at the wedding. Thank you very much. We're all looking forward to it.

Mr Hancock's room is the very last room at the end of the corridor, so I started my rounds there. After we straighten up their rooms we leave them to rest until lunchtime. Mr Hancock often took his lunch in his room. He didn't cope well with the noise levels of the sitting room – to put it mildly. Let's just say he was a rather solitary type. Timmy didn't find him until one o'clock when he went up with the tray. I'd just come back from my lunch break. He gave this high-pitched scream, like a lady who's seen a mouse or something, so we thought he was joking. Then we heard the metal tray hitting the floor and the emergency light went off on the switchboard. Mona and I hurried upstairs. Timmy was stood outside the door of room 214, very confused. When we pushed the door open, we understood why. There was blood and Timmy has haematophobia. A small fresh wound will throw him into a moderate panic. And this was a lot of blood. Mona went to fetch him a cup of water. Mr Hancock was lying on his bed, at a slant. His right arm must've got caught in the bars of the headboard, trapping the plastic tube of his IV drip, which had then jerked out of the vein. That's where the blood had come from. It must have been why his body was at such a strange angle, hard to piece it together, really, old people bruise at anything, even the adhesive pads of a necessary ECG will sometimes leave behind small circular bruises on their torso, sometimes in patterns similar to spread-out fingertips. It wasn't pretty, but dead old people are hardly ever pretty. It's a good thing we're used to it:

death midwifery is to hospice care what regular midwifery is to obstetrics. It's very much part and parcel of our line of work. We're professionals.

We called the surgery down the road and asked to borrow their emergency doctor. This wouldn't take a minute, we promised. It was the usual procedure but still. The doctor was in a huff when he arrived, obviously inconvenienced. He mumbled, 'Couldn't have picked a worse time,' then apologized, complaining of merciless cuts to public services. We tried our best to explain to the doctor that the old man had died while unsupervised, but he didn't seem keen to listen. 'Well, he definitely is,' he said. It was obvious he was in a hurry. His face was expressionless. He scrawled on his pad, 'cardiac arrest', 'ischemic hypoxia' – spasms not uncommon as an attack reaches its climax – and went back to his twenty-three five-minute appointments. Mr Hancock must've struggled as his heart stopped and it's not unlikely he had a fair bit of strength left in him. In his youth he had had a passion for bodybuilding. That's how his arm ended up in such an odd position. It looked worse than it was because of the blood, Mona and I concurred, because of the strange angle. And really it was only a bit of blood. Just a shame Timmy was the one to find him, because of his phobia. Time of death: approximately 10:30 a.m.

Over two hours before Timmy came up with the tray. But after I'd been to his room on my round.

I kneeled on the floor to clean it all up, picked up the chicken breast, the coleslaw, the bread roll and shoved them back into each individual section of the tray. Then I went over to the bin, stamped on the pedal and emptied it inside, tapping its back against the metal edge until all the food fell out. This is how we made a start on fixing the room. We called his daughter immediately, of course, but she was tied up. We didn't really get to speak to her. She'd put her phone through to her PA. Legally, we aren't allowed to share medical information on the phone with anyone who isn't a close relative, but we made an exception given the urgency of the matter. We were told by the assistant that Miss Hancock had been in a meeting in Noho for three hours. It didn't look anywhere close to finishing. Even if we'd caught it in real time, she would still have missed her father's passing. Nothing to be done. This made the circumstances of his death seem less unfortunate. Mona and I agreed on this point.

The doctor said he saw no problem in moving Mr Hancock. He'd send us a copy of the Cause of Death certificate digitally, he said. The two of us needed to compose Mr Hancock, but someone had to look after the rest of the patients and Timmy was still recovering in the staff kitchen. Besides, he was only a cleaner; we needed someone with the necessary expertise.

'Will you call Alanna in?' said Mona. 'We need some help sorting out this mess.'

'Alanna?' I replied. 'She isn't likely to be the most efficient. Why else would she take herself off the rota without saying?'

'Come on, Ruth, you want us to help you or what? I don't think you're in a position to be particular,' Mona said, though I hadn't considered I might be in need of help.

'It's just I don't have her mobile number,' I said.

Mona snapped open her phone and handed it to me without a word and I went down the corridor to make the call. The signal was better there and I needed to get away from the room for a moment. All that blood had started to get to me. The mobile rang a few times before Alanna picked up, her voice doughy with sleep.

'Yes?'

'Alanna? We need you at work. We are hugely under-staffed.'

'Who is this?'

'It's irresponsible.'

'Ruth? Is that you?'

'Yes, it's Ruth.'

'Ruth . . . Listen . . .'

'No. You listen, Alanna. You need to come now.'

'Come now?'

'There's been an accident.'

'An accident?' She was alert now.

That was a slip-up. We would never refer to it as an accident again. At Mr Hancock's age, anything can be 'natural causes'.

The girls arrived. They must've really rushed because they were wearing no make-up. They looked both younger and more tired. Just in time: Miss Hancock was due to arrive in less than an hour, and we needed the care home to look its best. Half of the patients were still waiting for lunch, and it was nearly 2 p.m.

Mona and I had bleached the blood from the floor, and the room, disinfected, was back to normal. The man's body lay under a white bed sheet. The girls seemed under-whelmed by the lack of action.

'So it's about Mr Hancock,' said Bex.

'Can we see him?' asked Emmy.

'Later, babe,' said Alanna. 'I'm sure everyone will get a chance to say goodbye to Mr Hancock.'

Bex looked up. 'No thanks.' She frowned.

Mona waved her hand in irritation. 'This is not the time, girls. This is about the worst time you could've picked.'

'We need some help, OK?' I said. 'To look after the other patients.'

Alanna said: 'OK.'

'Then go make yourselves look nice,' I said.

SOME KIND OF PUDDING

The Girls
Now

'Like, we always got on with her really well. She's a few years older so sometimes she wouldn't come out so much. Maybe, not often. But always in the care home she was good. Like, good with the old people. What do you call it? Always has a good word for everyone? The Samaritans? That was Jesus, right? Yeah, a bit like that.'

'She's the kind of person who's like that. She's always bringing in nice stuff from home, or if someone brings her sweets or chocolates, she shares, or even on her birthday if she gets any, she always shares with the rest of us, even when Mrs O'Toole's daughters bring the Godivas in at Christmas. Mrs O'Toole can't eat them because they're bad for her, so she's like, "I'm giving these to Ruth, she's the only one I can trust to teach you guys how to share." Good job for us girls because we can be piglets, we can.'

★

'Well, listen to me, dear, you have to listen. I've lived a whole lifetime before you were even born. And I've known girls like Ruth before. She's the kind of girl I would've taken out for a stiff Martini and a serious life chat. One olive, am I right, Constable? That's perfect, good man. I knew one like her when I lived out in Florida. Her husband died in a boating accident. On his own private yacht, can you believe it? Well, if I'm honest, I didn't think it the worst way to go. But I'm a romantic. In any case the man was a brute. What did you say you wanted to ask me, Constable?'

'I have never in my life met such an incompetent nurse. Appalling customer service. And the money I pay them.'

'Yeah, we knew she'd broken up with her partner. Not straight away, no, she didn't say. Yes, we are close. But she's pretty private even when she opens up, if that makes sense. It was hard to figure out what had happened at first, though in hindsight it all makes sense and it feels like any of us could've easily guessed it, if only we'd put our minds to it. She didn't have very many people in her life. There must have been a subtle change in her, but I think she was trying her best to conceal it. She's good at that – doing stuff without being noticed. Sometimes you forget she's even there until you notice that most of the work has been done. She works really hard. She's a good nurse. She can take a lot. But after a while she looked so skinny it was impossible not to see that something was up.'

'He had this disgusting joke that he played on the younger nurses. We'd all been through it so we had decided we wouldn't warn Bex and Emmy when they started working with us. It was a bit of a rite of passage for the new girls. We'd all gone through it. We're in it together, you know? He'd ask you to put his glass of water on the other side of the bed, so you had to bend over and then he'd sneak in a peck. It was nothing really. Just an old man desperate for attention.'

'Sometimes I found her sitting in the office, doing nothing, just staring at something: her can of Coke, the dark tea in her mug, the black computer screen. She didn't really see these things. She would be so lost in her thoughts she wouldn't hear you come in the door.'

'She was always tidying tidying tidying, doing all the jobs before anyone else could get there to do them. You couldn't figure out how she stayed standing. And I felt so bad for her, because I've been through stuff like that when I was younger. So I said to the girls, we should do something for Ruth – we should come up with some kind of plan to stop her from killing herself. They weren't so keen at first but it was easy to get them on board. The girls love projects.'

'You know that bastard kissed me once? On the mouth.'

'Alanna had the idea. She's really, really clever, you know?'

'It must've been the last week of January, she'd been acting weird for a while. I remember it was already dark outside. It was the end of the day and we were putting the meds in their little paper cups – you know the ones? Like the ones you get with a burger, for ketchup and mayo. And then we were meant to start the evening rounds. And I wasn't saying anything. I wanted to ask her what was up but I didn't know how to say it. I didn't want to scare her off. So I'm just flicking pills out of these blister packs and holding them up in my hand for her to choose from, and on the fifth or sixth round of doing this, she goes, "Mona, I'm so sad," and she starts crying.'

'Honestly, in my whole career as a personal shopper I have never met someone so awkward. It makes you feel good our service is free of charge. If you look at it that way, I mean, Topshop is an actual charity.'

'Paul was on board with it from the start. He loves it when I do good things. It's one of his favourite things about me, that I'm the kind of person who does that, so it seemed right to be doing a good deed by asking Ruth to be my maid of honour at the wedding. A good omen. And well . . . it might have helped that I asked him while we were in bed and I was doing a little something.'

'This whole place would fall apart without my Ruth. Little Ruth is a powerhouse. Does as much as two of those kids in a day. Probably in an hour! And she has time for everyone in here. She is kind to everyone – even that horrible man on the third floor. That man and his daughter, I swear to God, I've never seen anything like it. He spits his pills back out, if you can believe it. For the sake of it. He needs his meds, all right, that man.'

'At first she wouldn't even sit down. I insisted. I don't know why I did, I just had to start somewhere, so I just kept saying: Calm down, darling, have a seat, tell me what happened.

Eventually I kind of just picked her up under her armpits and physically lifted her to sit on the counter. That's when she really started sobbing, like she needed to make herself comfortable enough before she could really let go. "He's gone, he's gone," she kept saying, and though I asked her to tell me when it had happened, where, she wouldn't say, so I hugged her. Her sadness seeped right through my clothes. It chilled my bones: I can't explain it – it was a big, huge sadness. It was frightening.'

'She likes me to tell her tales of the sea. She says, Miss Phyllis, tell me a story, as if she were a child. She's never been to America and she says that the first time she does she'd like to go like I did, on a ship. She's a romantic, like myself, so I understand her well. So I say, dear girl, it is beautiful to see the Statue of Liberty as it approaches, but don't forget about all the puking. I could feel the ground rolling under my feet for days afterwards. I say, if you can fly, fly, don't you think, Constable? I say to her, my dear Ruth, why do you always have to do things the hard way?'

'She stares.'

'Honestly, I couldn't even believe she'd been with that sleazebag for ten years in the first place. That horrible man – so full of himself! Always putting her down. I'd been feeling so sorry for her! I think this is all for the best.'

'I'll say no one expected her to turn up like that. Like, she wasn't even writing in the group chat when we were discussing our outfits. Like, I knew what the other girls were wearing. I mean, she looked gooood. A little much maybe?

Catwoman-type thing, quite classic, but that V drop down the front, I don't know. I mean, don't forget this is someone else's hen-do. If I were Alanna, I would've been a bit pissed about it. But she said thank *God* she'd put in the effort and she would expect no less from her maid of honour. She's properly nice, you know, Alanna? Proper angel.'

'I mean, all Emmy's saying, right, is that we weren't going to a strip club.'

'I honestly was so proud of her. I thought she was going to wear these tailored trousers she'd texted me about. The girls get protective but personally I want my maid of honour to look her best. Ruth was doing mighty fine. No chance of her stealing my scene anyway, or that's what I thought. Although making out with the bartender was a bit cheeky, wasn't it? That was funny!'

'Well, I can't say I know her very well. She doesn't really come here for lunch with the others, only alone in the morning. Packed-lunch-type of girl. She comes in early though, before work, and she always looks half asleep. She stands next to the hot water dispenser. Sometimes I have to call her several times to hand her the cup. She takes her coffee black. Lots of sugar.'

'In the afternoon, I make us all coffee. She takes no milk, but I stir some into her cup anyway, for protein, then I pretend that I've made a mistake. I say, "Don't you dare get rid of it, it's perfectly good coffee." I watch her as she drinks it.'

★

'Listen, no one liked him anyway. What does it even matter? It could've been any day. That man had lived everything that he had to live.'

'Me and her go way back, you know? We've got history.'

'I'd love to take her with me to the piano bar. I'd buy her a stiff drink and we could have a game of pool with the soldiers. I fancy a little Martini, extra dry. A little toast to no one else but us: independent women. But I'm never allowed to go to the piano bar in this stupid hotel, Constable.'

'There's a place in this home that I like best of all. It's out the back, where the wooden decking descends gently into the garden and the trees that line each side lean inwards, giving it the look of an old, green theatre. It is really quite beautiful, out there. When the evening's sweet and all the patients have been put to bed, I come out to sit on the steps. I bring with me a piece of candy. I unwrap it, and hold it under my tongue, firmly, as the sugar melts.'

A Girl

A Year Later

Alarm goes off. 5:14 a.m. A day in the life. Hit snooze button once. +8 minutes. Hit snooze button twice. +16 minutes overall. Actual wake-up time: 5:30 a.m. Fifteen minutes allocated to peeing, shower with a temperature of 36°C, towelling. Towel around chest, tuck in, toe my way to the dark kitchen. Pros of the early shift? Making breakfast with no clothes on. Cons of the early shift? Noise pollution must be kept to a minimum. Toast. Two slices. One with butter, one with smooth peanut butter. Instant coffee. One small mug, one sugar, a splash of whole milk. Exercise shoulders with twenty inward rolls, twenty outwards. Breakfast while standing. Return to bathroom to complete morning routine. Clothes on the chair ready to go from the evening before. Wear uniform trousers but not the shirt. Regulation shoes: flats, black, strapped. The 149 leaves at 6:20 a.m. Sit at the back on the lower level for extra legroom.

Wait for keyholder at back entry. A day in the life. In winter, stand next to bakery exhaust pipe. In summer, stand well away from bakery exhaust pipe. It is winter. Keyholder arrives: 6:45 a.m. It's Malick. Malick is nice. Ten minutes allocated to changing into full uniform. Unlock locker. Blue polo shirt. Girl scout tri-coloured neckerchief. Clip magnetic nametag on pocket. Ponytail. Company visor. Why a visor? Reconvene in staff room. Time for one more hot drink, but no time to make a hot drink. Drink coffee if someone has made coffee while you were getting changed. Malick has poured a mug for you. He is nice. Jenny, Polina, Mercè and Kev are in staff room. Anya is late. It's the first time this week so it's OK with Malick. All march to safe to retrieve floats. No change is left in tills overnight. Occupy till at the back of shop floor. Pour change into correct slots: £2, £1, 50p, et cetera. Pull clear plastic bags out of dispenser box and shake open. Arrange to end side of conveyor belt.

'Ready, guys?' says Boris, the security guy. Inserts code and unlocks sliding doors.

First to come in are the office savvies. A day in the life. More choice from the meal deals early in the morning. They often buy fruit, like apples or bananas, rarely crisps. Save snacks for an afternoon spur of the moment. Keeps life exciting. Three items for £3.50. Beep. Beep. Beep. Usually take a bag. Don't bring their own. We charge 5p now. They don't mind. They don't care one bit about the environment. Sometimes they say 'hi'. Suits. Suits. Suits. Mostly men who tell the other men in the office early in the morning is the best time to buy a meal deal. Women come between 8 and 9 a.m. Mothers, car keys in hand, kids dropped at kindergarten, on their way to work or back to the chores. Baby-care items and health foods. Sometimes a baby perched on the hip. Always rushing. Beep. Beep. Beep. Beep. No more than ten items: no preferential basket queue required anyway at this time in the morning.

9 a.m. is when the unpredictable customers arrive. Now all of us are fully awake. This is when we keep tabs, anecdotes to share during the first break, 10:30 a.m. Today: a security man from the building site near by, with his safety jacket inside out, buying a six-pack of Peperami Hot; a slightly dishevelled, noble-looking old lady buying a microwaveable hamburger with bun and an orange Lucozade; a child with a mullet who asks me if I can call his mum on the interphone; and two very cute twelve-year-old twins with matching plaits but beads in different shades of pink and blue, clearly bunking off school and going to get in trouble. Mercè has already had security over to expel a drunk man buying a discounted six-pack of Strongbow. She's going to win this round.

In the break, Mercè relates her encounter with the homeless man. 'I thought he kills me, you know?' He was at least seventy years old and in a bad state. She, Kev and I return to the tills so the others can have their breaks. It's a long stretch until lunch, which is rush hour, customers fighting over the ready-meal aisle. This is the boring time, the store almost empty. Kev timed the morning slot many times. We get one customer every ten minutes between 10:30 a.m. and 1 p.m. Kev is very shy and obsessed with numbers and planes. One day, he'll be an excellent aeronautical engineer, but right now he's eighteen and working here to save money for college. Take my nail file from the drawer under my till and get to work on this cuticle that gives me trouble. Cashier's thumb. A day in the life. Serve three more businessmen. They are late for work, so I hurry for them. Beep. Beep. Beep. Beep beep beep. Beep beep

beep. Then this girl. Busy with her trolley. Hesitates at the till, picks up a packet of razors from the rack, puts them back. Makes eye contact. Says good morning. Small voice and face.

Not a woman, but not a girl either. I know how that feels. Awkward. That's an awkward age, I should know. Time to choose between one thing and another. But her outfit hasn't settled for formal or casual: little tailored coat, comfy shoes. Long straight brown hair, fringe too long. When she looks up, I am taken aback. Her eyes are like black pools: very wide and very wet. She stares at me.

I smile because it is my job to smile. She smiles back.

'You all right?' I say.

'You all right,' she says.

We both nod. She loads her shopping on to the conveyor belt. I put my nail file back. I scan her items.

'Got everything you need?' I say. She nods yes. I help her pack.

11:09   04/01/2017

- [ ] 6 LARGE EGGS
- [ ] COLA DIET 6 CANS
- [ ] PINK LADY 4X
- [ ] BASICS COTTON WOOL
- [ ] ROAST CHICKEN DELI
- [ ] HEINZ TOMATO SOUP
- [ ] PG TIPS FAMILY
- [ ] YELLOW TAIL PINOT GRIGIO
- [ ] OLIVIO PIMENTO 150G
- [ ] STRAWBERRY 500G
- [ ] GARNIER MOISTSR PEACH
- [ ] PEO CUT FLOWERS
- [ ] AUSSIE MIRACLE TREAT
- [ ] SINGLE CREAM 250ML
- [ ] SIRLOIN TOP SIDE 250G
- [ ] THICK BLEACH 1L
- [ ] GU 2X CHOC PUDDING

----

17 ITEMS
BALANCE DUE
DEBIT CARD
CHANGE

Did you receive great service today?
Visit our website to have your say.
Thank you for shopping with us.

Thank you.

ACKNOWLEDGEMENTS

Writing doesn't have to be a lonely business. (What a sad thing to want to believe.) This book would not exist without the help and support of other people.

I am hugely indebted to my agent, Zoe Ross, who believed in this novel fiercely from the beginning and pointed out the way, and to my editor, Lizzy Goudsmit, whose sensitive advice and genial intuition made it the best book I was able to write. Thank you, Alison Barrow, Bella Bosworth, Emma Burton, Sharika Teelwah, Antonia Whitton and the whole team at Doubleday/Transworld for making me feel right at home.

I am grateful to Sophie Collins and Wendy Jones, for taking my writing seriously, and to Tim Parnell, Jack Underwood and the English and Comparative Literature department at Goldsmiths, for putting faith in me and my research. A huge thank you goes to Alice Ash, Claudia Durastanti and Dizz Tate, for being this book's three Good Fairies and my best role models.

This novel owes a lot to the women in my life. I am

especially grateful to Charlotte Heather, for her unending support and real companionship, and to Sandra Neuburger and Caterina Pinzauti for teaching me everything about girls and friendship. Thank you, Anjalie Joseph, my number one, my compass. Thank you, Su Pereira, Sandra Rutten and Eilidh Urquhart, my warm-blooded sisters. Thank you to Khairani Barokka, Serena Braida, Emily Cooper, Sophie Corser, Marzia D'Amico, Silvia Della Porta, Tamsin Murray-Leach, Rebecca Tamás, May-Lan Tan, Francine Toon and Chrissy Williams for the gift of their intimate and literary friendships.

I owe a lot to the creative communities that have protected me over the years, allowing me space and time to grow: *Zamenhof Factory, DIY Space for London* and their brilliant associates – my beautiful friends, I love you. There's a chance I might still owe money on a Martini or two to famous local establishment La Tazza D'Oro – sorry.

Of course, I am most indebted to my family – both blood-related and acquired – and especially to my small and powerful grandmother, Maria Luisa Lavaggi; I am forever humbled by your tenacity and generosity. Thank you so much for supporting me, always.

Dario Franchini e Isabella Moretti, *mamma e babbo*: I suspect I'll never find the right words to express how thankful I am to have been born your daughter, but I promise I'll keep looking for them.

Francesco can have my green heart.

★

The 'grief booklet' Ruth reads from in 'Apples' (on pages 39 and 43–5) is based on the '5 stages of grief' model devised by Elizabeth Kübler-Ross in *On Death and Dying: What the Dying Have to Teach*

Doctors, Nurses, Clergy and Their Own Families (2014), NY, New York: Scribner. The TEAR model (on pages 46–7) is drawn from J. William Worden, *Grief Counselling and Grief Therapy: A Handbook for the Mental Health Practitioner* (2008), NY, New York: Springer Publishing.

'Lili Marlene' is a song written by Hans Leip and Norbert Schultze, famously sung by Marlene Dietrich. The lyrics to 'Wishin' And Hopin'', as sung by Dusty Springfield, were written by Hal David and Burt Bacharach.

ABOUT THE AUTHOR

Livia Franchini is a writer and translator from Tuscany, Italy, whose work has been published in numerous publications and anthologies. She has translated Michael Donaghy, Sam Riviere and James Tiptree Jr among many others. In 2018, she was one of the inaugural writers-in-residence for the Connecting Emerging Literary Artists project, funded by Creative Europe. She lives in London, where she is completing a PhD in experimental women's writing at Goldsmiths.